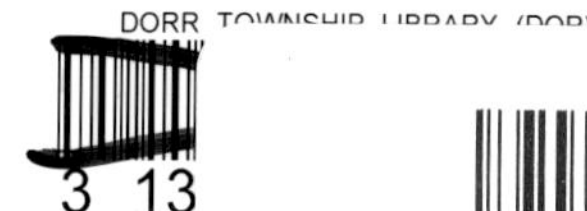

A COLD

A Cold Blue Killing

Book Three of the Del Sueño Files

ISBN-13: 978-1533674074

ISBN-10: 1533674078

Paperback Edition printed in the United States and published by Banty Hen Publishing in conjunction with Glair Publishing, June 2016.

For more about Banty Hen Publishing, please visit:

www.bantyhenpublishing.com.

For more about Glair Publishing, please visit:
www.glairpublishing.com.

Other Books from Banty Hen Publishing and Glair Publishing

By Sugar Lee Ryder & J.D. Cutler

Sagebrush and Lace

Six guns, whips and wild, wild women!

1876: Time to throw away the corsets
and draw down on the Old West.

When Horace Greeley said "Go West Young Man"
he never would have thought that two young women
would take his advice to heart. Striking out against all
odds and risking everything to be together.

Society calls them Sapphists.
Chief Sitting Bull calls them 'Big Magic'.
Buffalo Bill Cody and Wild Bill Hickok
call them friends.
Pinkerton's detectives want them alive.
Clarke Quantrill's gang of outlaws want them dead.

Two runaway women in a man's world
risk their very lives to be together.

See the full listing of J.D. Cutler
and Sugar Lee Ryder's works at:

www.JDCutler.com
~and~
www.SugarLeeRyder.com

Other Books from Banty Hen Publishing

Cowgirl Up

Part One of the 'Cowgirl Up' Trilogy
A hot romance with a young, independent
ranch woman that meets her match in this
novella about bulls, rodeo cowboys
and the difference between sex and love.

See the full listing of Sugar Lee Ryder's works at:
www.SugarLeeRyder

The Adventures of Amanda Love

Firefly meets *Flash Gordon* as con-artist and adventurer
Amanda Love travels the star systems of the frontier.
Her ample charms include the bluest eyes west of
Delta Vega, and a body that could give a pious man
a wet dream in a skin-tight spacesuit.

She and her crew of loyal misfits take their traveling
'pay to pray' Salvation Show out to the lonely, backwater
alien planets that dot fringe space. But her latest con
nearly becomes her last, when she and her crew are
attacked by Malco Trent, the man who runs the
galaxy's most corrupt company: Mal Corp.

See the full listing of Michael Angel
and Devlin Church's works at:

www.MichaelAngelWriter.com
~and~
www.DevlinChurch.com

DEDICATION

As always, my deepest appreciation to Sugar Lee Ryder. She showed me an article about a man and a car submerged for twenty-three years and started my evil mind working.

THE DEL SUEÑO FILES

Murder at the End of the Line
The Tattoo Murders
A Cold Blue Killing

OTHER BOOKS BY EUGENIA PARRISH

The Last Party in Eden
Eugenia Parrish's Baker's Dozen +2
He Had it Coming
Murder at the End of the Line
The Tattoo Murders

Prologue

Sheriff Pete Branson stood at the edge of the steep drop. Below him was a horseshoe-shaped cove in a forgotten part of Blue Lake. The sides of the cove showed a high-water mark not far down from where he stood, but it was well above the current level of the lake.

The area had suffered drought for more than a year. Above the horseshoe massive California Oak trees bent down thirstily, their leaves dark olive-green and their roots exposed to the air. Heavy thick branches hung out over the water, shading whatever lay in its depths.

The old Chevrolet rested below him, still half in the water with its front wheels on the stony bank exposed by the drought. Whatever color it had once been, it was bleached gray now. From beneath it a taut towing cable stretched upward to the top of the bluff where a cable truck sat waiting.

Pete watched as the police underwater diving team continued to scour the site. Their dripping wetsuits left trails of lake water on the small rocks lining the cove, turning them black in the sun. The men up on the bluff were busy and silent, preparing to haul everything up to the road. The car would go on a flatbed. The body would leave in a somber ambulance.

He wondered why the Seddleton police had called him to their jurisdiction to confer on the recovery of a long-submerged car and its luckless owner. The sergeant who called him had been vague, but sometimes the small town police forces in Riverside County gave each other a courtesy call if interests seemed to converge.

As if in answer to his thoughts, one of the divers removed his flippers and climbed up a steep path to stand beside Pete. He pulled off his mask and mouthpiece and looked down, scratching amiably at the police logo on his wetsuit. "No more bodies down there. Passenger musta got out before it submerged. Maybe thrown out. Dunno why we never got a report."

"Maybe they haven't had time?"

"That puppy's been down there for years. Maybe decades. Nope, whoever else was in the car, they didn't want it found."

"Maybe he was alone."

"Not official, but looks like there's a bullet hole in his temple."

"A murder, then. Or is it possible he killed himself?"

"And then got out of the car and pushed it in the lake? Or did he shoot himself, drive off the cliff, and throw the gun out of the car before it submerged?"

"Okay, no. I take it you haven't found a gun yet?"

"My divers have looked all around that cove. It's hard boulder all the way to the bottom. They haven't found anything but bait cans and fishing line. A 'course, they're still checking out the car itself."

Pete could see officers of the Medical Examiners Department with their heads and arms inside the vehicle.

"Decades," he mused. "And in all these years, nobody ever saw the car down there?"

"Not many people come up this way, and the water's usually a lot deeper," said the diver. "This old road's hard on a regular car. Could get here by boat, but those big oaks leaning right out over, they're usually touching the surface. Makes it hard to get a boat inside to fish. You risk tangling up your gear for nothing. I'll bet for years anybody who did come in here to drop a line never saw a thing, until the drought. Kid and his dad came back in here exploring the low water in their fishing boat, saw something and called the Lake Patrol. Just a fluke, really. There's not much fishing in Blue Lake."

"Why not?"

"Lake's never been stocked. Too cold for most fish varieties around here, so not much anthropophagy even after so long."

"Much what?"

"The body hasn't been eaten much. And there must have been some warmer summers before this one, enough for saponification to form and inhibit decomposition."

"Okay, what—"

"Never mind." The diver grinned and the sides of his tight rubber hood distorted his face. "I know, too much information. My boss is always on me about that. Anyway, the guy's pretty well preserved after all these years, and so's his I.D. Happens sometimes. That's assuming he went in the same time he was reported missing."

"He was reported?"

"That's why we called you. His wife reported him missing from Del Sueño thirty-eight years ago. Name's Betty Ann Stearns, now Betty Ann Beaumont. You know her?"

Pete's mouth went dry. "Yeah, I know her."

Chapter One

Outside the cave-like door of the End of the Line saloon, the sun heated the blacktop street, making it sticky and aromatic. It was unseasonably hot and dry for spring, even for southern California, even though the sun had spent itself and was working its way downslope. Patrons scooted gratefully in the door and paused to soak up the relatively cool air. A swamp cooler rattled in the corner. By August it would be exhausted.

The front of the barroom was long and dark. In the back, hanging lights gave a theatrical look to the two men playing a lazy game on one of the two pool tables. People sat scattered on the barstools, too numbed by the heavy air to carry on a conversation. Most just sipped and stared at the television screen hanging above the cash register.

Behind the bar Betty Ann Beaumont leaned one elbow on its worn surface and flexed an ankle. She didn't like admitting it, but at fifty-six years of age, it was getting harder to deal with the aches and fatigue of ten hours on her feet, six nights a week. Time was when she not only kept up with the bar patrons but was way ahead of them until deep into the next morning. Now it wasn't even sunset and she was thinking of sitting down on a stool next to Marilyn and letting the regulars serve themselves.

She had bowed to the heat enough to pin her short bleach-blonde curls high up off her neck and for once had gone light on the makeup. Since her teen years, she had depended on blusher, shadow and mascara to help her face the world with all flags flying. Now there were times when she arrived home at night to find that she had sweated most of it off anyway. Maybe it was time to accept that she would never look thirty again, no matter how much help she got from Maybelline.

"So when's Bill showing up?" she asked the woman perched on a stool across from her.

Marilyn shrugged. As usual, she was wearing a soft red dress and matching spike heels. Not for Marilyn the jeans and tee-shirts or cotton frocks of the local women. She loved dressing up and did it elegantly. Driving in to downtown Del Sueño, all six blocks of it, was only one excuse. Meeting up with a gentleman friend was another.

"He said he'd be here right after work." Her cell phone occupied its usual place next to her drink. She frowned at its screen. "He ain't called. Shoulda been here by now, I'm thinkin'. Well, if he ain't here in half an hour, I'm headin' over to the Jackhammer. And don't you go tellin' him where I went, neither!"

"Don't you want him comin' after you?"

Marilyn tossed her thick auburn hair. Betty Ann suspected she was on the high side of forty, but she wore it long like a girl, and there wasn't a sign of gray.

"Let him stew," she said. "I don't wait around for no man, and he needs to learn that right away. Anyhow, the Jackhammer ain't his sorta place. Them boys in biker leathers'd knock his blue serge butt right out the door."

"How long you been seein' him, now?"

Marilyn looked thoughtful, then surprised. "Y'know, it's been close to six months now! I can't remember the last man who I could stand for that long."

"Must be love," said Betty Ann. She figured Bill McAlister's plump income as CEO of a San Diego company might have had something to do with it, but the relationship was still on a high-swing, so why quibble.

Her attention sharpened when voices rose at the back pool table.

"Patsy," she called to the young woman at the other end of the bar. The girl had been leaning her plump breasts on the bar, chatting with old Josh McAfee and giggling at something he said. At Betty Ann's summons, she gave him a flirty slap on his wrinkled old arm and came over. Betty Ann wondered what lewd things the old coot had been saying to her.

"Go over there," Betty Ann directed in a low voice, "and settle those boys down before it turns into a fight."

Patsy looked at the pool table with alarm. Dirty old men were one thing, but the two pool players were sturdy young men, tall and hardened by ranch work. But she had asked for the job, had sworn she could handle it. Her chin rose a little, and she marched to the table, a pert smile pasted onto her face.

Pete Branson paused in the door, filling it with his large frame in sharp silhouette. He was still wearing the uniform of a Deputy Sheriff of the County, so she fixed him a Coke on ice. She had offered once or twice to slip a bit of something stronger into his Cokes, just to help him through his worst days, but he had declined. When he came in civilian clothes to shoot a few games of pool, it was a different story.

"Hey, Pete," she said, setting the sweating glass in front of him.

"Hey, Betty Ann." He didn't sit down or pick up the Coke. Standing with his thumbs hooked on his service belt, he let his eyes sweep the room cop-style. He said, still not looking at her, "Can we go in the back for a minute?"

She frowned. "Anything wrong?"

"Just need to talk. The office would be good."

"Office has a leak comin' from the ceiling pipes. Floor's flooded, and we had to throw out both chairs. Winston's been workin' on it, but there's no place to sit. We can go sit at the back bar, though."

She ignored Marilyn's inquisitive glance and led Pete past the pool tables and a rack of cue sticks. Unless there was something special going on, the tiny auxiliary bar at the back of the cavernous room was seldom used. It collected all the oldest bar stools, the ones patrons avoided because the torn tops of the vinyl seats could snag pantyhose or scrape bare legs. A stack of unused and ancient ashtrays sat forlornly on its far corner.

She stifled a sigh of relief as she settled her ample behind on one of the stools. Pete declined a seat. Betty Ann noticed a nicely ironed crease in his shirt and wondered if his new girlfriend had pressed it for him. She was a strong-minded college teacher, and she hadn't struck Betty Ann as the type for such old-fashioned duties. The heady beginnings of a love affair could have strange influences.

"Betty Ann," Pete said hesitantly, "the police over in Seddleton are saying they found Tom."

"Tom who?" she asked politely, one eye on how Patsy was handling the boys. The girl seemed to be doing alright, mostly because she was young and cute enough to distract their testosterone in a new direction.

"Your Tom," Pete said. "Stearns? That guy you told me about, that you were married to, thirty-some years ago."

Betty Ann stared at him. After a moment she felt the old bitter smile flicker across her lips. "You mean the sonuvabitch finally decided to show up? He's got a lotta nerve. Whaddya mean, *found* him? He get lost again tryin' to find his way home after all this time?"

He took a deep breath. "They found him in the bottom of Blue Lake, sitting inside an old Chevy about twenty feet down."

She stared at him again and her mouth opened slightly. Thoughts swirled in her mind but nothing came clear. He stayed silent, letting her take her time.

"Okay," she said slowly. "I'm sorry to hear that, Pete. But it ain't nothin' to me. He took off thirty-eight goddam years ago. Ain't nobody heard from him since, includin' me. I don't know why he'd even come back after all this time."

"The thing is," he said gently, "they're thinking he didn't come back. They think he never left. Looks like he's been there in the lake since around the time you reported him missing."

Betty Ann felt blood drain from her head, congealing somewhere near her heart. She pressed her fingers to her temples to stop the roaring in her ears.

"They sure it's Tom? How can they tell after all this time?" She tasted bile in the back of her throat and swallowed. "Listen, honey, would you go get me a shot of something? My stomach's feelin' a bit whoopy, and I'm seein' spots."

He went to the front bar and returned with a shot glass brimful of whiskey. Eyes followed him but no one said anything. She took the small glass from him and gulped half of it. It lit a fire down her insides, and her head began to clear a little. She sat quiet, with her head bowed, and heard more than saw Pete go back up to the bar, taking his time. He brought her back some cocktail napkins and she blew her nose on one, then furtively wiped her eyes. She made a gesture of apology, and he shrugged. Frowning at the glass in her hand, she sighed.

"Lordy, I feel right weird."

"I can understand that," he said.

"Funny thing is," she mused, "I always knew deep down that he never dumped me like they said. I just knew he wouldn't just go off like that and not say anything. I went to the cops. I *told* them assholes something bad must've happened to him. No offense, Pete, but them cops back then, well, they all but come right out and laughed at me. I was only nineteen, he was thirty-two, a hippie, an *artist*." Her lip curled as the word brought back memories of stiff police uniforms topped with sympathetic smirks. "They figured he just got tired of me, y'know? Found himself a new cupcake. They never listened to anything I was sayin'. I never saw 'em write anything down."

He was silent, letting her ramble. An image swam to her mind, of a tall man with soft black hair to his shoulders and a laugh that caught the sun. It was an image she hadn't let herself waste any feelings on for many years. She tilted the glass to her mouth, swallowed the rest of the whiskey and looked at Pete frankly.

"It was still hippie days back then, Pete, everybody sleepin' around loose, kinda, yeah. But old-fashioned Tom, he honest-to-

God married me down at the courthouse. Here I was, this silly little girl that didn't know nothin' back then, but he loved me like a fool. And them sumbitches looked at me like I was some kinda hayseed got took advantage of and too dumb to know it. After a while I guess they pretty much got me to thinkin' it too. A little bit." Her voice tightened in her throat. "And now you're tellin' me that all along I was *right*?"

"He didn't leave you, Betty Ann, not intentionally. They said it looks like he's been out there since right around the time you declared him missing."

"And they're sure it's him? I mean, that's a long time . . ."

"Divers found his wallet and everything, and the driver's license expired thirty years ago. They said it happens sometimes in cold mountain water. The cold kept everything, you know, preserved. And there's not much fish or...anything in the water. The car was spotted down in the cold rocks in a deep spot where the trees hang out over." He moved his hand in a descriptive arc.

"An' it took this long for somebody to spot it?"

"It's the drought we been having. Water's lower than it's been since the Thirties. I was standing on the rocks right over the water, and I still couldn't really see anything at the bottom. Car was all faded when they brought it up, kind of the same color as the water. Tree limbs hanging quite a ways above the water instead of dropping almost right in it like they usually do. I guess it's rare for anyone to fish back in that cove." He told her about the fisherman and his son in the rowboat and the call to the County's underwater dive team. About finding a wallet full of I.D. "Which is why they called me."

She had stopped listening. She thumped the shot glass down on the bar, got off the stool and dusted the seat of her jeans. "Well, hell, and guess what. It's still no matter to me. I forgot about him a long time ago. Even got married again, remember? I sure would like to get an apology from them sumbitch cops, but most of 'em are probably just as dead as he is by now."

Pete blew out a deep breath and glanced unseeing into the shadows at the back of the saloon. "The thing is, Betty Ann, they said they found what looks like a bullet hole in the side of his head. They're saying either he was shot and went in the water and the perp got free of the car, or somebody shot him and then pushed the car in. Either way, they want me to ask what you were doing back then, before you came to the police station to report him missing."

After a baffled moment, she barked a laugh. "You're kiddin' me!"

"Nope." He dug the toe of his black uniform shoe into the dingy linoleum and looked everywhere but at her face. "I'm supposed to find out what you can remember about where you were at the time in question—"

She slapped her palm down on the bar, stopping him.

"Now you just hold on one damn minute, Pete Branson!" she raged. "Are you tellin' me that after treatin' me like a damn fool because they didn't believe me, *now*, after thirty-eight years, they wanta know *did I kill him*?"

Everyone at the bar turned around. Hoping they had registered her volume but not the words, she scowled at them. To a person they went back to hunching over their drinks.

Pete cleared his throat. "Well, they ain't accusing you, exactly. But it is a murder now, and they gotta follow procedure."

"Procedure, my ass! And you can tell 'em whose ass they can shove their procedure up!"

She stormed back behind the front bar, to the farthest end, and began fiercely polishing the top of the bar with a limp bar towel. She deliberately fed the righteous anger, knowing by experience that it would help keep the tears at bay.

Pete came up and stood meekly on the other side. People watched the two of them while trying to look as if they weren't.

He leaned in and spoke low. "Look, Betty Ann, nobody here would ever take it seriously, but the cops in Seddleton gotta do what they gotta do. And so do I. So don't take it personal. Just try to remember where you were and what you were doing around that time, and the sooner you can give them an unbreakable answer, the sooner they'll go occupy themselves with who really shot Tom."

She stopped in the midst of polishing and looked at him with narrowed eyes. "An unbreakable answer, huh?" she hissed back at him. "How 'bout I break somebody's head, you come in here asking such a damn fool question again."

"Just tell me what you were doing right when he died."

"How should I know! When exactly did he die?"

"Sheriff said they can't be sure of the exact date after all this time, just approximate."

"Well, then, you tell 'em if they figger it out, I was *approximately* in the damn hospital. I don't remember where Tom was. Somebody else found me sick, took me to the hospital, and when I come back home, he was nowhere to be found. I never saw him again. That's all I know."

"Which hospital?"

"Valley Medical. The old one that burned down."

Pete sighed. "They might still have records in the new building. I'll see what I can find out. You remember who your doctor was, anything like that?"

"Hell, no."

"Anybody visit you there?"

"No."

"Your mother?"

"She had her stroke right before that. She could still take care of herself, but she couldn't leave the house unless I took her somewhere. Doesn't matter anyway. You know she died years ago."

"Who's the somebody who took you to the hospital?"

"Pete, you gotta understand how loose it was back then. People came and went. Last names weren't important. They might crash on your couch, they might find their own pad. You might see 'em every evening for a month. And then one day they'd just move on down the road. Ramona was around for a while, she 'n' Cowboy were datin'. He was just a kid, but he could ride a bull like a tick. They were always followin' the rodeo until they busted up. I don't even remember why she came to the apartment and found me sick on the floor. I was so pissed at Tom for disappearing, I just never thought back on it."

Pete scrubbed the fingers of one hand through his sandy hair. "That's just great. Possible witnesses are a buncha hippies comin' and goin' thirty-eight years ago, and you can't remember what you were doing the day he disappeared."

Betty Ann shrugged. "Check with Cowboy. Maybe he can put you onto Ramona."

"We ain't the best of friends since the time I locked him up for drunk."

"It gave him an alibi for that jewelry theft, didn't it? Try him."

"I will. And you think about it some more, will you?" he said. "Betty Ann, if it turns out I can't find any witnesses or any record of where you were, the Seddleton cops'll just come in here after you themselves. You think about it, okay?"

She picked up the bar towel and didn't look up as he went out the front door, disappearing into the glare of the sun.

Chapter Two

Once he was gone, a few people looked over at her, frankly curious. When she continued to ignore their interest, they went back to their drinks and the television. She knew they would try to get the story out of her later, when she had calmed down and had a few beers.

Marilyn moved from her stool to one across from where Betty Ann still savagely wiped at the same place on the bar top.

"You okay, honey?"

"I'm fine."

"You gonna rub a hole in the bar."

Betty Ann threw down the towel and blew out a puff of air.

"You remember me talkin' about Tom, that guy I was married to thirty-eight years ago?"

"The one that dumped you?"

"Hah!" Betty Ann's exclamation caused a few patrons to look up again. She lowered her voice. "I never said he dumped me! That's what everybody else said."

"Okay, okay," Marilyn said hastily. "So what about him?"

"They found him. At the bottom of Blue Lake. Where he's been, according to Pete, ever since he disappeared."

"Betty Ann," Marilyn said reasonably, "if they could tell it was him, then he ain't been in the bottom of no lake for thirty-eight years."

"Pete said he was 'remarkably preserved'." She ignored Marilyn's moue of distaste, adding softly, "And they found all his I.D. and stuff right there with him in the car. The thing is, I always knew he'd never leave me like that. Nobody ever believed me. Even you. You all thought I was a fool."

"No! Not a fool," said Marilyn. "We figgered he musta been a fool for leavin' a woman like you, so why should you care so much if he never came back? That's all."

Marilyn had never met Tom. She had no emotional connection to his disappearance, being younger than Betty Ann and growing up on the outskirts of Del Sueño, running with a different crowd. She was well into her thirties before she came into the End of the Line with a gentleman friend and started to be a regular.

"So, okay," she said now, "there's a reason he didn't come back, but after all this time, what's it matter? You moved on."

"Guess so."

"So, what happened, he drive off a cliff?"

"Yeah, maybe, but—looks like he was shot in the head first."

Marilyn stared, for once at a loss for words. Betty Ann considered telling her about Pete's other bombshell and decided the fact that she was suspected of murder would get around soon enough. She needn't be the one to start it along.

"Who the hell would shoot a guy that painted pictures?" Marilyn finally asked. "He into drugs or something back then? Seems like everybody else was."

Betty Ann shook her head. A few blonde curls slipped, and she pinned them back up absently. "He wasn't like that. He was never into that shit. Well, maybe smoked some grass now and then, but everybody did. We didn't see it as much different from tobacco back then."

"Then what the hell was he was doing gettin' himself shot out by Blue Lake?"

"How the hell do I know?" Betty Ann snapped. "That damn long ago, coulda been a hundred things going on that I can't remember now. Why's everybody want to ask me?"

She picked up the towel again and swept it viciously down the bar. Two people worked up the courage to ask for refills. She built their drinks and then made a martini and sat it in front of Marilyn. "On the house."

They both knew it was to make up for snapping at her. Marilyn sipped, mollified, while Betty Ann poured herself another shot of whiskey. It was a long while before she spoke again. "All I can think about is, instead of livin' the high life without me all this time, like I thought, he's been at the bottom of a cold lake right up there near Seddleton. In that old Chevy he bought partly with my money. Christ, he loved that car. Kinda fittin' he should die with it."

"Holy moley," Marilyn breathed. The alcohol was making her eyes shine. "Well, ain't it just gonna shove it up their noses, them turkeys that said you got dumped."

Including you, thought Betty Ann. But she didn't voice it, being abruptly reminded of the ramifications of the situation.

"Yeah," she said gloomily, "only now it looks like they're gonna be sayin' somethin' worse."

"Whaddya mean?"

Betty Ann debated again, but she wanted to tell someone. She leaned closer.

"Pete says now the cops want to know what I was doin', round about that time."

"What for?"

"Apparently they think maybe I shot him."

Marilyn sucked in her breath with a long hissing sound. "Jesus, Betty Ann."

"Yeah, ain't it a pisser? First they think I'm some pathetic little wife that got dumped, and now they think I'm a murderer."

"Well," Marilyn said, "all you gotta do is tell 'em where you were when he disappeared."

"Yeah. 'Cept I don't know where I was."

"Yeah, that's a long time to try to remember."

"No, I don't *know*. I was in the hospital for a few days, but I don't remember that either."

"You were in the hospital but you can't remember it?" Marilyn's tone was just short of skeptical.

Again Betty Ann hesitated. But she had already said so much. "Never could," she answered. "They told me my friend Ramona brought me in sayin' she came in the apartment and found me flopped down on the floor, out of it and hallucinating like I was on drugs. They couldn't find no drugs, I never did that shit. I couldn't tell 'em what happened, though. Don't remember fallin' down, or her findin' me, and don't remember goin' to the hospital. Never have."

"Well, it's still a pretty good alibi, isn't it? Lotsa people in the hospital who musta seen you."

"Maybe. Pete said he's gonna try an' find the hospital records, but it was the old place, the one that burned down back in the Eighties."

"The doctors and nurses might be at the new one."

"After thirty-eight years?" Betty Ann gave a hopeless shrug.

"So what the hell was the matter with you?" said Marilyn.

"They decided I got 'over-stressed', workin' two jobs an' my mother just had her stroke." She hesitated. "And some of it mighta been from me 'n' Tom fightin' all the time that year, but I didn't tell 'em that, and I ain't tellin' the cops either. Anyway, when I woke up in the hospital, they told me I'd been there for four days, talking and everything. I didn't remember any of it. I knew who I was. I remembered doing the dishes at the apartment, and then I was layin' in this hospital bed with bars on the sides, and some nurse I never saw before was sitting there reading a book. She said we'd had some nice long conversations."

"What'd they do about it?"

"Since I couldn't remember anything, they did a whole bunch more tests on me. They thought I might have had a brain aneurism or something. It's not so bad nowadays, but back then you had to lie perfectly still while they slid you in this big heavy-looking machine that almost touched your face. I remember some guy leaning down, peeking in to see if I moved."

Voices rose from a table where three young women looked up askance at the man who had approached them.

"Hey, Josh!" Betty Ann called. "You leave those girls alone. They're married."

He grinned at her toothlessly. "They're too young to be married."

"Then they're a damn sight too young for you! Now get away from 'em."

He gave her a desultory wave and shuffled back to his seat at the bar and leered at Patsy as she worked the beer pumps.

"Well, was you okay after all them tests?" Marilyn said, returning to a more interesting subject. She looked impressed.

"My brain was okay. Don't know what went wrong with the rest of me, but it was all working fine after I woke up, so when I got tired of the pokin' and proddin', I made a fuss and they let me go home with a prescription for blood pressure."

"Wow. So what'd Tom have to say?"

Betty Ann looked at her. "That's just it. He never came to the hospital, and he never answered the phone. I had to call a cab to get home 'cause I couldn't find Ramona either. Then I had to hunt through drawers and sofa cushions to find enough change to pay for the cab. Tom never did come home after that."

She took someone's payment, rang it up on the cash register and dropped the tip in her jar. She went back to lean on the bar. "I was runnin' around like a fool lookin' for him, but nobody'd seen him. I couldn't find him anywhere in town, and his car was gone. I got really mad 'cause I thought maybe he'd gone up to his studio cabin up in the hills to paint his damn pictures and just left me there in the hospital all by myself. Sometimes he did shit like that, not thinkin' it was important, not as important as his goddam art."

"Men are like that." Marilyn nodded.

"So I borrowed Sam's truck and drove up there, but the only person there was Barry. That's some guy Tom let sleep up at the cabin. He said he'd just got there himself, he'd been in San Diego with friends and hadn't seen Tom in a couple weeks. Our other friend, Louisa—you remember her, she's stayin' with me right now—anyway, she was outa town for some reason, I don't remember why. None of the other people we hung out with had seen Tom for days. Which wasn't exactly unusual, now I think of it. Most of them only showed up when he had beer and pot to share."

"Sounds like a nice bunch."

"Oh, don't get me wrong, that's just the way it was back then. People were kinda loose and drifty. Nobody except Ramona even knew I'd been in the hospital, so I didn't say anything about it. Anyway, I hung around the apartment until I stopped bein' mad at him and got worried. I mean, *nobody* had seen him for, like, three weeks by then. So finally I went to the cops." She scowled. "Like that did any good. First they told me we musta had a big fight, like maybe it was somethin' I hadn't noticed. Then they said he probably went on a bender and don't worry, he'll come home when he sobers up. Hell, I don't think I ever saw Tom drunk. Then when I finally told them about the hospital, they figgered some broad who'd been in a psych ward, they didn't blame him for leavin' me. He was in his own car, so it wasn't like he stole it or anything. I guess I'm lucky they didn't believe me. They mighta suspected me of murder back then."

Marilyn drained her martini and smacked her lips. "You tell Pete alla that?"

"Mostly. Told him about the hospital, didn't tell him I had a breakdown." She fixed Marilyn with a look. "And don't you go tellin' him or anybody else, neither. I don't need the whole town thinkin' I was in a psych ward."

"I wouldn't do that. But geez, Betty Ann, maybe Tom died while you were in the hospital. Then you'd be clear, at least."

"Problem is, I don't think they know 'zactly when he died. I gotta try 'n' figure it out myself, I guess. I gotta try 'n' remember, see if I can talk to a few folks. Like when did he leave town exactly? Right when Ramona took me to the hospital, or later? I wish I knew where Ramona is. Ain't seen her in years."

"You tell the cops about her, they'll look into it, now that it's a murder case."

"Yeah," Betty Ann said gloomily. "Now they'll be payin' all kinds of attention, won't they?"

"Hey, Betty Ann!" came a gravelly shout. "What's this I hear about you killin' your husband? Thought you only killed other women's husbands."

"Guess the word's already got around." Betty Ann sighed and turned to the old woman. "I never killed anybody, Nina."

She had been so engrossed in her own thoughts that she hadn't seen Nina Merryweather come in. The old woman was sitting in her usual seat full center of the bar, near the bar pumps. She had outlived four husbands, three of them lost to alcohol poisoning and one killed in a fight that she still blamed Betty Ann for. Her ancient voice screeched out of a face that was a map of the dead land around the San Joaquin hills and a record of decades of chain-smoking. Bitter and gaunt, dark and gnarled as a tree branch, her body in a perpetual state of emaciation, she might have stepped out of a sepia print of a warrior from the Indian uprisings of the nineteenth century. Newcomers often made the mistake of calling her "sir".

Old regulars still laughed when they spoke of the time Nina sat on the curb outside the End of the Line saloon to watch a Fourth of July parade. It was a hot day and one of her sons wanted to enter the bar for a beer, but the owner wouldn't let him in without a shirt. Nina whipped off her own tee-shirt and gave it to her son to wear. For over an hour she sat on the curb bare-chested until he returned. None of the tourists in the crowd noticed. None of the townspeople cared.

"Yeah, that's what them redneck cops put on their report," Nina said now.

"C'mon, Nina" called Brody from further down the bar. He was a huge man, as big-hearted as a Saint Bernard. "You know Betty Ann ain't never killed anybody, and even if she did, the sonuvabitch prob'ly had it comin' to him."

"My man didn't!" said the old woman. "Bitch got away with it then, too."

There was good-natured grumbling along the bar. Nina had been a fixture in town for decades, and no one took her seriously. Betty Ann sometimes wished someone would.

"You so sure," said Brody finally, "how come you never did anything about it? Seems to me like you was glad enough to be rid of him at the time."

"Maybe I'm waitin' till the right time come to do somethin' about it," she said.

Hoots and boos greeted this.

"How long you figurin' on waiting, Nina?" said Brody. "What's it been? Forty years?"

Her beetle eyes gleamed at him narrowly in the dark air of the bar. "You white-eyes are always in a hurry. Ten years is a passing breeze in the night."

"A dish best served cold. We heard that one," Joey Blankenship sneered. He worked on construction teams around the area when there was building going on. During the slow season, he wore his hair in spikes and spent his money going to Star Trek conventions.

"And where do you think they got it from?" Nina asked him. "Ain't no revenge like Indian revenge."

"Knock it off, Nina," said Marilyn. "You ain't that Indian, and you ain't scarin' anybody."

"You see the wall-walker behind you some night, you be scared enough."

"What'n hell's a wall-walker?" asked Joey. "Sounds like one a them fancy drinks."

Nina leaned forward to get a good look at him down the bar. "It's that shadow you see outa your eye-corners, some night when you's walkin' home all alone. They creep along the walls so you don't see 'em till they's on ya."

"Maybe one a them is what gotcher husband."

"It was a knife that got him." Nina dismissed him with a contemptuous look. "It was a knife fight, and it was this bitch started it! If she'd stayed away from my husband, he'd be alive today."

"Nina, I never was interested in your husband, or anyone else's either. I tried to stop that fight!"

"Only your word for it, since it was just you three drinkin' at three in the mornin'. But a'course, the cops took your word for it, little blonde piece a jailbait next to a couple of Indians. But don't you ever think I've forgotten, girly. If the wall-walkers don't do the job, I still got me my Julio's gun, the one he didn't have with him that night. I get it out now and then, just to stroke on it and talk to the wall-walkers."

"Time to go home, Nina," said Cowboy.

He was standing over by the juke box. Betty Ann hadn't seen him come in either. She was really slipping. Or Pete's news about Tom had shaken her more than she realized.

The old woman spun around on her stool to smile at him, showing teeth the color of old corn. "Is that an offer, boy? I still owe you three dollars, don't I? I reckon at fifty cents a shag, it might take us a while to work it off."

He took her by the elbow and steered her to the door. "You head that old pickup home, now, y'hear? Else I'll have to call up one a yore kids to come get you. Worse yet, one a yore daughter-in-laws. You know how they can be."

When her cackling had faded down the street, Betty Ann opened a beer and handed it to him.

"My hero," she said.

"Yes, ma'am. You need any more dragons slayed, this does go a mite further than a kiss." He tilted the bottle to his lips, drained half of it and strolled to the back to join the pool game.

Betty Ann shook her head at Marilyn. "He can be such a shit, and I wouldn't trust him any further than I could throw him. But he does come in handy sometimes."

"So what's that old broad's problem?"

"Oh, I was workin' over at the Jackhammer one night. Her first husband Julio got in an argument with some bruiser from off the reservation. I tried to stop it, but Julio got stabbed and the bruiser went to prison for manslaughter. Nina forgets about it until she gets drunk. I don't pay her no nevermind."

"Was that before Tom disappeared?"

"I think so. Yeah, it was. I remember, Tom was all pissed off for days, sayin' I shouldn't have been workin' in a bar that late by myself, and he was gonna get a real job so I didn't have to work at all. That notion lasted about a week."

"Maybe you should tell Pete. Maybe she figured an eye for an eye. Or a husband for a husband, if you see my meaning."

Betty Ann stared at her. "No. That ain't right," she said uncomfortably. "All these years that Nina's been threatening to shoot me, she's never even come close to doing anything. It's just drunk talk. She's okay when she's sober. And she wouldn't be still talkin' about it if she already got even, would she?"

"All-a same, you should tell Pete."

Betty Ann didn't answer. Nina was old End of the Line family. And she would be sure to let everyone know that Betty Ann had turned her in to the cops.

It was a hell of a thing when to watch your own back, you had to stab somebody else's.

Chapter Three

When the clock finally read midnight, Betty Ann ordered the remaining patrons out the door and locked up. If they were still thirsty, she told them, they could take a ride down to one of the saloons that sat along the river.

All the rage and distress she had felt thirty-eight years ago had come washing back into her heart and seething into her mind until she thought she would go crazy if she didn't get out of there.

The drive home in her powder-blue Thunderbird was usually a pleasure late at night. She had always had a skill with cars and used that skill to run the car smoothly through gear changes, slipping around curves like a ghost in the night. For years it had been a way to decompress after a night of riding herd on balky men and sloppy-drunk women. She enjoyed listening to the clean mechanical sound of the car's engine as she drove to Vista de Copa and the four-bedroom house that Jackson Beaumont had bought for her. It was a beautiful place, but after Jackson passed away, sometimes walking in the door made her shiver and turn the television on just for the company.

This night, she found herself putting off her arrival, taking the long way home, looping through the back streets of town and out to the still mostly undeveloped foothills where she could concentrate on the curves and corners sliding under the car and let it take her mind away from a night of horrifying new truths and ancient memories.

Sometimes she caught sight of moonlight glinting on roofs among the dark mysterious-looking California Oaks. By that time of night most houses were shuttered and dark, nearly invisible, and she felt alone in the world. Sometimes a house was still lit up, curtains left open to the street, glowing chandeliers visible and never a human being in sight. She wondered if, like her, they preferred to gather at the back, in smaller rooms stuffed with comfortable sofas and warm conversation, rather than sit in cold elegant rooms at the front of the house.

After Jackson's funeral, she had just lived through the days, wondering what she should do with the years she had left, wondering if she should move back to Del Sueño where people still sat out on their porch steps and watched kids play in the streets in the warm evenings. Loneliness had driven her back to the End of the Line, where old Mr. Meagan's son, for personal reasons, had given up wanting to run a saloon. He had turned over management to his cousin, Winston, and Winston had gladly hired her to tend bar, since she knew as much, if not more, about the place than he did.

It was a commute, but still she put off selling the house. It was a connection to a time when Jackson Beaumont had broken through her self-reliance and kissed her into accepting a life of ease and comfort. He hadn't meant for her to ever be lonely. He had sworn he would never leave her, and she had believed him, in spite of what Tom Stearns had done. Or, she corrected herself, what she thought Tom had done.

Two years later a ghost from the past showed up on her doorstep. Louisa Berringer.

Louisa had been a childhood friend of Tom Stearns. They had gone to the same high school back in New Jersey and hung out together afterwards. Then Tom moved to California and married Betty Ann. A year after that Louisa had got off the bus in Del Sueño and became an off-and-on presence on their lumpy couch, usually because she had broken up with yet another heartless boyfriend. Men were attracted to her dark prettiness until her mood swings and histrionics – what today they called being a Drama Queen – would finally drive them to decamp, leaving Louisa with empty bank accounts and past-due rent.

Back in the days of her marriage to Tom, Betty Ann had not minded having another woman around the house. She loved Tom, but he was thirteen years older, and sometimes his moods were morose or confusing to her, his sense of humor based in a different era. Louisa was closer to Tom's age than her own, but immaturity made her seem younger. She was an amiable friend, chatty and forthcoming about the civil rights protests they had been in back in the Sixties, until Tom grew bored and told her to stop raking up the past.

Louisa was, if anything, more upset than Betty Ann when Tom disappeared. After dealing with the disinterest of the police, Betty Ann found her obvious distress comforting, even steadying. It had pushed Betty Ann to stay calm instead of giving in to her own fears and confusion.

But Louisa became homesick and sullen, and after Tom's disappearance she moved back east. Two years later Betty Ann received a letter from her saying she'd gotten married and had a baby girl to support. Her husband had died of cancer, but not to worry, she and little Chloe were doing fine, but could she borrow a few bucks for rent? Betty Ann sent what little she could. Years later, when Louisa had a boyfriend who resented sharing her with a strong-minded sixteen-year-old, Betty Ann scraped together airfare and flew Chloe to California to stay with her for the summer.

She had enjoyed showing the girl around, listening to her vivid plans for college and a degree in graphic design. Chloe reminded Betty Ann of herself when she was young, full of passion and enthusiasm, with a strong streak of maturity that was understandable, considering she had always had to be the adult in the family. Betty Ann stayed in touch with Chloe, becoming "Aunt Bee", to her great delight. After college the girl found a job with a design firm in Denver and came to California for her vacations rather than going home to New Jersey. Betty Ann's contact with Louisa narrowed down to Chloe's vibrant, highly humorous anecdotes detailing her mother's latest peccadilloes.

Then Louisa had shown up a month ago in Vista de Copa, driving an old sedan that pumped blue smoke into the quiet clean street. The inside of the car had been piled high with grocery bags stuffed full of clothes. There were boxes of belongings, dozens of stuffed animals and a bewildering number of hats, sweaters and purses. The floor mats couldn't be seen for the fast-food wrappers and discarded drink cups.

"Me 'n' Chloe had a fight," she told Betty Ann as they pulled bags from the car. "A real big one this time. I don't know why she has to be so mean to me. Didn't I raise her all by myself, working overtime and scrimping and saving? I sent her to college, f'Chrissakes! She wouldn't be able to afford that fancy apartment if I hadn't. But I guess she's just like her father, selfish, allus has been."

"She'll get over it," said Betty Ann as she helped carry the bags to the spare room.

"She as much as told me to leave and never come back."

"She got a man in her life now?"

"Not since that guy a few years ago. Didn't last long. So it ain't like I was gettin' in anybody's way. But she up and says I gotta leave, just go somewhere else, and my bank account's all froze up because of the IRS or something. Couldn't find anyplace else to live and didn't think the car would make it alla way from Denver to Jersey. All of a sudden I thought of you. I mean, I'm footloose and fancy-free, so why not spend some time with my oldest friend?"

"Well," Betty Ann said, "sounds like Chloe just needs some time to herself. Anyway, there's plenty of room here. Stay as long as you like. It'll be a real pleasure to have someone else in this big ol' house."

After two weeks Betty Ann suggested that Louisa might like to find something to do besides watch television, just to fill the evenings while Betty Ann was working at the End of the Line. She offered to talk to Granny Jorgenson, get Louisa a job in Granny's café. She even talked to her boss about giving Louisa a job helping out behind the bar. But Louisa said she couldn't stand on her feet for that many hours. Gradually, the subject was dropped.

Betty Ann sighed and rolled down the windows of the Thunderbird—another gift from Jackson Beaumont—to let in the night air. She took deep breaths of bitter sagebrush, the rusty scent of oak trees and dry dust thrown up from the blacktop by cars long gone by. Finally she felt herself begin to relax and welcomed a feeling of knowing her place in the universe. Her pulse slowed. The desert valley dropped below, showing tiny lights glimmering along the black shadow of the river that curved around Del Sueño.

She turned up the clean driveway. Louisa's car sat in the driveway, not having been moved, as far as Betty Ann knew, since she had arrived. She clicked the garage door opener and drove in, wondering once again what Louisa's plans were. She didn't seem to have any. But then, Betty Ann reminded herself, she never had. Louisa was just one of those people who drifted along through life, accepting whatever people offered. Betty Ann didn't regret asking her to stay, but it baffled her that someone could spend their days cooped up in a house that didn't even belong to them.

Still and all, it was pleasant to come home late at night to lights on and the television talking away. She smiled through her weariness.

When she walked through from the garage to the kitchen, she was hit with the smell of cold grease. She encouraged Louisa to help herself to anything in the fridge while she was gone, and it wasn't like she expected Louisa to work as a maid, but, really, she could at least put her own dirty dishes in the dishwasher. She sighed and told herself that people like Louisa weren't used to having things like dishwashers, and anyway, what did it matter? After she had something to eat herself, it would be easy for her to clean up for the both of them.

"Louisa?"

"Back here."

She left her purse on the counter and went into the family room. 'Family room' was what Jackson had called it, although until she met his sister at the funeral, she hadn't known he had any family. It was her favorite place, family or no, and the best time of her days were when Jackson came home from work. He walked in the door and at his first sight of her, the taut look around his eyes eased. They ate dinner at the small table and then watched television, curled together on the soft leather couch. Nothing would ever make up for losing that.

She pushed the memory out of her mind.

"What are you doing up?" she asked as she always did.

"Couldn't sleep," came the invariable reply. Louisa insisted that she couldn't sleep at night until Betty Ann came home. "How late is it? Where've you been?"

Louisa was on the leather couch, half buried under a quilt. She struggled to a sitting position, dislodging at least two empty potato chip bags. Her hair looked like it hadn't been combed in twenty-four hours.

Betty Ann had a sudden memory of Louisa's glossy dark brown, almost black, hair back when they were young. Now it was dull, and gray was advancing through it like an invasion. She felt a rush of pity. It had to be depressing, getting to that age only to be rejected by your only child.

"I just closed the bar," she said. "A little early, in fact. It's only a little after midnight."

"Midnight! I don't know how you do it." Louisa gave a huge yawn and looked blearily around. The television was on, bleating an old forties movie, a melodrama, just the kind of thing Louisa loved. If Betty Ann remembered correctly, the main character in this one had an affair with a married man and got pregnant and then he died. Something like that. Betty Ann had never cared for manufactured grief.

A plate full of crumbs and a dirty fork sat on the end table. On the floor in front of the sofa was a bowl smeared with the dregs of milky cereal. Betty Ann picked them up.

"Got some news today, Lou," she said without looking at her. "Seems they've found Tom's body."

"Whose?" Louisa said absently. Then the word sank in. "Body? You mean he's *dead*? *Our* Tom?"

"Yes, my first husband. You remember him?"

"Of course I remember him," she snapped. "Why wouldn't I? Just because he wasn't my husband—"

"I thought you'd forgotten about him. You haven't mentioned him since you got here."

"Never mind," Louisa said impatiently. "What happened to him?"

"They found him at the bottom of Blue Lake. Sheriff Branson said he was shot through the head."

Louisa stared with her mouth open. Distractedly she punched the mute button on the TV. "Y'mean somebody *killed* him?" she said into the silence.

"Looks like it. It wasn't suicide. Couldn'ta been, Tom wasn't like that, was he. Anyway, he couldn't shoot himself in the head and then drive into the lake." She looked at the plates in her hand, set them back down and dropped onto Jackson's oversized La-Z-Boy lounger. "The thing is, it didn't happen recently. It happened 'way back when he first went missing. Lou, he's been dead all these years, and I never knew it."

Louisa eyes filled with tears.

"Oh my god!" She clapped her hands to her mouth. Her voice was muffled as she cried, "Tom! Oh my god. All this time – down there. At the bottom of a lake. Oh my god. All this time I thought he'd—" She slid a look at Betty Ann. "I mean, we thought he'd just gone off somewhere." She picked up a corner of the quilt, pressed it to her face and started to sob.

You'd think it was her damn husband, Betty Ann thought irritably. Then she wondered why she had no urge to cry herself. Maybe Louisa's tears were the more admirable reaction.

Louisa lowered the quilt to ask between choked gasps, "Who killed him?"

"They don't know yet. They might want to talk to you. What were you doing when Tom disappeared?"

"Me!" Louisa spluttered. "I wasn't doing anything! I didn't have anything to do with it!"

"Oh, Lou," she said, exasperated. "I mean, do you remember where you were, what was going on? What either of us were doing at the time?"

Louisa thought for a moment. "What day of the week was he killed?"

"Hell, I don't know. I don't think the cops know. I remember I didn't start thinking anything was wrong for days. I thought he was just bein' his usual self, getting all absorbed in painting and not bothering to check if I was okay. So I drove up to the cabin. Barry was there, and he said he hadn't seen Tom in over a week. Over a week! Neither had anyone else, so that's when I got scared. Where were you that week? I seem to remember you weren't around for some reason right then."

"I was up in Riverside. I had a doctor's appointment. When I came back, you were all freaked out, yellin' stuff like 'Where'n hell's Tom?' I couldn't tell you and that's all I remember."

"A doctor's appointment? Why'd you go clear to Riverside? Cheaper here in town."

"I knew the doctor. Friend of a friend. It was nothing, really. Some kinda stomach flu. He gave me some prescriptions."

"How'd you get there?" Betty Ann asked curiously. "Tom took his car."

"Borrowed Granny's Buick."

Adele 'Granny' Jordenson had been running the oldest cafe in town for fifty years. She was known for hiring people with no skills or experience and even sometimes hired recovering addicts, alcoholics and ex-cons. Granny had helped found the local pet shelter and always had an empty pickle jar on the counter next to the cash register, for folks to donate their change to one cause or another. More than one battered woman had found safety in her tiny anonymous bungalow hidden out in the eucalyptus groves.

Louisa had sometimes waitressed for her back then. Betty Ann didn't doubt that Granny had loaned Louisa her car; she was an easy touch for just about any down-and-outer who needed a temporary set of wheels.

"Anyway," she asked Louisa, "where were you staying when you came back? I don't remember seeing you at the apartment."

"No. After I went to the doctor, I stayed with some friends up in Riverside for a while."

"I didn't know you knew anybody else around here."

"Yeah, well, they was just out from Jersey, visiting with a cousin or something. Since I had Granny's car, I drove over to say hi. Ended up spending a couple weeks. Granny got a little bent outa shape, me bein' gone so long." She shrugged.

That sounded like Louisa. In a way, it sounded like everyone she and Tom had hung out with back then. Betty Ann sighed. Such lackadaisical behavior had seemed fine at the time, but it made things like memories and people hard to track down.

"Tom was acting kinda funny that summer," she said, picking at a bit of mustard on one of the plates. "Lotsa times he went up to the cabin alone. Said he had to 'have some peace an' quiet', remember? You even asked him once if he had a girlfriend. So finally I asked him myself, and we had the biggest fight up to then. Ramona was going down to Baja to visit her folks, so I went along. Me an' Tom made it up when I got back, and things were fine until what? Couple months later? Anyway, in July—remember? It was hotter than a chili pepper—he went up to the studio to do some painting. I was working two jobs right then. Next thing I remember, I was in the hospital, and he never even came to see what happened to me. And when I finally could go looking for him, he was gone. Maybe that's when he ran into something bad up there at the lake. Maybe that's why," she added thoughtfully, "he never came to see me. He wasn't being selfish—he was already at the bottom of the lake. But how'n hell did he get there? Why?"

Louisa peered at her. "Do they know that? I mean, do they know for sure he was killed up there? Not shot down here, or somewheres else, and then taken up to the lake to hide the body?"

Betty Ann was silent. This possibility hadn't occurred to her. Nor, she was fairly certain, had it occurred to Pete. At least he hadn't mentioned it. She wondered if it had occurred to the Seddleton police.

"Shit, if Tom was shot in Pete's town and taken to the lake, just how involved is he going to have to get? Wonder what pressure that'd put on his loyalty to me? Well, anyway, I'm gonna need to remember what in hell I was doin' right then, so I can bust up any goofy notions the Seddleton cops have. Problem is," she added with a frown, "all these years I worked so hard at forgettin' the whole thing, I can't rightly remember much that happened that whole summer."

Louisa glared at her. Her cheeks pinked slightly.

"Betty Ann Stearns!" she snapped. Betty Ann opened her mouth, but Louisa rode over her. "You can go tellin' everybody else you was in the hospital, but you don't need to play that game with me!"

"Now what are you talking about? And don't call me Stearns. I'm Mrs. Jackson Beaumont."

"Oh, go ahead," Louisa said with scorn, "put on your airs, the poor widow over 'n' over. But if you think I didn't know what you was up to that summer—if you think everybody didn't know that was a lie about you goin' to Baja! That's why I said what I said about him havin' a girlfriend. I figgered he had a right to one."

"A *right*?" Betty Ann glowered at Louisa. "Just what bullshit are you pukin' up now?"

Louisa tried to get up from the sofa. Her feet caught in the quilt, and she yanked at its folds. Betty Ann couldn't help the grin that twitched at her lips. Louisa always managed to look silly in an argument, no matter how hard she tried to take the high road. Finally she got free and kicked the quilt out of her way. She was wearing the same sweats she had worn to bed the night before.

"You go right ahead and laugh, missy," Louisa said, "but we all knew you was carryin' on with Barry behind Tom's back!"

Chapter Four

Betty Ann gaped at her. "That's a lie!"

"Everybody knew that was why Tom finally left you for good. He took off and you was gone too for a while, so we figgered you was up at the cabin with Barry!"

Betty Ann stood up and braced her own hands on her hips. "Who's *we*? You mean *you* figured, dammit! Nobody else ever said such a nasty thing to me, not even the cops, and they'd have loved throwin' another reason at me for gettin' dumped!"

Louisa sniffed. "Maybe they was just bein' nice."

"Exactly," Betty Ann said meaningfully.

"Exactly what?" Louisa said. Then she exclaimed, "You think I'm not being *nice*? Well, I'm being honest! I woulda thought you'd want me to be honest. 'Specially right now! Maybe you need to know what people was thinkin'."

"Oh, Louisa." Betty Ann felt her anger drain out of her and sat back down with a sigh. "Honesty isn't always the best policy, but maybe you're right. Maybe now isn't the time for makin' nice. We gotta try and figure out what happened to Tom before the cops make up their own theories. I need to know what folks were thinking. But f'Chrissakes, I never had anything to do with Barry! He hung around the cabin 'cause Tom let him camp there rent-free!"

Louisa humphed and crossed her arms.

"Honestly," said Betty Ann. "When was I supposed to be havin' an affair? I was fed up back then, feelin' all insecure and worryin' about who Tom was with while I was workin' my ass off at two or three jobs, and gettin' paid under the table 'cause I was only nineteen. No health insurance, nothing, just his damn paintings that never sold. We had a huge fight, but it didn't mean anything. And then Ramona finds me on the damn kitchen floor and takes me to the hospital. Remember her?"

"She took you to the hospital? What for?"

"Doesn't matter. That's where I 'was gone' to, as you say. I don't remember the exact, y'know, sequence of things. I just know I sure as hell was never anywhere with Barry that summer, or any other time either."

Louisa looked at her with disbelief, but something in Betty Ann's face appeared to shake her conviction.

"For true? You was in the hospital? You sayin' you and Barry never . . .?"

"Oh, hell, no! We never did like each other that much, to tell the truth. But I never said anything. Tom was always tryin' to help him become a real artist."

"I never understood why they painted that stuff." Louisa said as she sat back down heavily. "Them crazy big black and red things. Hard to sleep sometimes with 'em hangin' over the sofa. Barry did the same sort of stuff as Tom, didn't he, only worse. But most of the time it seemed like Barry just mooned around doing nothing but whine 'cause he never got shows in galleries like Tom did, and when was he supposed to be a great artist? I figgered he was moonin' over you. So – what? You sayin' you didn't even like him?"

"I think I felt like he resented me being there. He acted like I'd come between the two of 'em, which was crap. Tom and I were married before he came to town and started hangin' around with us."

"Yeah, I remember when he got here. I hadn't seen 'im for years, and lemme tell ya, seein' him drive up in that old secondhand hearse was a hoot."

"Tom let him park it up behind the cabin and sleep in it, so he was always there when I went up. But so was Tom, Lou, every time except that last. I even complained to Tom about him always bein' around. He told me not to be so jealous. Jesus." Betty Ann massaged the nape of her neck. Memories were piling a huge weight there, and for the first time in years they were starting to feel like something that had happened to her yesterday.

Louisa was saying, "I heard Barry got himself a gallery down in San Diego. He even sold a couple of them god-awful paintings to some college for a lotta money. So I guess somebody liked 'em."

Betty Ann picked up an ashtray that Louisa had filled with cigarette butts and put it on top of the dirty plates. A thought struck her. "Oh, Lordy, I suppose I gotta try and find Barry now. Tell him they found Tom."

"I wouldn't bother. He was a jerk, and he never cared about Tom. He let me think you and him was having it on."

"I thought you all were friends from way back when."

Louisa stared at the floor for a moment. "All this time," she said to her bare feet, "I thought you and Barry was carryin' on under Tom's nose. I felt so sorry for Tom. I thought you and Barry was up at that cabin alone when Tom was at his gallery shows. It seemed like such a nice private place for a . . ."

"A shack-up?" Betty Ann said caustically. "Not hardly, way up there with no electricity or air-conditioning. It was a damned uncomfortable shack, as I remember, and the ceiling leaked whenever there was a good hard rain. Come to think of it, those leaks were the only thing Tom tried to fix. Didn't want his paintings to get ruined. Other than that, he didn't give much of a damn. I think some aunt left it to him when she died, and he said it gave him inspiration to be up there amongst all the weeds and coyotes. Back then the rich people hadn't started building any of those fancy weekend places up there. Lemme tell ya, it was secluded! Too secluded."

More and more vividly the memories were creeping back in. She had never wanted them before. She wasn't sure she wanted them now, but Pete did.

Louisa said, "I remember the gang of us hanging out up there sometimes, smokin' pot and cookin' weinies in the fireplace. Me 'n' you 'n' Tom, of course, and Barry and Sam the bartender, and Ramona and Cowboy sometimes when he wasn't rodeoing. And some other girl, what was her name, the one with the hair down to her butt?"

"Celeste. Some friend of Sam's. She didn't like us much and made Sam stop coming up. Seems like they all left, one way or another."

There was a moment of silence. Louisa looked up at her through oily dark bangs.

"So it belongs to you now, that place? The cabin? Mebbe—" Louisa licked her lips. "Mebbe I could go live up there. You know, sorta be a caretaker for you."

"Lou," Betty Ann said with exasperation, "it was crap back then. The roof's probably fallen in by now. And how would you live? I mean, food and all. Closest town's Seddleton, and you don't want to drive that old car of yours back 'n' forth a lot. It might not even make it up there in the first place. And it's colder'n shit up there this time a year. Won't be warm enough to spend the night for another month at least, and then it'll be too damn hot."

Louisa said stubbornly, "I'll get Chloe to send me some money for food and firewood and such. She owes me somethin' for raisin' her. Our whole fight was about me supposedly crowdin' her, so I expect she'd be glad to pay for me to stay out of her life." Louisa's eyes became wet again. "Maybe she'll send me enough to buy it from you, even. I need some place to live, don't I? And I could raise chickens, something like that."

"What do you know about raisin' chickens?"

No answer.

Betty Ann sighed. "It's too late to talk about anything like that tonight. Maybe in the morning. I don't know about you, but I've had about all I can stand for one day. I'm goin' up to bed."

The doorbell rang. With an ugly feeling that it might be the police coming to arrest her, Betty went to the front door and looked through the peephole. She threw the door open.

In the strong glow of the porch light, the woman's black bob looked like she was wearing a shiny bowling ball clapped around her head. Pearls dotted her ears and hung in a rope across her pale sweater set. An expensive-looking car sat in the driveway behind Louisa's heap. She could hear its overworked engine ticking in the cold air.

"Greta?" Betty Ann said blankly.

Greta spoke through the storm door. "I saw on TV about them finding your late husband in Blue Lake, so I came here as soon as I could. Saw all the lights on in front, so I decided to stop now and get it over with, instead of waiting until tomorrow."

"Get what over with?" Betty Ann hesitated, but her upbringing was too ingrained. She ignored the urge to slam the door and opened it instead. Greta walked in, followed by a man Betty Ann had never seen before. Before she could decide to take them to the back, Greta stuck her head in the cold living room and then helped herself to a seat on the pastel sofa. The man with her took up a stance beside it.

Louisa poked her head in curiously.

"This is Jackson's sister," Betty Ann said to her by way of introduction. "Greta, this is my friend Louisa."

Greta lifted an eyebrow. "I thought maybe the police were here. Might have made things simpler."

She had a look in her eyes that made Betty Ann sorry she hadn't slammed the door. "What the hell's that mean?"

"I been talking to my lawyer," Greta said with a gesture to the man behind her. "He's real knowledgeable about California law, since he used to practice here before he moved to Phoenix."

Betty Ann folded her arms across her chest. "So?"

"Well," said Greta virtuously, "My brother was a real moral person, so I always assumed he knew what he was doing when you insisted on marrying him—"

"I didn't insist on nothin'. He didn't want us just livin' together. He told me that. He insisted we have a real marriage ceremony—" Betty Ann raised her voice to carry over Greta's snort of contempt. "I told him I didn't think it was necessary!"

Greta sneered. "I'll bet you didn't think it was necessary, not wanting to admit that you had no legal right to marry him! Not until you decided you wanted his money, of course."

Betty Ann stared at her. "What kinda shit is that? Why wouldn't I have the right to marry him if he wanted to? He told me he'd never been married before in his life!"

Greta's smile got wider. She was beginning to remind Betty Ann of a small shark she had watched some kids catch over at the San Clemente pier.

Greta said, "That's right. Jackson was never married."

"Well, I sure as hell wasn't either!"

"Oh, yeah? In the state of California—hell, in every state that I know of, including Utah—you can't marry someone else if you are already married and never got a divorce. That's called bigamy, and that's illegal."

"A divorce! What the hell I need a divorce for?" Betty Ann demanded. "I was a sure enough widow! Didn't you just say you come here because you heard about it? My first husband was dead long before I married Jackson."

"Maybe he was." Greta sniffed. "And maybe he wasn't. Personally I don't see how he coulda been dead all this time and still sitting in that car in that horrible lake. I think the whole story of him being dead for thirty-eight years is a load of bunk. But that's up to the cops to figure out. The point is, my lawyer can't find any evidence that you ever filed for divorce or desertion or—"

She glanced up at the man.

"Death in absentia," he offered.

"Right. Before you married my brother. So unless you have proof of that—"

"I don't have to prove it!" Betty Ann said through bared teeth. "Jackson and I was legally married long after my first husband was dead, even if nobody knew he was dead."

"Including you?" Greta jumped up. "Which makes your marriage to Jackson a deliberate fraud. I said at his funeral that I'd take you to court to get what's mine, and I'm sure as hell gonna do it now. You're a fraud and a cheap gold-digger and maybe even a murderess, and you got no right to his money or this house or anything else!"

Betty Ann's mouth fell open. "F'Chrissakes, even in a common law marriage, *which it wasn't*, I got the right to inherit Jackson's property! That's California law too, if you ain't aware of it!"

Greta stepped toward her and pointed a bony finger. "You made no effort to get a divorce or declare your first husband dead. You *say* you didn't know he was dead, so that means you entered into a marriage with my brother with intent to commit fraud. Phil, here, says I can break that will!"

Betty Ann glanced at him. He nodded and spread his feet farther apart, as if to brace himself against an attack. She opened her mouth, but no words came to her mind.

Louisa had not spoken a word, obviously taken in by the drama. Now she said to Greta, "You're just plumb crazy, bitch! Tom disappeared thirty-eight goddam years ago, and if that ain't reason enough for considering a marriage over, I don't know what is!"

Greta huffed, "We'll see. As far as I'm concerned, as far as the *law* is concerned, you were never legally married to my brother, and that just makes you his whore. You got no right to his bank accounts or his insurance money. Whatever money you've spent since he died, you will damn well pay back. But first, I want you out of this house! Lock, stock and barrel, and all of your shit, outa this house. Or I will bring the Sheriff up here to throw you out! That's if you aren't put in prison for murder first!"

Betty Ann felt the blood rush into her face, down into her hands, the fire of it pounding in her fingertips as she clenched her fists. She advanced on Greta. For the first time Greta lost her confident look. She stepped back.

"Don't you touch me!" she screeched. "Don't you dare touch me! I'll have you arrested for assault! Phil! Do something!"

Phil hesitated.

Betty Ann glared at them both. "I don't care what crazy notions you got in that stupid head of yours. This is my home, and if you don't get out now, I will be the one doin' the arrestin'. For trespassin'. This is the house Jackson bought for me because he wanted me to have a nice place to live in for the rest of my life, and no greedy little shit of a sister is gonna take it away from me!"

"I looked it up!" Greta shrieked, still backing up. She came up against the edge of the sofa and clutched her purse with both hands, not taking her frightened eyes off Betty Ann. "This house isn't in your name."

"He put it in his name and mine, together. When he died, I put it in mine."

Greta shook her head wildly. Her black bob waggled like a loose football helmet. Her chest panted under the sweater set. "The name on the deed is 'Beaumont'. If you were never divorced from your first husband, then your name is not legally Beaumont. It never was!"

"Beaumont's my name, and it always will be my name. We were married before a Justice of the Peace, and you are not taking my home away from me! Now get out before I pick up your skinny ass and throw it out!" She advanced another step.

"Fine! I'll go! But I'll be back with the Sheriff tomorrow, and we'll just see what he has to say about it! C'mon, Phil!"

She bolted to the front door, tore it open and ran out. Phil straightened his suit coat and followed at a more dignified pace. Betty Ann watched as Greta jumped into the passenger seat, barely waiting for Phil to get behind the wheel before screaming at him to take off. She was still screaming as the car backed out of the driveway and took off down the street.

Chapter Five

Betty Ann blew out a breath, gently closed the door and returned to the family room.

Louisa had settled back on the sofa with her feet up. "I can't believe that silly bitch thinks she can walk in here and take your house away from you. Don't family always seem to come outa the woodwork as soon as they smell somethin' in their favor. She's tryin' to take advantage of you in your hour of grief, and that's just mean and hateful."

Betty Ann wondered for a moment if Louisa was referring to her grief over Jackson's death two years before, or the loss of Tom after thirty-eight years.

"Greta never did like Jackson marrying me," she said. The adrenalin rush she felt as she had faced off Greta was now draining from her. Tension had racked up a headache in the back of her neck. She sat heavily in the brown lounger. "She never cared that he was happier with me than he'd ever been in his life. I think until he met me, she figured he was a life-long bachelor and she'd get everything he had when he died. Musta been a pretty nasty shock when I come along and busted up all her plans for a juicy retirement. I wonder how she found out so fast about them finding Tom. You s'pose it's nationwide news already?"

"Don't worry," said Louisa, her eyes on the television. "If you and Jackson was married, ain't nobody gonna take anything away from you. Wives always inherit. Just like you inherited that land up there from Tom."

She paused and picked up the remote to mute the sound. "You did inherit it, didn't you?"

"Yeah, but I guess I better go get it put in my name, now that I know Tom's for sure dead."

"You ain't never done that?" Louisa looked shocked.

"I never wanted to see it again. I don't think I even cared back then if the state took it for back taxes. Might have been simpler if they had. What a mess. But at least that's something Greta can't take away from me, even if the government already has."

Louisa was silent for a moment. "If you did lose this place, then, you gonna go up there to live?"

Betty Ann rubbed fiercely at her temples, willing the pain not to migrate forward from the back of her head. "I ain't gonna lose this place, Lou. I'll burn it down before I let that woman just take it from me."

"Really?"

"Oh, hell, no." She sighed. "I ain't goin' to jail for arson just because of her. But no matter what, I'd move down into town, not up in the hills all by myself."

Louisa picked at the stitching on the leather sofa with her bitten nails. "Betty Ann, *did* you file for divorce from Tom?"

Something in her voice got Betty Ann's attention through her headache. She looked up.

"I—to be honest, I don't rightly remember for sure. I know I was going to. I remember intending to. So I must've!"

"So how come that she-bitch said they couldn't find any record?"

Betty Ann hit the padded arm of the chair with her fist. "I don't know! My head was so screwed up at the time. For years I just sorta moved through each day without thinkin' about it, without thinkin' about Tom or the cabin or *anything*. You and Barry and just about everybody else took off, seemed like. I had nobody to talk to about it. Mama had had her stroke, and I had to take care of her, so there was more important things to worry about."

She slumped back and rested her head on the back of the chair. "You know, I do remember talking to some guy in the End of the Line, years before I met Jackson. He was a lawyer, or said he was. Anyway, he seemed fairly sober at the time. Told me that after that much time had passed—" She frowned. "Don't rightly remember how much time it had been. Anyway, he told me there wouldn't be any problem about me filin' for desertion and gettin' married again. I didn't pay all that much attention because at the time I didn't think I'd ever want to get married again. I wasn't even thinking about the property. I guess I still felt like I was married to Tom."

"All them years?" said Louisa.

"Yeah." She sighed. "Greta's right—I didn't know Tom was dead. Maybe I thought that enough time made it the same as divorce, but what if she's right! What if I go to court, and some stupid judge that sees it her way?"

"Sure would be better if you had some papers or something to show that you tried."

"Yeah. Listen, I think I did at least part of what that lawyer told me to. I went up to Riverside and got some papers to fill out. But I got to feelin' so bad about it, I guess I just kept putting it off. Goin' and gettin' a divorce woulda been like sayin' they was right, all them assholes that told me he dumped me. Jackson didn't come along until thirty years later. By then, it was all like a movie, or somethin' that happened to somebody else. It just never occurred to me that marryin' Jackson might not be legal."

A silence fell. On the television screen talking heads came and went silently.

"What was it he told you to do?" Louisa asked. "That lawyer guy. He tell you to make a will or anything?"

After a moment, Betty Ann grimaced. "I can't remember, Lou. It was too long ago. But Jackson and I made wills. Now that he's gone, anything happens to me, it all goes to my niece, along with Mama's house."

"Includin' the property up there?"

"I guess so." Betty Ann's sat up and her eyes sharpened. "Oh, my God."

"What?"

"Lou!" She felt excitement starting to mount. "I remember now, he told me I should make sure that piece of land would be listed in any papers I filed for divorce. He said with Tom not there to contest anything, I should ask for everything to be put in my name, even that property whether I wanted it or not. I think...yeah! I remember havin' to go to Seddleton to the courthouse to look up the lot number! I needed to know exactly what parcel to put in the application so the judge would grant me title to it. And then on the way home I was passing the studio, so I stopped. Carried the stuff up to the cabin to look it over." She fell back against the chair again, her headache forgotten. "Oh, sweet Jesus, I'd forgotten that. It was spring, and so pretty up there."

"So you did do it," said Louisa. "You got a divorce. For what? Desertion?"

"No, nobody does that anymore. In California there's only two ways to get a divorce — irreconcilable differences, or declare the guy insane. Couldn't declare Tom insane, no matter how crazy he was, 'cause he wasn't there. So..." Her brow knotted. "So I must've used 'irreconcilable differences'. If I got a divorce."

"But you don't remember," Louisa said.

"It's comin' back," Betty Ann said, a trifle defensively. "All this time I was thinkin' I never went back up to the studio again, but I guess I did, just that once. Before that I worked and waited for Tom to come back. Then somewhere along the line I stopped waitin'. Just put it all further and further back in my mind. When I stopped at the cabin on the way back from the courthouse, all of a sudden he was real again. The smell of the trees and the sound of the crick—it was early enough there was water in it. I could almost hear Tom talkin' about the colors of the leaves and all." She closed her eyes.

Louisa said, "So you think you mighta just never finished getting a divorce after all? Like that she-bitch said?"

Betty Ann felt tears come into her eyes, tears of weariness, tears of frustration, tears of grief. Tears she had never let herself shed for Tom out of anger that he had left her, whether on purpose or not. Tears that she thought she was too philosophical to shed for Jackson, at their age. Tears that she had been too stubborn to shed for herself, getting left behind yet again.

She clenched her teeth and forced herself to overcome the urge to self-pity. She had never had any use for it, and she wasn't going to start now.

"I did *something*, Lou. I at least did part of what I was supposed to. I'm sure of that."

"Well, I think you oughta make damn sure of what you did do. You must have some kinda papers layin' around to prove it. Would you of packed anything away somewhere? Where would they be? A closet? Desk drawer? Or maybe some box out in the garage?"

"I'm pretty sure I didn't bring anything like that with me when we moved in here."

"Well, you wouldn'ta just throwed 'em away. Where else would you have stuck something like that? You got a safe deposit box?"

"Sure. At least, Jackson did. But I never got into it until after he died. I'm sure I never put anything like that in it."

"Well, dammit, Betty Ann. You stash anything at your mother's house?"

"Cleaned everything out when she died. Gave the house to my niece, she's got three kids and her old man skipped. I didn't need it, I had this place."

"Shit, you sure you didn't leave something there just for safe keeping? Maybe we should go look, see if there's a box you stuck up in the attic and forgot about."

"Louisa, that bungalow doesn't have an attic. I'm tellin' you, there wasn't nothing like that when I gave the house to Sherry! I took all Mama's records with me, and there wasn't anything amongst it that had anything to do with Tom."

"Then where the hell else would you have put it? You didn't leave them up at the studio, did you?"

"I dunno. I don't actually remember having them with me when I got back to the apartment. So maybe that's what I did. Maybe I stuck 'em somewhere up there so I could forget about it."

"Worked good," muttered Louisa.

Betty Ann ignored her. "Tomorrow's my night off. I think I'll just take a drive up to the cabin in the morning. You wanta come along? You can get a better look at this place you think you're gonna fix up with some paint and a mop rag."

"Whatser-face said she's comin' back tomorrow. With the Sheriff."

"Well, we'll see if she can talk Pete into breakin' in, 'cause we ain't gonna be here to open the door!" She paused on her way to the stairs. "Ain't this the pits, Lou? I go from having two husbands to having none, from owning a house but maybe I don't, and from thinking Tom still owned the property, and turns out it's been mine for thirty-eight years. And people callin' me a murderess, to boot!"

Louisa called out, "I guess I'll finish this movie. Anyway, I didn't eat much for supper. So maybe I'll fix myself a snack."

"Help yourself, but put some of that stuff in the dishwasher, will you?" She made her slow way up the stairs, pulling herself with one hand on the bannister. It seemed like the stairs were getting steeper all the time. It was another reason to think about moving to a smaller place. Something all on one floor and down in Del Sueño so she could walk to the End of the Line. She would need someplace with a garage, so she could lock up the Thunderbird. She could afford somewhere nice now, thanks to Jackson. She owed him so much, she thought as she changed to pajamas and washed off her makeup. Bless him, he was still taking care of her. If only he hadn't left her to enjoy it by herself.

She fell wearily into the massive, cold and lonely bed.

Betty Ann was up early, cooking bacon and eggs. Louisa stumbled into the kitchen with her hair looking like a cat had been licking it.

"Hurry up and eat," Betty Ann said. "We need to get on the road."

"Why we gotta leave so early?"

"It's seven o'clock, Lou, and it'll take around three hours to get there. We don't want to be finding our way back down after dark. We can stop at a taco place I know of for lunch."

Louisa made a face. "Never did like that Mexican food."

"How'd you grow up here and not eat Mexican food?"

"I didn't. If you remember, I grew up in Jersey, Betty Ann, same as Tom. I didn't come out west 'til after you guys met."

"That's right. I forgot."

"And soon as you met him, you quit school to marry him." Louisa sounded oddly resentful.

"Funny the things I've forgotten," said Betty Ann. She slid the food onto two plates. "I can't remember when you weren't hangin' around with the rest of us. You were what? Twenty-six? You looked like you were about fourteen. Old Mr. Meagan kept carding you down at the End of the Line."

"Stupid," Louisa grumped as she sat down at the table. "I didn't never drink anything but Coke anyway."

"Didn't you ever drink anything stronger?" Betty Ann set a plate in front of her.

"Nah. I never liked beer or whiskey. Still don't." Louisa slurped up her scrambled eggs and crunched into a strip of bacon. "That's why I never got a job bein' a bartender, y'know. Who wants a bartender that don't drink?"

"Most owners. At least you won't drink up their profits. When you're done eating, get some Cokes outa the fridge and put 'em in that little cooler over there, will ya. I can make some cheese sandwiches to take along if you like."

Louisa wrinkled her nose. "Cheese makes me burp. Aincha got no peanut butter?"

"No. I guess you'll have to suffer or eat tacos." Betty Ann had not slept well and was not in a mood to cater.

The drive up into the foothills took longer than Betty Ann remembered. By the time she was on the right road, Louisa was hungry enough to nibble at one of the tacos they bought at a stand just outside of Seddleton. The small town's courthouse was on the main street and shared a long one-story building with the police department. Betty Ann looked at the low brick wall enclosing the entrance in a simple half circle.

"I think this is it. There's the police station at the other end." She made a small face.

"I thought you said you been here before."

"That was a long time ago. It was a different building. They musta built a new one."

The woman seated at a desk behind the counter looked bored until they walked in. She jumped up with delight. Upon hearing what Betty Ann wanted, she pulled out a plat map and found the property.

"How long since anyone's looked up the deed?" she asked.

"I'm not sure. I couldn't find any papers."

"Well, it's public record. Is it in your name?"

"It's still in my husband's, I think." Betty Ann spelled it out. "My late husband's. He died thirty-eight years ago."

"Oh my, sweetie. That goes back a long ways. It won't be in the computer, that's for sure, so I'll have to go down to the basement. Haven't been down there since I started working here. Might take me a while."

"I don't know when I can come back. How long do you think?"

"Haven't the faintest," the woman said cheerfully. "Why don't you go on across to the cafe and have lunch?"

"Already had it," said Louisa grumpily.

"Here." Betty Ann gave her some money. "Go get some dessert and bring me back a donut."

As Louisa disappeared out the door, the woman said, "My name's Dorothy, sweetie. You make yourself comfortable on that bench over there."

Forty-five minutes later Louisa had not returned. Dorothy came puffing up from a stairway almost hidden behind the file cabinets, holding a fat file.

"Found it, dear. Looks like the taxes have been paid regular, at least."

"Really?" Betty Ann said blankly. "By who?"

Dorothy peered at the papers. "Somebody named 'Abigail Hoffman'."

"Never heard of her. So she owns it now."

"Oh, no, dear. The deed's in your name. You sure you don't know this woman? Don't seem right some stranger'd pay taxes on property she don't own. Maybe a rich aunt you never met?"

"Tom's aunt, maybe, but that name doesn't sound right. And she died, that's how he got it. Wait. Did you say it's in *my* name? Not Tom's?"

"S'right. Betty Ann Stearns, right?"

"It's Beaumont now. Betty Ann Beaumont."

"No problem. Just bring in a copy of your marriage certificate and we can change it." She frowned. "You thought it was in his name?"

"Well, I never changed it. You sure it hasn't got his name on it?"

"Nope. No Tom or Thomas or anything. He musta put in your name before he died."

"Could he do that without telling me?" Betty Ann felt dizzy. Tom had never said a word about putting the property in her name.

"Oh, sure, sweetie. Bein's you're his wife. You just get yourself a title agent, bring in the original papers from when you bought it or inherited, and pay the court fees. Then sign over the deed in the presence of witnesses. Usually the person you're signing it over to is there, but I don't guess they have to be. People put things in their kids' names all the time to avoid the death taxes after they're gone. So long as it isn't done for purposes of fraud, it's perfectly legal. Makes it nice, doesn't it – you didn't have to go through all the rigmarole to get it put in your name when he died. Even though you're his widow, probate's still kinda a pain in the patoot, know what I mean? Anyway, this year's taxes aren't due until November, so you're good, sweetie."

"What about the taxes? Is that legal, for someone else to pay, who isn't on the deed?"

The woman snickered. "Sweetie, the government don't care who pays it, long as they get the money. The trick is making sure it goes to the right property, if the name on the check is different. Like I tell people, always put the lot number on the check. Could save you a lot of grief."

"Is that how she paid, this Hoffman person?"

"Ahh...yep, says here by check, every time for the last thirty-some years or so, looks like. The tax statements were sent to..." Dorothy lifted a faded yellow form from the pile, frowned at it and then frowned at Betty Ann. "Here's the change of address form that you signed."

Chapter Six

Betty Ann stared at the form in Dorothy's hand. "Me! I've never signed anything like that!"

Dorothy pushed the form across the counter and pointed. "Isn't that your signature?"

Betty Ann stared. "It doesn't look like it."

"Well, sweetie, it sure don't make much sense for someone to fake your signature just so they could pay your taxes for you," Dorothy said reasonably. "The tax statements been sent to the new address for... looks like at least thirty years. You think maybe you just forgot about it?"

She thought of that lost week, that forgotten time before she woke up in the hospital.

"What's the address it got changed to?"

Dorothy read it off and Betty Ann wrote it in her purse notepad. It was an address in La Mesa.

"I don't remember ever knowing someone from there. But if this Hoffman woman paid the taxes last year, then she's probably still at that address, right?"

Dorothy shrugged.

"Did she pay in person?" Betty Ann asked. "Do you happen to remember what she looked like?"

"Oh, sweetie, taxes have to be paid by November first, and I didn't start workin' here until last December, after old Mrs.

Reynolds died. Before that I was in Cal-Trans in Riverside. So even if she did come in personally, I wouldn't have seen her." She flipped through the papers in the file. "Doesn't say anything about whether the checks came by mail or in person. I guess nobody ever cared, why would they? Well, just the same, I'd go through all the rigmarole to get the property put in your new married name just to be sure. And put in another change of address, I should think."

When she left, Dorothy seemed genuinely sad to see her go. Betty Ann crossed to the café to find Louisa had engaged a young couple in conversation. They looked rather desperate, so after she got a coffee and donut to go, Betty Ann said it was time to hit the road.

"What's wrong?" said Louisa as they walked back to the Thunderbird.

"Nothing. Lou, did Tom ever say anything about putting the property in my name?"

"Not that I recall. You mean you own it straight out?" Louisa frowned.

"Apparently. But I don't remember anything like that. Why would Tom do that?"

"Dunno, sounds kinda crazy to me. So if anything happens to you, it goes to your next relative, not his?"

"Well, that's a nice thought."

"Sorry." Louisa got in the passenger side of the car. "But I still wanta live there, okay?"

"Lou, you ever heard of someone named Abigail Hoffman?"

"Shit, no. Sounds like one a my great-aunts from Jersey. Who is she?"

"Apparently she's the person who's been paying the taxes on the place for thirty-eight years. Could she be somebody Tom knew?"

Louisa's brow wrinkled. "Well, if she was, I never heard of her. 'Course, after this many years I prob'ly forgot. But how come she never let you know she was payin' for it or even get it put in her own name?"

"Beats me. I don't know how she would get it in her name unless she bought it at a tax auction, but it looks like she didn't do that. She just paid the taxes for thirty-some years and left it in my name. It's weird."

For the next few miles, Betty Ann listened with one ear to Louisa's chattering about her great-aunts. It occurred to her to wonder if they would find some crazy woman had taken up residence in the cabin. If so, what could she do about it? Would she have to pay back the money the woman had spent, in order to get her off the property?

Ms. Hoffman might have been part of the week of her collapse, the days she had never remembered. Maybe she had met her then; maybe Tom had introduced them. But in that case, why hadn't the woman let her know that she was paying the taxes? Why had she never been in touch?

She sipped on her coffee and drove with one hand until the road became so full of potholes that she needed both hands. She put the cup in a holder and eased her hips where they felt like they had become embedded in the seat. The smell of the leftover tacos had started to permeate the car.

"What were you were figurin' on eatin' up here, anyway?" she asked when Louisa paused for breath. "Roots and berries?"

"I saw a store in town. I can stock up on bread and milk and stuff."

"Lou, there's no refrigerator, remember? We always brought ice up with us and kept it in that old cooler. And it barely lasted a whole weekend. When Tom was up here longer than that, he ate beef jerky and drank warm beer."

"I can buy ice," Louisa said stubbornly. "Anyway, how much longer? I gotta pee."

"Shouldn't of drank so much ice tea."

"Gotta wash that Mexican food down with something, and Coke gives me burps nowadays."

After a moment Betty Ann said, "Lou, what kinda stuff did you and Tom do together? You ever get in any trouble?"

"What'dya mean, trouble?" she said warily.

"I mean all that stuff you guys used to talk about. You and Tom and Barry. The protests and everything."

"Oh, that. Not much. Marched. Waved signs. Called the cops pigs. You know."

"Were you in that march with Martin Luther King? In Selma?"

"Shit, Betty Ann, that was in '63. I think I was twelve, 'n' you were what? Four? Five? I think Tom was outa high school by then. We was in the same neighborhood, but I didn't start hangin' out with them till after I left school. Not that there was much hangin' out at first. Tom met Barry after college and both of 'em was piss-poor, so they was workin' two jobs when they wasn't goin' to SDS meetings."

"SDS?"

"Students for a Democratic Society," Louisa said in a mincing tone. "Said they was 'organizin'." She snorted. "More like smokin' weed 'n' gettin' laid alla time."

"You guys were part of all that? Tom ever get in any big trouble? Like those riots in Chicago?"

"Him? Nah, of course not. Dick talked about doin' something radical, sometimes, but you know Tom, he don't even like bein' around violence. I think Chicago scared him. Me, I just hung around, made sandwiches for the meetings."

"Who's Dick?"

"Just one of the guys in SDS. Why? Where were you in '68?" Louisa's shift in conversational direction seemed overly casual to Betty Ann, but it could have been because she really hadn't had much to do with the serious events. She was far too lazy and fearful.

"I was about ten years old," said Betty Ann, "and a million miles away from anything that was happening. Watched the war on TV, thought it was cool until we started seeing the bodies. So you guys were at that Chicago thing?"

Again Louisa sounded cautious. "We was there at first. We thought it was going to be a peaceful protest. Then Jerry Rubin and them guys got crazy, and the pigs started crackin' heads, so we split. Hey, didja know I met Tom Hayden once?"

"Jane Fonda's husband?"

"Yeah. It was some meeting with a bunch of SDS people, and I fixed him a sandwich. He said 'thanks' and gave me this really big smile," she said proudly. "He was nice."

Betty Ann drove for a moment, running thoughts through her mind.

"So you guys weren't mixed up in any of that nasty stuff?"

"Hell, no. None of us did anything all that bad. It's not like we were really part of the Weathermen or anything."

Betty Ann took her eyes off the road to glance at her. "What'dya mean, you weren't *really* part of the Weathermen? Were you or weren't you?"

"I mean we weren't really, that's all." Her wariness became defensive. "SDS was okay, but those Weather guys were losers, even most of the SDS didn't like 'em. I told Tom they was gonna end up in jail, they hang out with that bunch." She snorted. "Barry said I didn't understand what they was tryin' to do."

"I heard they were tryin' to kill people. Blew up buildings."

"Blew themselves up, more like. They were stupid. That's why Tom and I didn't like 'em. So we took off."

"Together?"

"Not really. I mean, we kinda stuck together for a while after Chicago. Tom was datin' a friend of mine and they let me sleep on the couch."

Of course.

"Then he said he wanted to go California, see Haight 'n' Ash. Took off with a bunch of hippies in a camper truck. There wasn't enough room for me, and anyway it looked like a long trip with nothin' to eat but Cocoa Puffs. I went to up to Woodstock with some friends and nearly caught pneumonia. Bummed a ride back to Jersey, to my folks' house. Why you so interested in that shit?"

"I dunno. I thought maybe something happened in Chicago or somewheres else, somebody would come back and shoot him for, that's all."

"Ten years later?"

"I'm grasping here, Lou, okay? Why would anybody else kill him? You got any ideas?"

"I don't remember him ever doin' anything that anybody'd shoot him for. Even back in '68, let alone ten years later. Is that the bridge we gotta cross?"

"Shit." She had almost driven past it.

"This has grown up a lot," Louisa said nervously.

"Thirty-eight years' worth." Betty Ann turned the nose of her car onto the tiny gravel turn-out, wishing she'd borrowed or rented another car. This was no place for a pampered low-slung sports car. As if in agreement and complaint, a loud scraping groan came from underneath. Betty Ann winced. "Shit. Hit a rock."

Louisa scowled at the bridge. "You ain't gonna drive over that thing, are you?"

A weedy ditch made a gully between the turnout and the tangled brush on the other side. The short bridge that spanned it wasn't much more than wooden planks on a frame stretched across the gap, connecting the turn-off to a rutted lane that disappeared over a rise. Betty Ann remembered the bridge being solid enough for a car to cross over, but now it sagged to one side and looked loose enough to slide into the ditch at the slightest touch.

"There's planks missin' off it," said Louisa.

"Just the one." But it made for too narrow a width for any car to pass over, even one as small as the Thunderbird. She stared at it and pondered.

"We used to drive Barry's hearse across that thing," she mused, "loaded up with a bunch of construction wood the boys boosted from midnight lumber supply. Or cans of old paint that people gave us. Near as I could ever tell, Tom's improvements just made it look worse. I guess the first thing I'll have to do is have that bridge replaced. I wonder what the roof on the cabin looks like."

She pulled the Thunderbird forward, as far off the road as she could get, yanked on the parking brake and killed the engine. It gave a sigh of relief and settled to pinging away in the cool air.

"C'mon," she said. When Louisa sat looking doubtfully at the path up the hill, she added, "It's just over that ridge a bit. The bridge looks strong enough to walk across, and the path isn't too overgrown. You can sit here and wait if you want, but I expect to spend some time up there, checkin' out the damage."

Grumbling under her breath, Louisa slid out of the car and let the door slam shut. Betty Ann started across the bridge and then turned back to make sure the car's doors weren't locked. They hadn't seen anyone in the last hour, but kids had been known to stop by a lone car out of mischief. If the doors were locked, the cloth top of the convertible might prove too much of an invitation for serious thieves to slice through. She would rather they helped themselves to the custom CD player than have to replace the ragtop.

Louisa followed Betty Ann, mincing across the boards in her soft tennis shoes. Betty Ann plunged on up the hill ahead of her.

"Ouch," said Louisa, pulling away a bramble that had caught her ankle.

"Shoulda wore some boots," Betty Ann called over her shoulder.

"These are all I have," came the plaintive reply.

"First thing you'll need to invest in, then, if you're planning on livin' up here." Betty Ann knew she sounded cold-hearted and didn't care. All the way up into the hills, Louisa had been full of ideas, babbling about how much fun it would be to chop wood to cook and to live by kerosene lanterns at night. Livin' up here for free sounded good until she got here, Betty Ann thought sourly. They hadn't even reached the cabin, and she was already crabbing.

Betty Ann felt more sympathetic half an hour later, when she realized her memory had played her false. They had tramped up and down and then up again, fighting sagebrush and small manzanita saplings that had snuck into the rutted twin tracks. They paused at the top of the third rise, puffing and wiping their forearms across their sweaty faces.

Below them, what looked like a small frontier homestead lay quiet in the tiny valley. Betty Ann felt a small smile touch her lips. She had forgotten just how pretty the place was, as long as you liked what Tom had called 'rustic' and Barry had called 'American primitive'.

The small cabin, what Tom always called 'the studio', had survived better than Betty Ann had expected. It still looked whole, and the tiny outhouse down in a gulch hadn't fallen over. Beside the humble cabin was a large corrugated tin shed. It had held anything Tom didn't want to risk keeping inside the cabin, where in cool weather they relaxed by an evening fire. Things like cans of paint, cleaning fluids, turpentine, kerosene, fuel for their secondhand bushwhacker, along with tools for fixing plumbing or walls, oily car parts in case one of the vehicles broke down, and various bits of junk that had caught Tom's eye along the road. He had sometimes, she remembered, thought of joining the "trash art" school and had spent money on arc welders and hammers. Nothing had come of it.

With a sigh she led Louisa down the lane to the flat weedy dirt pad that stretched across in front of the cabin's roofed porch. There were some faint oil stains in the dirt, evidence of the days a vehicle could get up there.

The porch ran the length of the front of the building, and it was where they had congregated after a long day of artistic creation. She ran her hand along the bannister. The thick red paint had peeled and faded until it was nearly the same color as the manzanita wood underneath. She thought of how they had spent many hot nights sitting outside, contemplating a clear black sky packed with stars, conversation drifting easily from one topic to another.

Tom had called it solving the mysteries of the universe, and he and Barry had done most of the talking. She was too young then to formulate many opinions of her own, other than a few vague political ideals. She had, she realized now, sincerely believed in those ideals at the time and felt strongly about them, though she had been awkward and inexperienced in expressing them. The two men had scoffed at her every urgent pronouncement.

"Baby doll," Tom had said her, "you're wastin' your time worrying about who gets elected president. Whoever it is will be just another political crank like the rest of 'em. And in the end the results will be the same. The rich will get richer, and the poor will keep on working in the factories of the rich 'cause they ain't got no other choice if they want to feed their families. Either that, or fighting their wars. That's why I ain't gonna add to the population problem or the employment problem. I am a free artist or nothing."

"Here, here!" exclaimed Barry as he saluted Tom with a beer bottle that glinted in the moonlight. His usual spot was on the top porch step, his skinny back against the bannister, one foot up on the porch and his knee supporting the hand holding the bottle. He brushed his long blond hair back. "If this were a decent self-respecting country, we artists would be revered and provided for, instead of having to suck up to a bunch of rich assholes who think owning what we've created makes them something special."

"Well, we ain't in no country like that," said Betty Ann, "so just how in hell would you two manage to drink beer and live on your artistic talents, if I didn't work in a goddam bar all week for one a them paychecks you got such a low opinion of?"

"You are my patron, my sweet young thing, my muse, my rich and beautiful inspiration." Tom had pulled her onto his lap and kissed her until she lost her angry tautness and laughed. Barry brooded until their groping got intense. Then he murmured, "G'night," and slipped off into the dark in the direction of his hearse.

Louisa's voice brought her rushing back through the years with a whoosh.

"Door ain't locked." Louisa had pulled the dusty screen door open and was pushing on the knob of the heavy wooden door, forcing it inward an inch, where it stopped. "Sump'n is blockin' it, though."

Chapter Seven

Betty Ann helped her push, and with a grinding rush they pushed the door back far enough that they could enter the tiny front room. The blockage was a dead tree branch. It wasn't large, but Betty Ann looked up to see a gaping hole in the roof. It hadn't been visible from the path.

"Well, hell, I guess that's another thing that'll have to be fixed right away. Lucky the last years have been dry, or the whole roof probably would've fell in. Be careful where you walk, though," she cautioned as Louisa went through to the kitchen. "Floor boards might be rotted like the porch steps."

She glanced around the front room. It was roughly twenty feet by twenty and took up the most floor space in the cabin. Beside the door was the only window. Against the back wall leaned the back seat of a Dodge van, rescued from a curbside dump and put into use as a sofa. Its upholstery looked tired and the metal crosspieces were powdery with oxidation. In front of it was one of the ubiquitous cable spools used in the Sixties and Seventies for coffee tables.

She had gotten many a vicious splinter, and Tom had promised to sand it down, another bit of improvement that never got done. Instead, in the evenings, he and Barry worked on a project to turn the table into "living art" by setting cigarettes to smolder around the rim. She could still see the dozens of burn marks making a pattern around its edge. It appalled her now that they could have been so careless in brushfire-menaced southern California.

The small stone fireplace in the right-hand wall was heaped with dirt and leaves that had drifted down the chimney onto the ashes left from old fires. She would have to make sure nothing had built a nest further up the chimney before they tried to light a fire.

She dropped her purse on the cable spool, crossed to the bedroom door and pushed at it gingerly. It swung inward. The windows in this room were so dirty they blocked most of the sunlight, and the little room swam in permanent dusk. A double-sized bed filled one wall.

She felt her breath catch in her throat. The sagging mattress was still covered with a faded, slightly tattered red and orange Indian blanket. The bed showed little sign of being used by wildlife, two-legged or four. She was glad. Under that blanket was where, on cold nights, she and Tom would cuddle after working up an envelope of body heat by making love.

In the wall above the bed was a long window. When the moon was up, Tom had lulled them both to sleep by drowsily describing how he would paint the sky, using dark orange for the moon with maybe titanium white to paint it in a midnight blue sky, with a touch of mars black along the horizon, or maybe raw umber if the light called for it. Tom's favorite colors had been red, orange, and intense black. Her eye had become surfeited with hues of strident emotion, when she would have preferred the soft silver moonlight outside the window.

"Hey, Betty Ann, there's still some cans of food out here. But the stove don't work."

"F'Chrissakes, Lou!" she called. "Don't touch that stove. It's propane, and the damn canister's probably dangerous."

"Don't look that old. I think I can hook it up."

Betty Ann turned her back on the little bedroom and went into the kitchen area. It was only a kitchenette, with sink and cabinets tucked under a long wall that contained windows looking out at the hills behind the cabin. The two-burner stove occupied the west end. Louisa was holding an ancient canister of propane.

"Put that down!" Betty Ann ordered. "Don't you dare try to hook it up."

With a pout Louisa complied. "Well, how else you gonna find out if it works?"

Betty Ann ignored that and looked around. There was no table or chairs – they had eaten from battered tin plates balanced on their laps in the front room in winter, or out on the picnic table in summer, batting away the few insects that thrived on the dry mountain air.

Across from the kitchen windows, a set of shelves hung on the wall, full of cans with faded labels. A crushed cereal box lay flat on the floor, it's corner chewed off. Small creatures had had a tasty breakfast of Kix. Otherwise, the wildlife seemed to have left the place alone.

"Where's the fridge?" Lou asked.

"I told you, we never had one. We brought up bags of ice when we came here and kept it in a cooler. That should be around here somewhere." She groped under the cast iron sink and pulled out a plastic tub that had been lying on its side. "Wonder what happened to the lid. Just as well it was tipped over, I guess. Wouldn't want to find some poor dead squirrel that couldn't get back out."

"You see anything interesting in the bedroom?" Louisa put a chipped mug back on a shelf and dusted her hands.

"No."

So many memories. It was more overwhelming than she had thought it would be, and just as bad as she had always feared. It was why she had never managed to talk herself into returning once she had given up on Tom. Eventually the reasons not to return had seemed insurmountable.

Suddenly the years were like a pressure in her chest. She couldn't breathe. She yanked at the little hook lock on the back door, dragged it open and shoved the screen door wide on its shrieking spring. Heedless of the state of the tiny back stoop, she flew down the steps, put her hands on her knees, coughed and waited as the faintness faded away. Wearily she straightened up and stood for a moment, catching her breath.

"You okay?" Louisa called anxiously from inside the screen door.

"Fine," said Betty Ann.

Louisa disappeared back into the cabin. Betty Ann was loath to join her. There was a slight buzz of insects from spindly trees at the side of the yard, but she could hear no traffic, no passing thump of music from a car radio. No children called out in their high voices; there was not even the underlying almost subconscious sound of the modern electronic world with its humming telephone wires and buzzing traffic lights.

The silence lay gently on her ears, and gradually her pulse and her mind settled. There had been times when she had enjoyed the peace and quiet in spite of Tom's irritation when other people invaded his "studio" space.

She heard the echo of the rifle report before she registered the thud in the shingle wall near her head.

For one instant she froze, baffled. Then anger surged and she shouted at the hills, "Hey, you damn fool! There's people down here!"

Silence. Then another *pock* splintered the shingle an inch closer, sending wood dust stinging against her cheek. She started to shout even more fiercely than before and then felt her throat dry up. There was no wind, no noise, no answering call. No movement. Whoever had fired the rifle had to have heard her cry out. It was possible they had run when they heard her. It was possible they were standing up there, too appalled at the near accident to react.

On the other hand, there was the second shot. The trees, the brown grasses, the hills seemed suddenly to have a taut feeling, and she felt that primitive awareness that signifies to the senses that someone is listening, waiting. An odd shiver went through her, and her heart started to pound in her throat. She grabbed at the screen door and rushed through the kitchenette. There was no sign of Louisa. The front door was ajar.

"Louisa!" she cried, yelling as much for the unseen watcher as for the woman who had gone who-knew-where. "Louisa, stay away! Go down by the car and call the police! Someone's shooting a gun up here!"

Again the silence. There was no sign of anyone. Then Louisa appeared through the trees on the far side of the house, carrying the bag that still had tacos in it.

"Who you shoutin' at?" she called plaintively. "Whaddya mean, someone's shootin'?"

"Get in here!" Betty Ann yelled as she flung the door wider. In an agony of impatience, she waited while Louisa made her wincing way across the stony ground. At the bottom of the steps, finally caught by Betty Ann's urgency, she climbed quickly to the porch. Betty Ann dragged her through the door.

"Get down!" she ordered as she slammed it shut. "Stay away from the window! Somebody's shooting at us!"

Louisa stood in the living room, looking mildly puzzled.

"Whaddya mean—"

"I said get down, dammit!" Betty Ann shoved her to the floor and squatted next to her. Louisa straightened into a sitting position with an irritated grunt.

"Don't move." Betty Ann crawled to the cable spool. She thrust her hand into her purse.

"Damn. Where's my phone? I remember puttin' it in there. Wish I had a gun."

"*Gun*? Whatchu want a gun for?" Louisa started to get up.

"You go ahead and stick your head up again," Betty Ann advised, "if you want to get it shot off."

Louisa sank back to the floor and began to protest again. Betty Ann shushed her with a downward snap of her hand. She hissed, "There's someone out there with a gun. Took two shots at my head. And one of 'em was *after* I yelled to let 'em know I was there."

"They probably didn't hear you. It's just somebody out deer huntin'—"

"Deer season's over a long time ago. Anyway, don't matter what they're aimin' at, if they hit one of us."

"Squirrel, then—"

"Will you shut up! I need to hear if whoever it is, is trying to get closer to the house. And there ain't no squirrels climbing five feet up the outside wall. They were aimin' at me."

"Aw, Betty Ann, c'mon. If the idjit realized he almost shot you, then he prob'ly took off. He'll be halfway outa the county by now."

"I said shut up." Betty Ann duck-walked back through the kitchen to the screen door and peered around the jamb, trying to see as much of the yard and hills as she could. Everything looked empty. Felt empty. After a moment she stood up and walked back into the front room, dusting her hands.

"I guess you're right," she said ruefully. "Just some damn fool shootin' out of season. I should've known that might be a regular pastime up here, with nobody ever around to object."

Louisa grumbled, "I got me a whole new set of bruises, Betty Ann. Hell of a way to treat a friend."

"I was tryin' to keep you from getting your head shot off," Betty Ann snapped. "What were you doing over in the trees, anyway?" She motioned toward the side of the house. "I thought you'd gone back to the car."

"I did. I got hungry again, and that taco stuff's all there is. I know how you feel about that car so I figured I'd gather up the trash and throw it in the garbage up here. I was looking for some kinda garbage can out by the shed. Couldn't find one, though."

"Garbage cans draw coyotes and varmints. We threw everything in a bag and took it back home with us. Unless we built a fire outside in the ring and burned it."

Louisa lit up. "A fire! What fun! Too bad we didn't bring some wienies with us. And marshmallows."

"This ain't the Girl Scouts," Betty Ann said sourly. "And we ain't gonna be up here that long. We didn't bring any water or anything either. Besides," she added with a frown, "I don't think I want to be up here after dark, with some asshole out there firing a rifle."

"How close they come?"

Betty Ann took her outside and pointed to the fresh holes high up and a little to the left of where she had been standing. Louisa peered up at them doubtfully.

"Don't look like bullet holes to me. You sure it ain't, like, a woodpecker or somethin'?"

"I know gun shots, Lou. I can't believe you didn't hear 'em." A thought struck Betty Ann. "Maybe we should dig the bullets out and take 'em to the police. Maybe they could identify the gun. Or no, I guess we should let them dig 'em out. But we'd better hurry and report it so they can. Pretty soon it'll be too dark up here to see your hand in front of your face."

Louisa shivered in spite of the heat. "Why don't we just call 'em and have 'em come up here right quick?"

Betty Ann went back to her purse and finally found her phone hiding under a wallet packed with grocery receipts. She poked at the screen and sighed. "No bars."

"How'n hell did you ever live up here with no bars?"

Betty Ann rolled her eyes. "Lou, cell phones didn't exist the last time we was up here."

"Oh, yeah. I forgot."

"C'mon. No point in looking around anymore. Let's just get the hell out of here."

The sun was sitting on the top of the western hills when they drove back into Seddleton to the courthouse. A black and white patrol car was sliding silently into the evening-lit street at the other end of the building. She pulled into a space in the visitor's lot, two down from where she had parked only that morning.

"Why do I gotta come in?" Louisa whined. "I didn't see anything."

"I showed you the damn holes in the wall. You can verify that I didn't imagine somebody shooting at us." Betty Ann scowled as Louisa struggled out of the car. "You sure you didn't hear anything? Those shots were loud."

"I keep tellin' ya, I didn't hear nothin' that sounded like no shots. Sure seems like if somebody was shootin' a gun up there, I'da heard somethin', doesn't it."

"Anyway, the main thing is the holes," said Betty Ann. "Once they send someone up to look at them, they'll know. You can't miss bullet holes, especially with the bullets still in 'em."

She led the way along the flagstoned path to the glass-fronted police station. The lobby was stuffy with the sun's heat. Along one side of the room was an enclosure with thick glass above a counter. Behind the glass a woman sat sideways to the talk-hole, typing intently on a keyboard and did not look up when they approached.

Betty Ann cleared her throat. There was no reaction.

"'Scuse me. I need to report a shooting."

Without looking up from her computer screen the woman said, "Drive-by? Or a domestic quarrel?"

"Neither. Somebody took pot-shots at us from the trees."

The woman raised her head at that, squinting at Betty Ann doubtfully. But she said nothing, waiting for more.

"There's bullet holes in the wall of the studio," Betty Ann persisted. "The cabin, I mean. If you send somebody up to investigate, they'll find 'em."

"When did this happen?"

"About three o'clock, I think. I didn't make a note of the time."

"You mean today?"

"Yes, I mean today! You think I'd wait a couple days until I felt like drivin' in to report it?" Betty Ann brought her voice back down and added, "It was this afternoon."

"Is the alleged perpetrator still up there?"

"The—? Oh—I don't know. I don't think so. At first we hid in the house. Then, when he didn't shoot anymore we came down here to report it."

"Are you saying it's a cabin or a house? Are we talking about your home of residence?"

"No, I live in Del Sueño. It's an old cabin on some land I own up in the hills, up off Old Seddleton Road."

The woman pivoted back to the computer and with a sigh began to enter information. She asked for their names and typed them in. "Was anyone injured?"

"No. Just scared to death."

"The person who was shooting, it was someone you know?"

"Hell, no! It was some person I never saw. He musta been behind a tree or something. When I realized he was taking potshots at me, I ducked back in the house and stayed down outa sight!"

"Then how do you know it was a he?"

"I don't, I guess. Can't picture a woman shooting at people for fun, can you?"

"You'd be surprised what some women do," the woman said wearily. She asked for the address of the cabin, which Betty Ann had to read from the copies of tax assessments that she had gotten from Dorothy.

The woman nodded toward Louisa, who was hovering behind Betty Ann's shoulder. "They shoot at both of you?"

"I don't know. I don't think so."

The woman paused. "You don't know if she was shot at?"

"I didn't hear any more shots after the two hit the wall near my head, so, no, I don't think she was shot at. Listen, could you send somebody up to look at the bullet holes?"

The woman looked past Betty Ann's shoulder. "You see anyone?"

Louisa shook her head.

"What did you hear?"

When Louisa hesitated, Betty Ann said, "She'd gone back down to the car and says she didn't hear any shots. Listen, can you just send somebody up to look? The sumbitch might still be around. If not, they can dig out the bullets for proof."

The woman hardly seemed to register what Betty Ann was saying. She paused in her typing to check a roster of some kind.

"Take a seat. I'll see if Sergeant Lopez can take your report."

"It's going to be dark soon. There's no lights up there right now, no kinda power, and I didn't bring a flashlight with me."

"Please take a seat. Sergeant Lopez will be with you as soon as possible."

Betty Ann sat next to Louisa on the hard wooden bench and gazed through the wall of windows. The town of Seddleton was at a lower elevation than the cabin. The trees were larger than the ones in Del Sueño, and there were firs mixed in with the oaks, but they were widely spaced, with scratchy ground underneath. Wide lots separated most of the buildings, and the cracked asphalt road was edged by soft sand. The last of the sun's rays fell like a golden veil on the buildings, and the flagstones outside the glass doors began to glow like a campfire carefully banked for the night.

It would be useless to return to the cabin now, she thought bitterly. Suddenly she wished they hadn't come and wondered if she should just get in the car and go home. It was likely nothing could ever be proved, especially with Louisa being useless as a witness. Even if they found out who did the shooting, what was she going to do, sue the bastard for a bad aim?

Louisa started to complain about not having had much to eat since her 'snack' in the car. Betty Ann suspected she was just bored, but she pulled some money from her wallet and sent her across the street to where golden arches caught the last of the sun. She watched Louisa's stocky body fade into the long shadows of the trees, wondering if they should have just gone home.

Chapter Eight

"Ms. Beaumont?"

She looked up. He was young. They always seemed to be young these days.

"I'm Officer Lopez. You're reporting a shooting?"

"Actually, what I wanted was for somebody to come up to my property and investigate it," Betty Ann said and knew she sounded petulant. "Look, I know you guys are probably busy, and I don't mean to be rude. It's just that it's nearly dark now. I don't know what you could see up there now, and I for one don't feel like wandering around in the dark even if the shooter's gone. And there's no real guarantee of that. He stopped shooting and that's when we took off. But somebody that careless or that crazy probably oughta be stopped. I just don't know what you can do, now that the sun's gone down."

"Okay," he said with professional calm. "Why don't we finish filling out the report, and then we'll have somebody go up and check it out first thing tomorrow." He led her over to a heavy door. "Like you say, it'd be hard to find anybody up there now, especially if it's somebody what don't want to be found. Did you see the person? Were they shooting at something specific, or was it just random shots? Mighta been somebody after squirrels. That's legal outside of the city limits."

"Not on my private property, it ain't. And they were shooting at *me*."

He looked startled. "So you know who it was?"

"No! I never saw 'em, got no idea who it was. But the bullets hit the wall right next to me. Two of 'em, in broad daylight, a foot from my head."

"Okay, that does sound like it might be some serious negligence." He swiped a card through a reader and held the door open, waiting for her to precede him through it.

Betty Ann shot a look through the glass windows. In the darkening street, she could see no sign of Louisa returning. She was probably scarfing a Big Mac and large fries without thinking about anyone else. Betty Ann hadn't eaten in a while either, and it wasn't helping her attitude.

"Listen," she called to the woman behind the glass barrier. "When my friend comes in, would you bring her back to wherever we're going?"

Apparently sound carried through the Plexiglas only sporadically. There was no sign she had been heard.

Lopez said, "She'll let me know if your friend comes back and asks for you."

With a grunt, Betty Ann went through the door. It hissed shut behind them. He led her to a small cubicle with shoulder-high fuzzy blue walls.

"Now, let's take care of this," he said. He motioned for her to take the other chair and settled in front of the computer screen. "You believe they were shooting at you? And you don't think it was someone you know?" He clicked the mouse and began to hit the keyboard with two fingers, one eye checking the form the receptionist had sent him.

"Whoever it was hid up in the trees above our place," said Betty Ann. "I don't know anybody anywhere in the neighborhood. Haven't been up there in years. I s'pose it coulda been kids thinkin' it was funny to scare somebody. It might even have been a stray bullet from a hunter, but nobody should have been shooting in that area. There's not many houses, but there's some."

"So they were trespassing? Where is your property, exactly?"

She described its location and added, "The property's still under my former name of Stearns."

His fingers paused over the keyboard.

"That name sounds familiar. You been in here recently?"

"No. It might be because my husband – my first husband – was found dead the other day at the bottom of Blue Lake."

He stared at her. Then he mumbled, "'Scuse me, ma'am," and bolted from the cubicle.

In a short time he returned with another officer. The new man was solid-looking across the shoulders and older, with gray starting to take over his chocolate-brown hair. A dark mustache hid his upper lip, making the lower one appear truculent. He seemed to fill up the cubicle, even when Lopez remained respectfully outside.

"You're Betty Ann Stearns?" he asked in a tone that wasn't strictly unfriendly. She wondered if his voice was really that deep or if he practiced it for effect.

"No," she said. "I'm Betty Ann *Beaumont* now. Stearns was a long time ago."

"Branson said he was going to talk to you."

"He did."

"He was supposed to send his report to me, then." He said brusquely to Lopez, "Take her report and don't let her leave. I'll have some questions."

Betty Ann jumped up and found that she still had to look up at his face. "Wait a minute! I'm here to report a shooting!"

He fixed her with a look. "Is it connected to the first one?"

She gaped at him. "Connected? How could it be? This shooting happened today."

"Who was shooting, and why?"

"Dammit, that's why I'm here! I want you people to find out."

"What kinda gun?" the man asked, and Betty Ann got the feeling that his mind was still on the shooting that happened thirty-eight years before.

"How the hell should I know?" she snapped. "Musta been a rifle, or he'da been close enough for us to see 'im."

"Us?"

"My friend was with me. She's across the street right now."

"Why didn't she come in with you?"

"She was hungry," she said, knowing that it sounded lame.

"Coulda been a hunter," Lopez interrupted. "Or stupid kids that ran away when they realized they'd nearly shot someone. Playin' around with their old man's gun."

A feeling of futility rose within Betty Ann and threatened to swamp her. The long day had made her more tired than she realized. She sighed. "Look, never mind, no one was hurt, so let's forget the whole thing. Can I go home now?"

"Aside from whatever happened today, we are investigating your husband's murder." He studied her from under his eyebrows, as if taking her measure. "We don't get many murders up here. Folks don't get used to them like down in the valley. Up here, they get damned upset and expect us to wrap it up quick. Which means we generally need for folks to come in and answer our questions. Or at least make a report to the local police. Among other things, I need to know where you were at the time of the shooting. The first shooting. Which story Branson was supposed to fax me."

"Look, I only came here about the shooting today," she said, ignoring his use of the word 'story' She may have imagined his slight emphasis. "Somebody shot at *me*."

He had turned to speak to Lopez. That stopped him. "Why'n hell's somebody shooting at *you*?"

"Well, that's what I'd like to know, isn't it!" She was finding it difficult to control her temper. "That's what I'd like for you people to find out!"

He crossed his arms. "Alright. 'Sposin' you tell me about it."

She hesitated and then gave him a quick description of what happened. "We didn't want to hang around after that, so we came here to report it."

Lopez had squeezed between them to sit again at the tiny desk and was tapping her words into the computer. There was barely room for the three of them. To Betty Ann, the tall man seemed to be standing uncomfortably close. She was grateful that he wasn't the type to wear a lot of cologne. His brown and beige uniform smelled only of a man after a long working day. She wondered what she smelled like, after the day she'd had.

"Print that out," he said. Lopez clicked his mouse, and Betty Ann heard a hum outside the cubicle. Somewhere a printer rolled out sheets of paper.

"So you think it was a hunter."

She returned her attention to the big man. "No, I ain't sayin' that. I didn't hear any shots before the shingle next to my head exploded, and no voices either. It was perfectly quiet before that. And too damn quiet afterwards."

"Well, sounds like before you hollered, he didn't know there was anybody around. Potshottin' at squirrels, most like, but we'll go up there and look around, see if we can find out who it was. Whoever they are, they got no business firin' off where there *might* be people."

She knew she could not explain it to these two men, but she couldn't get rid of the strong feeling that the shots were deliberate, not just "fired off". She had tried to describe the heavy pause after she had shouted, followed by the second shot. It had been a very deliberate-feeling second shot.

But maybe fright had made her over-react. Maybe the man was right, and the shooter hadn't heard her. Maybe they had just been shooting at a squirrel, not realizing people were in the area. Or maybe they were just trying to scare her for fun. It was a crazy world, where too many people had taken to shooting at total strangers. Some did it out of anger at the whole world, but some, she suspected, had picked up gun fever from television shows and decided to take gleeful shots at some unsuspecting person and then fade away, to chuckle about it later over a beer. It was hateful, but it seemed to be a fact of life nowadays.

So she remained silent. The man wasn't listening anyway. This shooting had nothing to do with the murder he wanted to solve. He went out in the hallway and picked up the freshly printed report.

"Right. If you'll come with me, Ms. Stearns—"

"Beaumont."

"Sorry." He paused to look at her. "You remarried?"

"Some time ago."

"Okay. We need to get straight just exactly what you were doin' at the time of your husband's murder."

Feeling that she really had no choice and she might as well get it over with and the day was shot to hell anyway, she followed him to a glassed-in office where he held the door for her to enter. The nameplate beside the door said, "*Lieutenant James Kovacs*". Beyond the far windows a wide grassy area stretched through trees to what might have been a small creek.

A large metal desk hunkered across the corner. Behind it a large chair sported tufts of white stuffing that puffed from splits in the faux leather. He motioned her to another chair in front of the desk. She sat down wearily, hoping it wouldn't take too long to convince him that she had very little to offer.

"So, since I haven't received Branson's report about your whereabouts when your husband was killed, how 'bout you just give it to me."

She felt the weight of his gaze like a tangible thing, compelling her to answer, and she stiffened with resentment.

"Look, Lieutenant," she said firmly, "like I told Pete Branson, Tom *disappeared* a long time ago. I don't remember what I was doing at the time. I remember what I was doing afterwards. Tryin' to get them assholes—'scuse me, them *officers of the law*, to look for him. I mean seriously look, not just go through the motions."

"Why would they do that?" he asked sharply.

"They didn't believe me. That something had happened to him. Thought he'd just run off with a new girl or something. They thought it was funny."

"Go on."

"Well, I spent a lot of time tryin' to find him myself, but after a while I had to give up."

"Give up? Why?"

"My mother had had a stroke, and she got worse after he disappeared. It shocked her. They were close. Caring for her took all my time outside of my job."

He studied her again. It was a moment before he spoke. "What was your job?"

"Bartender at the End of the Line. That's an old saloon down in Del Sueño. My mother didn't have any money saved up, and me and Tom never had much. So Mr. Meagan, he owned the Line back then, he knew I needed a job, so he hired me to tend bar."

He quirked an eyebrow. "That was thirty-eight years ago. You had to be just a kid at the time. They let you work in a bar?"

"I've always been older than my age."

For a moment he looked like he might smile at her phrasing. Then he leaned back in his creaking chair and frowned.

"End o' the Line. I've heard of it. You still work there?"

She nodded.

"Weren't there a bunch of murders there last summer?"

"Not a bunch," she said, bristling. "Somebody got murdered in the alley outside. But Pete caught the guy who did it. He's a good cop."

"Mm. And you're sayin' you don't remember what you were doing before your husband was killed."

"I didn't know he *was* killed. There was no reason for me to make a point of rememberin', so I never did. It's all muddled up with what I was doing afterwards, when I couldn't find him. At first I thought he'd gone up to the studio for a few days. Then I got worried he was in an accident and was down in a ditch or something. Then after the cops stopped half-assed looking for him and he never came back...I just stopped thinkin' about it."

"Who else knew your husband back then? Who might remember things from around that time? Your boss?"

"Mr. Meagan passed years ago. His son owns it now, but he has a friend running it, and anyway, he wasn't even born then. I guess most of our friends were pretty transient."

He said nothing, but she knew how empty it sounded. If she had ever wondered what happened to all of Tom's friends, it hadn't been until long after there was no way to look them up. She told him Louisa's name and what she had said about Barry's gallery in San Diego. "They were the only ones who might have been around the studio at the time, and come to think of it, Louisa said she was in Riverside that week."

"The studio—that the place you were today? Where you got shot at?"

She nodded.

"How often do you go up there?"

She hesitated. "Truth is, today was the first time I been up there in about thirty years."

He made a small sound which could have indicated disbelief. Or acceptance.

"I had no reason to go up there by myself," she persisted. "That was Tom's workin' studio, where he did his paintin'. He didn't like to be bothered when he was paintin', so I hadn't been up there much anyway, and then afterwards, well, I just never wanted to go back. I didn't like bein' up there anymore."

"Bad memories?"

"No. Just...memories." She peered through the inner glass to the heavy lobby door. Still no sign of Louisa.

Kovacs pinned her with another look. "You haven't been up here at all until today?"

"Just the once. On my way back from a trip to Riverside. That was a few years after. Like I said, it felt...lonely, so I never went back."

He interrupted. "But you still own it?"

"Yes." When he said nothing more, she continued, "I guess you're right. I should have paid more attention to it."

"You were only—what? Sixteen?"

"Nineteen."

"I've been wondering why no other family members showed up in the original reports of him missing. I mean the ones your *officers of the law* filed." He pulled a file over from the side of his desk. "Nobody's come looking for him in all this time?"

"I never heard about it if they did, and I been right there in town all along."

"You never thought of moving away? I mean, after your mother passed?"

"Why would I do that?" she asked, baffled. "I grew up there. I could always get a job somewhere in town, so I never had any reason to move. When I met Jackson Beaumont, we bought us a house up in Vista de Copa. I never thought about the property until Louisa started askin' me about it the other day. That's why we drove up there."

"Mr. Beaumont up at the property with you today?"

"He passed two years ago."

For a moment he looked at her, his dark brows twitched in a slight frown. Then he flipped through the file. "Says here that at the time you reported Stearns missing, you also reported a stolen watch."

"Did I?" She looked at him blankly. Then a memory floated to the surface. "Oh. Yeah. My father's watch. Did you find it in the car?"

"Why would you think that?" he asked sharply.

"I don't know," she said with exasperation. "Maybe because you're bringin' it up? I couldn't find it after he disappeared."

"If you believed something had happened to him, not that he took off, why claim he stole the watch?"

"Because I thought maybe the cops might look harder for him if they thought it was a robbery and not just that he dumped me!" Betty Ann swallowed her irritation. "Look. I was sure Tom would never do to me like they were sayin'. He just wasn't the type. But nothin' I could say would convince them. So I figured that telling 'em he stole something might give 'em whatchucallit, incentive. If they weren't interested in huntin' down some poor schmuck that ran out on his wife, then maybe solvin' a robbery—well, they *had* to do that, right? It was their job."

"So what happened? You're saying it wasn't stolen?"

She felt the blush rise up from the neck of her blouse. "Fact is, it belonged to Tom. I gave it to him for his birthday after we married. I always figured he had it with him and whatever happened, if they found it, they'd find him. But they never did."

She stopped, remembering that 'they' had indeed found Tom. Thirty-eight years later.

"Well," he said, "they must have believed you about that. Says here they checked the local pawn shops with no luck."

She snorted. "Shoulda known that's as far as they bothered. Tom wouldn'ta pawned it. The watch wasn't worth much, just something my Pop got for thirty years on the railroad. But see, that was the thing—I always felt if Tom was dumpin' me, he wouldn't have taken the watch. That was just his way."

"If it was his, then I don't see why you think he wouldn't take it with him."

"He wouldn't have taken it if he was leavin' me, knowin' what it meant to me. Like I said, it wasn't worth much. Tom liked having it because it was part of my family. I think because he never had one of his own. He and my mom always got along good." She paused, remembering her mother, so torn between fearing something bad had happened to Tom and assuring them both that he was still alive. Which would mean that a beloved son-in-law had abandoned her daughter—in a way, had abandoned them both.

Betty Ann shook off the memory and said firmly, "Anyway, later I forgot about the watch, and I tried to forget about him too." She took a breath. Too much talking on an empty stomach always made her short of breath. After a moment she said, "So, did you find it? I mean, when you found him?"

He stared at her with his impenetrable eyes for a moment, then left the room without a word. When he came back, he was carrying a brown paper bag marked "Evidence". He opened it and tipped out the contents. Something heavy fell onto the desk.

Chapter Nine

This time Betty Ann's breathlessness didn't come from talking. She was assailed by memories and feelings that predated her relationship with Tom. Most of them predated every memory in the vast vault of her fifty-six years.

Her earliest memories were of her father's hands, already scarred and gnarled from working the gears and levers of the locomotives that he had tended most of his life, first in Arkansas and then in California, where he moved with his young wife in search of a better life. He had become a railroad foreman in time, but was still known for jumping in and getting his hands dirty. She could hear her mother's voice after he died, filled with pain, not for herself but for the man who had given his life to the railroad and in return had gotten a gold-plated watch.

She had never heard her father complain. A simple man with a simple education, he had often sat her on his lap and brought the huge watch out of his pocket to let her see the tiny sliver of a second hand as it went around. Sometimes he opened up the back to show her how the gears worked together to make it move. She had felt as though he were showing her the workings of the universe.

She reached across the desk for it and then pulled her hand back.

"Go ahead," Kovacs said flatly. "No prints. Too much time in the water."

She nodded for some reason she couldn't explain and picked it up. It still felt heavy, although her hand was now much larger and much stronger than it had been at the age of five. After her father died of pneumonia, she found he had left it to her in his will, with a request that she give it to the man she married. There had been nothing else for him to leave her.

She blinked against the stinging in her eyes and rubbed her thumb on the corroded metal. The etched design had almost disappeared. "Yep. This is Pop's watch. So you found it with Tom."

"In his pocket. What sort of things did he keep in it?"

"Keep in it? What's that mean?"

"There's room under the cover for something. Most people put a picture there. What we found had been pretty much destroyed by years in the water, but it looks like it was a piece of folded paper with some kind of drawing on it. What would that have been?"

She stared. "No idea. Maybe a draft for a new painting."

"Funny place to keep it. Did he own a gun?" Kovacs asked bluntly.

"Hell, no, he hated guns. Shoulda heard him hollerin' at the hunters that came by the studio sometimes, looking for mule deer. He called 'em so many names, I got scared a couple times that they'd get mad enough to shoot *him*. He didn't exactly hold himself in about it, Tom didn't."

"A bit violent, was he?"

"No! Just cared a lot about some things. Like painting and guns."

"You remember anybody in particular? That got upset with his name-calling? Anybody who mighta come back around to get even, when there weren't any witnesses?"

"Oh," she said. After a moment, she added, "I never thought about that. Could he have been shot by one of those hunters? But why would they have shot him out at Blue Lake?"

"Somebody might have followed him, forced him off the road. How about you? You own any guns?"

"Well, ain't that subtle. The answer's no, and I never did back then either. I mean, I don't hate 'em, not like Tom did. I've even fired some, you know, out in the desert takin' potshots at cans. But I never owned one. Tom probably woulda divorced me if I'd tried to have one around, that's how strong-opinioned he was about it. After he was gone I never felt the need."

This seemed to get his attention. He studied her for a moment. It seemed to be something he liked to do, putting his gaze on someone until they couldn't help but wonder what was on his mind. Betty Ann considered telling him it was annoying, but then he leaned forward and when he spoke, there was belligerence in his tone.

"You never felt the need for a gun after he was gone. How about before, maybe when he was being...strong-opinioned? Was there ever any confrontation about the watch? Any reason you might have been upset that he took it with him when he left you?"

"He didn't leave me. And he had every right to take it with him, wherever he was going that day. I told you, it was his. I made up that part about him stealing it." She felt him waiting for her to go on and set her lips. It was like a stare-down in the schoolyard. She won.

"Ms. Stearns—"

"Beaumont."

"Beaumont." He nodded. "And you're a widow. Again." He was playing with his pen and glanced up at her from beneath his eyebrows.

"My second husband died of a heart attack," she said stiffly. "You can ask his doctor."

"I'm very sorry."

"Thank you." She wondered if he was expressing sympathy for her loss or regret that she couldn't possibly have killed Jackson too.

"Where do you think he was going that day?"

"I have no idea. I didn't know he knew where Blue Lake was."

"Are you planning on going anywhere?" he asked.

"Subtle again. You sayin' 'don't leave town'?"

"Something like that." His lips relaxed in a small smile, and she realized that the sternness of his features came more from the work he was in than from his personality. He wouldn't be a bad lookin' guy if he'd lighten up, she thought.

"I won't go so far as to say you're a suspect right now," he was saying, "but we need to get to the bottom of where you were when your husband—your first husband—was killed. For now, I'll accept that you don't remember. It was a long time ago. But I will be having to ask you more questions, and I'd appreciate it if you would try to remember the answers. And not leave town. That's for your sake as well as ours. The sooner you come up with an alibi—"

"The sooner you guys can start looking for the real killer."

He ignored that. "For now, you can go back to Vista de Copa. Tomorrow I'll go up myself and check out those bullet holes."

She gave him directions to the property and cautioned him about the bridge before getting up. Marilyn's words suddenly came to her.

"Listen," she said and stopped.

"What?"

"This is stupid. I mean, there's no way she'd know where the property is. I don't think. Anyway, if she was gonna take potshots at me, she'd do it down in town."

He waited patiently, his eyes on her. This time he won.

"Okay, there's an old woman who nursed a grudge against me after her husband got killed in a knife fight. That was before Tom disappeared. I'm sure she's all talk, but, well . . ."

"Name." He wrote that down too, along with everything Betty Ann could remember about the old bar fight, while she squirmed with a feeling that she was betraying a harmless old resident of Del Sueño. But she had opened her mouth. Damn Marilyn anyway.

He snapped his notebook shut. "You told Branson about this?"

"Um. No. I never took her seriously, so it didn't occur to me to tell Pete about it. I don't know if he's heard any of Nina's stupid talk."

"I'll mention it to him when I talk to him. We need to know more about this. And maybe having the cops question her will make this woman back off."

"Doubt it." Feeling that everything had been covered that could be, Betty Ann stood up, moving slowly so as not to betray how stiff her back had become. All the tension of the day had done its work. She didn't offer to shake his hand and merely said, "You want me, you should find me at the End of the Line. I work there most nights. When can I have my father's watch back?"

"Unfortunately, not until we find out what happened to your husband or declare the case closed. I promise you we're working on finding out."

When she left through the lobby, the receptionist was nowhere in sight. The lights inside the glassed-in enclosure were off, giving it a shadowy, secretive look. Betty Ann stepped out into the evening and spotted Louisa walking across the road toward her.

"Where the hell have you been?" she snapped, releasing the tension of the interview.

"Stopped to talk to somebody. Folks are friendly in this town," Louisa said and added sullenly, "Anyway, I don't like cops. Why'd I gotta come in? You're the one thought somebody was shootin' at you."

"I didn't think it. They were shootin' at me. And you were there, Lou, even if you didn't see anything. They might still want to talk to you, but it can wait, I guess."

She led Lou to the car and drove them back to Vista de Copa, to the house that didn't seem like such a refuge any more.

"Wonder if the she-bitch showed up," said Louisa as she got out of the car.

Betty Ann shrugged, faking an indifference that she really didn't feel. "Obviously she didn't get in. She'da had to break the door down, and Pete wouldn't let her do that."

She turned the heat up as soon as they walked in and fixed spaghetti for dinner. Afterwards she loaded and started the dishwasher, and found she wasn't ready to sleep. Restlessness crawled through her.

"I'm going down to town for a beer. You wanna come?"

Louisa declined, saying that her favorite sitcom was on in ten minutes. Betty Ann left her wrapping herself back up in the quilt, jabbing the remote at the cable box, and reaching for a half-empty potato chip bag.

The Thunderbird growled pleasantly down the steep night road to town.

After old Mr. Meagan had died, his son took over running the bar for over a decade. Then family problems had taken his heart out of it, but he couldn't bring himself to sell outright. A year ago he had hired his cousin Winston to run the place while he lived in Arizona.

Thanks to too many years of haphazard care, the End of the Line was just short of decrepit. The front door had a familiar kicked-by-too-many-boots look and was set deep into the front wall. She parked the Thunderbird in its usual place in front of the door where she could keep an eye on it. The bar sat backed up on a municipal parking lot, but Betty Ann refused to use it, declaring she wasn't getting conked on the head for the buck-fifty in her wallet.

The city council hadn't gotten around to putting lights up in the parking lot itself, and the ones on the street didn't reach the Line's back door. And sometimes the street people used the fence at the end of the alley for a handy latrine. Even on a cold night, the smell was nothing to start your evening with.

As she got out, she checked out how many people were hanging around outside. If no one was there, it meant something was happening. Either everyone was inside so as not to miss anything, or they had all gone home to avoid getting entangled in it. Everything looked quiet, with several people leaning against the wall.

The night was warm, and the heavy front door was propped open with a sand bucket that was probably older than the bar itself. Aside from a door prop, it served as the only butt can, and at nine o'clock at night it was already overflowing. Winston considered it fitting that something intended to put out fires in the building fifty years ago now served to put out the tiny fires that he was forbidden to allow people to enjoy inside.

She would have to speak to Patsy, get her to clean it out before it made a mess on the sidewalk, giving the city fathers something to complain about. Maybe she could get one of the regulars to do it. About time one of those dead weights earned his bar stool.

"Hey, Betty Ann," said Cowboy. He stood hunched against the wind just outside the door. His hard-knuckled hand held his cigarette cupped against his pearl-studded shirt. He tipped his head back to look at her from under his huge Stetson hat. "About time you showed up to take over. That girl in there ain't got no business behind the bar, y'know."

"I'm sure she's doin' just fine, Cowboy. Lighten up. She'll learn all the ins and outs eventually."

"Ins 'n' outs ah'm sure she can do," he leered. "It's pourin' a beer without gettin' her tits in the way thet's botherin' me."

"Gimme a break. Since when did you ever object to a bartender with tits?" She brushed past him and through the door. "Anyway, I ain't workin' tonight, so you'll have to put up with her."

Several people greeted her, and Marilyn waved from her favorite stool halfway down the bar. Betty Ann sat down next to her, and Patsy brought her a bottle of beer. Ice crystals slid down the side of the bottle.

"Gimme a glass, honey," Betty Ann said. When the girl set one in front of her, she added below the hum of conversation, "Always bring a woman a glass with her beer, kiddo, don't make her ask for it. It's up to her if she wants to use it, but most appreciate it, especially if they're with a date. It's more ladylike."

Cowboy came up to stand beside her. He gave her an "I toldja so" look and ordered another beer. "*Without* the glass, darlin'. I ain't wearin' no brassiere."

"Cowboy," said Marilyn, "you're just a class act, you know that?"

"Hey, Cowboy," Betty Ann said, "you remember Ramona? That long-haired girl you dated for a while?"

Patsy set a bottle of beer in front of him. He took a long swallow and looked thoughtful. "Ain't thought of her in a long time. One of the few I didn't end up marryin'. Why?"

"Do you know where she is now? We lost touch, and I kinda wanted to talk to her about something."

He shrugged. "Last I heard, she went back to Zacatecas. Married some cholo an' had a passle o' kids. Then he got in trouble with the Federales. If she was smart, she woulda come back up north, but I ain't heard about it."

Betty Ann spotted Winston sitting in the back and carried her beer back to join him. The railroad spur that the bar was named for had been closed for sixty years, but on the wall hung a faded painting of a locomotive toppling off the end of broken railroad tracks into what looked like a bottomless canyon. It was a long-ago donation from a local artist with a sense of humor.

The manager of the End of the Line sprawled in his usual place in the evenings, on a padded banquette where he could nurse his whiskey and watch the pool games. When she sat down next to him, he peered at her owlishly, which told her she would probably have to find someone to drive him home. She found herself longing to be able to talk with her old boss.

Frank Meagan had been able hold his liquor no matter what, and he might remember where she had been and what she had been doing just before Tom disappeared. Frank never cared that much for her first husband, never liked what he called "hippie-dippies". But he had an amazing ear for the local gossip and kept tabs on local kids like Betty Ann. If he had lived, he would be in his seventies by now. Sharp old codger, he'd remember things even that long ago. Most people in the Line probably couldn't remember their own movements thirty-eight hours ago.

"Hey, Winston, your Uncle Frank ever talk to you about when my husband disappeared?"

She waited while he stared into space as though her words were butterflies dancing in front of his eyes. It looked like it was a struggle for his mind to catch them.

"Jackson disappeared?"

"No, I mean my first husband. Tom Stearns. He disappeared thirty-eight years ago. Caused quite a stir at the time. You remember your uncle ever talking about it?"

After a moment of thought, he said, "You was married? Before Jackson?"

"Yeah, long time ago. You remember your uncle ever talking about him disappearing back in the late seventies?"

A longer pause. "Hell, Betty Ann, that's before I was born."

She gave up and went back to sit beside Marilyn. "Where's Bill?"

"Some male-bonding dinner," said Marilyn. "So whatchu been doin'?"

"Running around up in the hills gettin' shot at."

Marilyn turned to stare at her with her green eyes. "What for?"

"Whaddya mean, what for?"

"I mean what's somebody shootin' at you for? What'd you do?"

Betty Ann sighed. "Who knows? It was probably some hunter gettin' his jollies after a slow day. At least, that's what the cops think. They're gonna go up and check it out in the morning, they said."

"Pete's goin'?"

"Naw. We went to the Seddleton cops."

"Who's we?"

"Me 'n' Louisa. She went up with me."

"Oh, yeah. How come she's never been in here? Too fancy-schmancy?"

"Hardly. No, she's just not the bar type, never was. I've only ever seen her come in with me 'n' Tom 'n' Barry, and that was forty years ago."

"Who's Barry?"

"This guy used to hang out with us. He was an old friend of Tom's who just showed up one day wanting Tom to help him become a famous artist."

"So where is he now?"

"Bein' a famous artist down in San Diego, apparently." Betty Ann took a thoughtful pull off her beer. "I should probably try 'n' break the news to him before the cops do. I didn't know he was still around until Louisa told me. Maybe I can find him in the phone book."

"If you can find a phone book. They still make those things? Look, let me see if I can find him." Marilyn pulled a red patent-leather bag from under the bar overhang, where she had hung it on one of the purse hooks. She threw back the flap and pulled out something that looked to Betty Ann like an overlarge smart-phone.

"It's an iPad," Marilyn said happily. "Bill bought it for my birthday."

"You never said it was your birthday. Happy birthday."

"It was a month ago, but thanks. I don't usually say anything. After a while, they're only good for getting presents." She tapped at the screen. "Okay, I'm online. Gimme his last name."

Betty Ann thought for a moment. "I think it was Freid. Or Freidman." She spelled it.

Marilyn tapped some more. "Oh, boy, lots of 'em. Pretty common name. Wait. You said he's an artist. Look, this guy has a website. And his own gallery." Her voice went to neutral. "Geez. Does that look like his paintings?"

Betty Ann peered at the small screen. "Could be. That looks like the stuff Tom used to do."

"I wonder why anyone would want to buy something that looks so pissed off. It'd give me a headache. But it says here some of his stuff is hanging up in Pashington College, wherever that is."

"Is there a phone number? Address?"

"I'll write it down, you can send him an email. Or, I don't know, maybe that's a shitty way to tell him. Well, you can send an email and ask him to call you. Here, do it right now."

Betty Ann drew back as Marilyn pushed the device toward her. "I've never done an email. That's okay, I want to go down to La Mesa tomorrow anyway. I'll stop by the gallery."

"Betty Ann, you need to come into the twenty-first century."

Betty Ann eyed Marilyn's dress and hairstyle with its faint whiff of the Fifties, and said defensively, "I still got Jackson's laptop, I just don't use it much. Anyway, I'm not looking forward to meeting up with Barry again, but I think it's something I should do in person. We had some nasty words last time I saw him. I think I accused him of lying about where Tom went. He drove off with the tires sprayin' gravel, and I never heard from him again."

"Listen," Marilyn's face brightened. "Maybe you could ask Pete about it? You said the cops probably would want to talk to this guy, right?"

"That's an idea." Betty Ann finished her beer. "I gotta ask Pete about my sister-in-law anyway. I'll call him tomorrow."

"I saw him go in Granny's before I came in. Bet he's still there." With a flash of thigh, she hopped off the bar stool. "C'mon, let's go."

"You don't need to come," said Betty Ann as she followed her out the door.

"Wouldn't miss it for the world. When did you acquire a sister-in-law?"

"Recently."

Chapter Ten

The little café was humid with the smell of fried food. Through the kitchen door they could see Granny Jordenson berating one of her new hires for letting the biscuits burn. Pete sat at the counter, finishing up what looked like a plate of chicken-fried steak. He sipped at his coffee cup, eyeing them warily as they sat down, one on either side of him.

"What?"

"Jeez, Pete," said Marilyn, "you don't hafta look so scared. We ain't gonna bite."

"The Lieutenant up in Seddleton called and chewed my ass today," he said to Betty Ann. "I was supposed to send him details on your whereabouts at the time of Stearns' death. This damn new meth cartel has got us running around with our thumbs up our—anyway, he said you went up there yourself. You coulda let me know so I didn't look stupid."

"I'm sorry, Pete. I went in there to tell them about something else, and he jumped me about Tom's murder. Listen, did my sister-in-law bring you up to my house today?"

He stared at her. "Sister-in-law? Didn't know you had one. Which husband?"

"Jackson. I didn't know about her either until after he died. She came to my house last night with a lawyer and said since she and him couldn't find a record of a divorce from Tom, that I married Jackson bigamist-ly and she's gonna sue and get everything he left me. Can she do that?"

Pete thought for a moment while Marilyn sat with her mouth open.

"I wouldn't worry about it," he said finally. "Seems pretty evident that Tom was dead a long time before you got married again."

"She says unless I knew for sure Tom was dead, by which she means I killed him, then I married Jackson with intent to defraud him, because the previous marriage never was ended. Thing is, I'm not absolutely sure I ever did anything like that, Pete. Isn't there something about after so many years of being deserted, it's the same as a divorce?"

"I think you have to file for desertion or such-like anyway. You never did?"

She shrugged. "I remember getting some papers for something like that, but I don't remember going through with it. And Greta says her lawyer didn't find a record of it anywhere."

"Well, figuring it was thirty-eight years before you married again, even if you never got around to filing, I don't think a judge would believe you intended to defraud anybody. Hell, Betty Ann, anybody with any sense would figure you—" He stopped.

"Figure I knew he was dead? Because I'm the one who killed him?"

"No," he said patiently. "Figure you were really upset at the time, that's all. Not thinking straight. But better not take my word for it. I'm a cop, not a lawyer."

"Okay. Guess I better get a lawyer myself, then, in case Greta decides to actually go through with it." It was time to change the subject. "I wanted to tell you, I remember there was a guy that hung out with us before Tom disappeared. He might remember something."

Pete pulled out his notepad. "Name?"

She gave it to him. Marilyn told him about the website they had found.

"But listen, Pete," Betty Ann said. "I think I should go down and talk to him first, tell him they found Tom. They was pretty good friends, so I'd like to be the one to break the news."

"If he's got any information, the cops'll want to go talk to him first, before he can think about it. People have a tendency to start organizing their memories and then believing what they've decided they remember. I'll have Rodgers call SDPD first thing tomorrow."

"That seems awful cold," Marilyn said sadly.

"So's being in the bottom of a lake for thirty-eight years."

Betty Ann pushed that out of her mind.

Granny came over, poking a pencil into her hair bun. "You girls want something to eat?"

"No, thanks, just came in to talk to Pete. Granny, you remember anything about where I was when my first husband disappeared long time ago? About what I was doing at the time?"

Granny shook her head. "Kinda remember he just wasn't there anymore, but I don't remember anybody in here talking about it."

"Yeah, nobody was much interested," Betty Ann said bitterly. "Do you remember my friend Louisa? She told me that back around when Tom disappeared, she borrowed your car and drove it up to Riverside for a couple weeks."

"Oh, hell, yes, that I remember. Took me another week to clean it out. That damn car was a mess, fast food junk and even blood."

"*Blood?*"

"Yeah, looked like she killed a chicken on the front seat. Probably just her period, but it looked like she never even tried to clean it up." At the look on Betty Ann's face, she said, "Why? You think she murdered somebody in my car?"

Pete broke in. "That's not likely. Tom was shot in his own car up by Blue Lake. What happened to your car, though, Granny? You still got it?"

She looked at him with derision. "Pete, that car was on its last legs forty years ago. I don't remember who I gave it to, but I reckon it's been smashed and melted down into scrap a long time ago."

She went back into the kitchen.

Betty Ann said, "I was wondering if the Seddleton cops would want to talk to Lou, that's all. But if she really was in Riverside for two weeks, then she prob'ly won't have anything to tell them. Listen, Pete, can I just go down and talk to Barry? Maybe he can trigger a memory in my head. Besides, I got something else I need to do down in that area."

He pulled money from his wallet, dropped it beside his plate and got up. "Tell you what, you do what you need to do, Betty Ann. I'll do what I need to do."

They watched him go out the door.

"Well." Marilyn looked put out. "That sure wasn't very friendly."

"Last time it was just you, me and him together, we tossed him into a storage room, remember?"

"'Zactly. We saved him from his own police department knowin' he'd been in a bar fight. You'd think he might owe us one. So, who else you lookin' up in San Diego?"

"Nobody. There's somebody I wanta talk to in La Mesa." For some reason she felt a deep reluctance to tell anyone that a stranger had been paying her taxes for the last thirty-some years without her knowing. "Listen, I'd go tell Winston I need another day off, but I don't think he'd remember. You gonna be in the Line tomorrow?"

"I can. I'll tell Bill to meet me there after work and catch the boss before he starts drinkin' again. You want that girl to cover for you?"

"Yeah, she'll do. I guess I'm all tired finally. I'm goin' home."

Marilyn walked her back to the Thunderbird and then went inside the End of the Line. Betty Ann waved at the smokers and drove home.

The next afternoon Betty Ann pulled into a parking spot in the Old Town part of San Diego and stared at the long window that said, 'Revolution Art Gallery'. Inside she could see framed paintings hung to cover the walls. The sight of them hit her with feelings she had been fighting for thirty-eight years. Barry obviously had never felt the need to change the style Tom had taught him. Angry reds, acid greens and eye-watering orange put Tom in the passenger seat beside her.

What happened to you? she thought. *This should be your place.*

Tom said nothing, he only smiled in a way that used to send her heart racing. Now the memory brought nothing but empty sadness. It replaced the furious anger and frustration that had driven her from La Mesa after her futile visit to Ms. Hoffman's address.

It had taken an hour and a half to drive to La Mesa that morning, and she had used it to rehearse what she wanted to say when Ms. Hoffman opened the door to her knock. But the address she got from Dorothy of Deeds and Records turned out not to be a residence. "Discretion Home Mailbox Inc." arched in a business-like font across the wide window.

When she pushed the door open, it struck a little bell hanging above her head. A voice called from somewhere in the back, "Be right out!"

She studied the cork board covered with business cards and personal ads, and a coin-operated copy machine squatting beside a table holding a tiny postal scale and a business-size stapler, along with what appeared to be a lending library of the latest bestsellers. Under the table was a cardboard box full of well-used toys. A tall rack held greeting cards designed by local artists.

One wall contained rows of retro-looking brass post office letter boxes, numbered from 100 to 345. She looked at the address she had scribbled in her notebook. Dorothy of Deeds and Records had said nothing about a box number.

A young man bounced out to the counter. "Good morning. What can I help you with?"

"I think a Ms. Abigail Hoffman has a box here. I need to find out her home address."

"Sorry," he said. "We never give out that information."

"But, look—" She hadn't rehearsed for this contingency. "I need to talk to her. It's very important!"

He looked at her with professional sympathy and a complete lack of interest.

She went on desperately, "Apparently she's been paying the taxes on a property I own for some years, and I have no idea why! I've never even met her. I really need to at least leave her a note, maybe thank her?"

She ended on a somewhat pleading note. Obviously her story wasn't one he had heard uncountable times. Almost with admiration, he said, "Well, that does sound mysterious. Maybe you're the recipient of some eccentric billionaire benefactor."

"Well, I don't feel benefacted! I feel obligated. I can give you to a note to slip inside her box, and then she could contact me. You can read it, make sure it's not a threat or anything."

"Nope, sorry, that's not something we're allowed to do either. The whole point here is our folks don't get bothered unless they want to be. If it doesn't have the box number, I can't put it in the box."

"But I know she's been getting mail here. Can I leave it with you, then, and you give it to her when she comes in?"

"Sorry."

She stood in complete bafflement. He took a moment to think. "Only other thing I know would be to get a court order, I guess."

After several fruitless attempts at persuasion, she stalked out. Maybe she could ask Pete how to get a court order. After all, she shouldn't be forced to accept someone's largess without even knowing why. There could be something criminal going on. Although, she had to admit as she drove to San Diego in search of Barry's gallery, it might be difficult to explain to a judge why she waited thirty-eight years to start looking for this woman.

Sitting in the Thunderbird now, staring through the window at paintings that had brought back Tom's memory in a rush, she considered just pulling back out and driving home. After all, the police had probably already informed Barry about Tom. There wasn't much she could add. On the other hand, there might be things that Barry would be willing to tell her and not them. She sighed and climbed out, massaging tension out of her hip.

The place had a musty smell that matched the shabby-chic neighborhood, but she wasn't sure if the mustiness came from old paint and canvas, or if it was a part of the building itself. One full wall was devoted to the paintings that in her heart she thought of as purely Tom's influence. From front to back, the paintings grew in size, and the colors grew in their disturbing affect. Louisa was right, she thought. You would have to have a strong constitution to walk in and see those in your living room every day.

A number of large framed photographs hung on the other wall, and one caught her eye. It was a peaceful black-and-white shot, a perspective from the underside of an ocean pier. Soft ocean flowed outward and blended into a misty horizon. The contrast with the paintings was startling. She reflected that if Jackson had lined their front room with something like this instead of giant cool flowers that looked like genitalia, she might be more inclined to spend time there. Her own taste ran more to portraits of horses and John Wayne, but that didn't go with Jackson's soft pastel furniture.

She bent to read the price on the discreet card and drew back with a suck of air.

"They'll be worth a lot more someday," said a friendly voice behind her, "after he dies. That's usually the way it works, isn't it?"

She turned to find a young woman standing behind her. Betty Ann took in the crop-top and belly-piercing and wondered if she would ever have worn a ring in her naval, even if such things had been accepted when she was a girl.

"After who dies?" she asked.

"Barry, of course. The artist."

"He did all these?" Betty Ann swept an arm around, indicating the walls crowded with frames.

"Every single one," said the girl with obvious pride. "They're just cool sweet, aren't they? So ripped and exciting."

"He seems to have moved toward a little less exciting. I mean, the paintings look angry, but the photographs are rather nice."

"The photos belong more to his later period. He quit the paintings a long time ago to try a new media, something with a little more subtlety. I guess some artists do that when they get old. Personally, I think the paintings have a lot more feeling, don't you? They really hit you in the hizzazz."

"Well, they do hit you. Why 'Revolution Gallery'?"

"Barry says he's just an old revolutionary at heart. You know, protesting against the Viet Nam war and all that. The emotions expressed in some of his paintings is really awesome-stokken! So, are you interested in the photography or the older stuff? It's a great time to buy, because most of his paintings were on display at the university all last month. They'll probably have to go back into storage now, and that would be such a shame. Barry was just saying the other day—"

"Is he here right now?"

The girl pouted. "Oh, no, sorry, you missed him. He had to go out of town for a funeral."

"Funeral?"

"Yeah, he said he had to go 'pay his respects'." She giggled, and the belly ring bounced. "I just love the way he talks sometimes. Anyway, I stayed to mind the store. I'm expecting him back this evening. I could have him give you a call, if you prefer to buy from the artist himself. It's no problem."

"I wasn't really looking to buy," Betty Ann said hastily. "Maybe I'll stop in another time."

"If you'd like to leave your number—"

"No, really, I wouldn't want to waste your time. Are you his assistant?"

"Well, some people call me that," the girl said with another giggle, "but we're really more than that, if you know what I mean. Like, we've been together forever, ever since I left college!"

Was that last year? Betty Ann wondered. "I'll be back sometime soon."

She fled out the door while the girl was still asking her name. Her errand now felt doubly foolish. She should have done as

Pete said and left it to the police. Her visit might seem suspicious to them, a need to get with Barry to compare notes.

She arrived home in Vista de Copa to find Louisa had felt generous and ordered pizza. There were greasy paper cartons and napkins all over, and the air stank of cold pepperoni, but after the first slice, Betty Ann realized part of her depression had been low blood sugar.

Speaking around her fourth slice she asked, "Did Barry come here today?"

"Barry? I thought you went down there to see him."

"His assistant said he went 'up north' because a friend passed away. Thought he might have come here."

"He knows where you live?"

Betty Ann paused to chew pizza. "No, I guess he wouldn't know that. Maybe he went up to talk to the Seddleton police after San Diego P.D. told him about Tom."

She cleaned up the mess, poured herself a glass of cabernet and enjoyed an old Bette Davis movie that Louisa found on TCM.

CHAPTER ELEVEN

By Friday evening Betty Ann was glad to walk into the End of the Line and have a thousand things to do while Patsy presumably slept off the shock of running the bar by herself. She was building a whiskey and soda for Marilyn's friend Bill when a shadow appeared in the door, disturbing the sleepy air of the evening. At first she merely registered that he was not a regular. So did the other patrons, judging by their raised eyebrows. It wasn't often that strangers ventured into the End of the Line. They were welcome enough, but definite curiosities.

Marilyn twisted around on her bar stool and recrossed her legs. Bill put his hand on her arm to draw her attention back to him.

The newcomer paused as though unsure of being in the right place. Soft lights from the jukebox touched his dull thick hair. It might once have been blond or brown, but had long since faded into the indeterminate shade of middle age. His slacks, polo shirt and loafers clashed with the flannel shirts and boots that lined the bar.

His face lit up with a broad smile.

"Betty Ann! Hell, girl, you don't look a day older!" He came to the bar, swung a leg over a bar stool and leaned on his elbows, grinning at her.

"Hey, how you doin'?" she said. "Long time no see."

A good bartender never let on that she didn't recognize a patron. She searched through memories, years of customers, drunks and laughter.

His light-colored eyes crinkled, telling her that he had registered her false bonhomie. He said with more than a touch of challenge, "Have I changed that much?"

"Ain't changed at all," she said, refusing to back down. "What'll you have?"

"And you don't remember that I always had a Corona in my hand," he said softly. "Now, that just about breaks my heart."

It took a moment for what he had said to register. Betty Ann stopped in the act of pulling a bottle of Corona from the cooler.

"Barry."

"Sure, it's me."

His smile swept her back to a misty past, as nearly everything had done for days. She was back at the studio in the hills, in the hot bug-filled summer. Not as it appeared when she and Louisa were there, but as it had been years ago, smelling strongly of dry cedar-shake roofing. All of them, Tom, Barry, Louisa and herself, sitting at the sagging picnic table out under the sparse trees. Each of them holding a bottle of beer, trying to outdo the others in outrageous stories, killing the evening until the cabin lost the day's heat, and she and Tom could go inside to sleep. Louisa would curl up on the car seat that served as their sofa. And Barry would finish the last of the Coronas from the cooler and climb into the back of his hearse.

She opened the bottle and slid it across the bar. He smiled, and her breath caught. She was hit with a sudden clear memory of his young smile and how his mouth had always gone down on one side even as it went up on the other. He raised the bottle in a salute to her and drank, never taking his light eyes from hers.

"I guess I was expecting you to have long hair," she said.

He set the bottle down and pounded a fist lightly against his chest. "Wow, that tastes better than I thought it would. It's been a while. Yeah, I remember having a lot of hair in those days, but that was the way we all wore it, wasn't it? Wild and uncombed. Anything not to look like our parents. Except you. I remember your hair always fell in these smooth blonde waves down your back, no matter what."

"Ain't so smooth anymore. And the blonde needs a little help." Betty Ann waited a moment. When he didn't say anything more, she said, "I guess you heard about Tom. Cops come to see you?"

"Yeah. Told 'em what I could remember from back then. Not much, I guess. I was real sorry to hear about it." He chewed his lip. "Pretty weird, huh? I guess when he never showed up, we all thought he'd gone off to live up in the woods in Oregon, or something like that. That's sure what I figured. It must've been tough, findin' out after all this time that he got mugged or something."

The sympathy in his eyes, the comfortable familiarity of it, filled her with warmth. She realized she had been feeling cold since Pete came into the bar to question her about her alibi.

Get a hold of yourself, she thought. A little bit of sympathy and you fall apart.

For something to do, she started sudsy water in the bar sink and washed some dirty glasses. Like him, she ignored the glances being thrown their way, especially Marilyn's. "What brought you up here? You supposed to go talk to the cops in Seddleton?"

"Actually, B.A., I just drove up to comfort an old friend, didn't I?"

She stopped with her hands in the water. "You're the only person who ever called me 'B.A.' and that was a long time ago. Sounds kinda funny."

"Funny nice, I hope."

Marilyn signaled, and Betty Ann went over to make her another martini, avoiding her questioning look. To give herself time, she made the rounds of the bar, making new drinks and picking up old glasses. She put them in the sudsy water and started washing again.

"It has been a long time," he said. "How'd you know where to send the cops to find me?"

"Told 'em about your thingee on the internet. Website."

"I paid enough for it, glad to know it worked."

"Marilyn over there found it for me," she said. "I don't do that stuff much. Jackson – that's my husband – he bought a computer but the darn thing makes me nervous."

"So you married again. That's good, I'm glad. I guess there was no sense in you waitin' around forever for Tom. Life's too short."

"I waited a long time, Barry." She turned to stack the clean glasses on the back bar and wished he hadn't said it. "Don't think I didn't give him a hell of a long time to come back. After you and Louisa left town, seemed like it was just me who gave a damn. The cops sure didn't."

"I get it," he said ruefully. "It was wrong of me to leave like that. In my own defense, I didn't really think anything had happened to Tom, and I knew there'd never be a chance for me as long as he was in your life. So I finally gave up and split."

She stared at him. "What kinda bullshit is that, Barry? A chance for you? Shit, you never liked me. We never liked each other."

For a moment he looked disconcerted. Then he flashed the crooked grin again, and she thought about how much difference such a grin might have made all those years ago if she had seen more of it. It was rather attractive.

She went on, "Anyway, it's all water under the bridge, ain't it."

"Mmh." He took a sip and glanced around the bar room. "Is your husband here? I'd like to meet the man who could knock Tom outa your mind, since I obviously never did."

"He died two years ago." She was getting mighty tired of saying that.

"Oh, hell." He put the beer bottle down with a thump. "I'm sorry, B.A. Really. I guess I'm not managing to be real sensitive tonight. Here I was hoping to make a good impression. Put it down to the shock. The cops came out of the blue, wanting me to remember what was going on back then. What I remember most is that those days were some of my happiest."

She rinsed the last few glasses and wiped her hands on a bar towel. Those days had been her happiest, too, but over the years

Tom had become a soft ghost, their marriage like something that happened to somebody else. She accepted the bald truth about his death, but sometimes it felt as though it had nothing to do with her.

Now in the shadowy light from the backlit bar, Barry's features slowly sharpened, coming clear like a ship appearing through a fog bank. Yes, this was the boy – man – that she had competed with for Tom's time and attention. With a pang, she realized what she had not admitted before, what Tom had recognized without effort. She had been jealous of Barry. How ridiculous it seemed now.

Barry had been studying the room, his gaze roaming over the worn banquettes, ramshackle cocktail tables, the pictures of centerfolds tacked to the walls that had probably been there long enough to be valuable. Unidentifiable emotions flickered across his face. He raised the beer bottle to his mouth again and nibbled on it, his eyes on her.

"So how have you been, really?" she asked to break the silence.

"Been doing alright. I live right over the gallery, so life is pretty simple."

She tilted her head. "Barry, really, how come you never came back just to say 'hi' in all these years? San Diego ain't that far. How come none of the old gang has ever heard from you? Or have they, and I didn't know about it?"

"No, I haven't been back. Pretty much cut all ties, I guess. Painted a lot at first, hours and hours of it. It came so fast and felt so glorious, I didn't want to stop." He leaned forward and spoke earnestly. "It's like I never could get going when I was up here, B.A. I mean, every time I tried, Tom just pointed out what was wrong with everything I painted. I don't mean to speak ill of him, I owe him a lot. But he wasn't much for simple encouragement, was he? Always the disputed passage, that was him. Sometimes it seemed like he did his best to suck the creativity out of everybody around him. Including you."

She snorted. "What 'creativity' was he supposed to encourage me at? I was never an artist, never wanted to be, he knew that.

You were different, though. He gave you a place to live, let you use his paints, even gave you some canvases when you couldn't buy your own. Always talked you up to the buyers and collectors that came around to look at his stuff."

"Did he, now? I don't remember much of that."

She said hotly, "Then your memory's mighty weak. What do you remember about those days, anyway?"

"Hmm." He rolled the base of the bottle around on the bar top, leaving wet circles. "That's what I was thinking about on the drive up here. Listen, can we go somewhere and talk without people watching us?"

She shook her head. "I can't leave here. But we can go sit for a spell." She called to the large black-haired man who was staring at the TV above the bar. "Hey, Mason, anybody needs another beer, you take care of it for me, okay?"

Mason nodded without taking his eyes off the TV.

As she led him to the rear of the room, she said, "Mason's got him a crush on that weather girl, so if nobody else cares, I put the weather channel on. It's usually worth an extra beer sale."

She gestured him to a stool at the same small back bar where Pete had given her the bad news about Tom.

"You the only one working here?" he asked.

"Don't take more'n one, most nights. On weekends, Patsy's here to help out."

He gave her a look of admiration. "You always did well in these kind of places. You got a touch with people, B.A." His voice took on an intimate tone. She could smell some male cologne, a heady rich scent. "I always admired the way you had with people, the way you could connect with them. I had a hard time of it, back then. I don't know if you realized it, but I was pretty shy."

"You seem sociable enough now," she said dryly.

Another flash of the grin. "I never did get to be very good with women, though. I think I always had you in the back of my mind, to compare them to. You were a hell of a woman. Still are, I'd say."

"Barry, cut the crap. You never showed any interest in me."

He drew back and looked hurt. "Hell, B.A., you were married to my best friend. Doesn't mean I didn't notice you. With that gold hair and trim figure. Still trim."

"Not hardly. I ain't gonna blow over in a stiff wind. But thanks anyway. Been a while since somebody said something nice about my figure. What I want to know is what you remember about Tom back then. Anything he was doin' before he disappeared, anything he mighta got in trouble for."

"Trouble?" His wary look uncannily echoed Louisa's.

"Yeah, like, was he doing something illegal back then that I didn't know about?"

"Illegal?"

"You know," she said impatiently. "Like sellin' drugs."

"Oh. Hell, no. Not straight-arrow Tom. I don't think so. Come to think of it, on the trip up here, I was remembering, he did act odd that summer. Secretive like. Sometimes when it was just him and me up there at the studio, he'd moon around all day and never speak more'n two words. And then there was those times he'd just up and drive somewhere. He liked to go down to the beaches in Mexico, didn't he? I always wondered why he never tried to live there. A lot cheaper."

"I don't care for beach-bumming myself."

He nodded. "Yeah, that was probably it. At least up here he had you and a roof over his head."

"The trips to Mexico, could that have been drugs?"

"I don't know. He never liked drugs, did he? Smoked dope, of course, like we all did. But I don't remember him dealing, even back before—" He stopped. "Before he moved out here. He did say once he was worried about you having to work so much. Do you think maybe he was doing something like selling drugs? To get money?"

"I don't know. And the cops seem as stumped as I am. Except for suspecting me of murdering him, that is."

He started to laugh and stopped when she didn't join him.

"You serious? They didn't say that."

"That's why I need to remember where I was and what I was doing back then, I mean real clear. Otherwise, they're not gonna bother looking anywhere else."

"Jesus, B.A., I had no idea." His eyebrows came together. "What did you tell them? I mean, about where you were."

"Told 'em I was probably working in one of the bars most of the time, but I'm damned if I can even remember which one. I had a sick spell before he disappeared, and my memories are mostly a jumble in my mind. It might take another thirty-eight years to sort 'em out."

"Nah," he said with confidence. "We'll just work on it together. Anything comes up in your mind, you tell me and we'll compare it with what I remember and figure it out."

"It ain't gonna happen tonight."

"That's fine." The intimate tone returned to his voice. "I'm a free bird right now. Nothing on my calendar, so I can drive up any time you like. Unless you got a spare room I can use."

She hesitated for only an instant. Barry's very male attention was surprisingly pleasant, she ruefully admitted to herself. But after so many years they were virtual strangers, and to have him sleeping in a bedroom right across the hall was something for which she felt completely unprepared.

"Louisa's got the only spare room right now," she lied firmly. "Her daughter threw her out, so she came back to Del Sueño."

"Boy, that sounds like Lou. As I remember, that girl never did anything but live on other people."

"She hasn't changed. Well, this is where you'll find me most nights. We can talk as long as it's slow. Maybe it'll help."

"Let's give it a try, anyway. We gotta get the cops off any silly notion that you're a murderer. Have you been up to the studio lately?"

"Drove up a few days ago, but we didn't stay long. Somebody started shooting at me with a rifle."

She had expected him to be shocked, but he simply shook his head.

"I remember Tom hated all the hunters prowling around," he said. "Always ran them off, didn't he? You run them off too?"

Before she could answer, there was a commotion at the front of the room. A group of people had come in. Still absorbed in the weather girl, Mason made no attempt to get up from his stool.

"Looks like it's time I got back to work." She stood up.

He put his hand on her arm. "When's your next night off?"

"Monday."

"Okay, let me pick you up first thing in the morning, and we'll take a drive up to the studio, see if anything shakes loose in my head. Nobody's going to shoot at you if I'm with you. We can stop somewhere for lunch. How about it?"

She hesitated.

"Yo, Betty Ann!" one of the group called. "It's been a long day, darlin'. How 'bout some service?"

"I'm comin', Ricky, hold your britches on."

Barry followed her back to the front bar where she scribbled her address on a cocktail napkin. He entered it into his smartphone and showed her that he had marked it as a "favorite". Then he lifted a finger to his forehead in a cocky salute and went out the door.

"Wow, girl," Marilyn said to her as she went behind the bar. "Who was that hunk?"

"That's Barry, the guy we were looking for."

"Looks like he found you first. I didn't realize you knew him that well."

"Hardly knew'm at all, as I remember."

Marilyn tilted her auburn head. "Sure looked like he remembered it different."

"Yeah," she said, feeling baffled. "It did seem that way, didn't it?"

Chapter Twelve

Sunday night Pete came into the End of the Line in civilian clothes and settled on his usual stool. She opened a beer and took it to him.

"I should tell you, I talked to Barry last night," she said.

"Who?" He took a long pull from the bottle, his eyes checking the room cop-like.

"The guy I told you about, that old friend of Tom's and mine."

"Sorry, things have been busy. I told Rodgers to look him up, but then I forgot."

"*Forgot.* Jesus, Pete, I'm suspected of murder here. I was counting on you to help me find a witness to anything going on back then." She decided not to mention her foolish trip to the gallery, since she hadn't found him there anyway.

He scratched his sandy hair, looking like a guilty child. "I'll see if Rodgers talked to San Diego PD yet—"

"Never mind," she grumped. "They already told him about Tom, that's why he came here. I don't know if it was Rodgers called 'em or that Lieutenant Kovacs, but they must've mentioned the End of the Line, 'cause he knew right where to find me."

"Okay, so, what did he have to say?"

"That he doesn't remember much more than I do."

"Doesn't sound like he'll be much help. I think I'll have a talk with him anyway. Is he still in town?"

"I don't know. He never said."

He threw down some money and got up. "Keep the change, girl. I guess I owe you."

"That's a thought." She put the money in the register drawer and dropped the change in her tip jar. When she turned around, he was gone. She hadn't gotten around to telling him that she was going up to Seddleton with Barry the next day.

Betty Ann spent the night punching her pillow, mulling over Barry's plans for her day off. It wasn't that she was against the idea of having someone along, especially someone more sensible than Louisa. But she was still feeling ambivalent about his effect on her. This new Barry was strange and at the same time strangely familiar. Actually seeing him in the flesh had brought back more memories of good times, but also of the worst time in her life.

By morning she was wishing they had not set up the trip to the cabin, but Barry arrived promptly at eight with a small bouquet of roses and a six-pack of Corona for the trip. She had accepted the flowers reservedly and let him peck a kiss on her cheek, aware of Louisa watching from the hallway. As she took him back to the kitchen, she saw him glance into the front room.

He said nothing about the flower paintings hanging on the walls, and his silence had given her the uncomfortable feeling that he didn't think much of them. What she had told herself was cool and relaxing now struck her as perhaps a little too unexciting. Maybe even dull or stodgy. But at least, she told herself stoutly, Jackson's choices were not made up of violent orange and red slashes that gave a person a headache.

After dressing in some old jeans and a flannel shirt, she dug the old picnic cooler out of the garage.

"I don't know why we can't take peanut butter sandwiches," said Louisa for the fifth time.

"When people got so sick from salmonella, I quit eating the stuff," said Betty Ann. "Get the tuna salad out of the fridge."

"Well, what about mayo in that? Don't it go all funny in the heat?"

"Actually," said Barry, "store-bought mayonnaise is completely safe even at room temperature, with all the vinegar and things like that in it. I'd be more worried about the fish."

Louisa shot him a filthy look. Neither of them had seemed happy to see each other and had been circling like wary hounds. After hinting broadly and ineffectively that Louisa should stay home, Barry had spent some time roaming the outside deck and then returned to the kitchen. He poked a finger in the mayonnaise-tuna mix and stuck it in his mouth.

Betty Ann slapped his hand away from doing it again and said, "Tuna is all I have, and Louisa here doesn't like tacos. I don't know what'll be open in Seddleton on a Monday morning."

She shoved another sandwich into a plastic bag and shut the lid of the cooler. Barry carried it to the back of his Ford F-150 truck while she locked the door. Louisa grumbled about needing a step ladder to climb up into the back seat.

"Hush," Betty Ann said. "At least this thing won't drag its belly on the rocks. You like big trucks now?" she asked him. "Seems like I remember you making fun of them before."

"They come in handy for off-roading."

"Oh, you like that?"

"Now and then," he said evasively.

It wasn't summer yet, but balmy breezes blew in the windows as he drove up into the hills. Betty Ann watched uneasily as he let the truck's outer wheels drift onto the accumulated grit that lay in the shoulder. She clutched at the grab handle.

"Whoo-hoo!" He laughed. "This is more fun than city streets, isn't it?"

She smiled politely. Slaloming around on blacktop was not her idea of fun, but men with trucks always wanted to show them off.

He took the next curve close to the center line. An oncoming sedan shot by them, too close and fast to see anything but a glimpse of the driver's horrified face. Barry jerked on the steering wheel, overcompensating, and the tires spun toward the shoulder again, this time inches from a ditch. When he finally got the big vehicle back in the lane, she testily asked him to slow down.

"Yeah," said Louisa. "You gonna kill us actin' like some kinda hot-dogger."

He flashed her a smile in the rearview mirror. "Guess I'm more used to fast driving than you are."

"Yeah?" she repeated. "You so used to it, why're you sweatin' like a pig?"

"Let's just take it easy," Betty Ann broke in. "We got all day, and it's too nice up here to rush through it."

"If you like," he said indifferently. But he slowed, and the feverish excitement in his eyes went away.

Once again she almost missed the gravel pull-out beside the rickety bridge. It took Barry several tries to get the big truck parked far enough over to be off the road. Betty Ann was relieved to see that he had no trouble carrying the cooler up the long path, even with the weight of all the bottles of ice tea that Louisa had piled in on top of his six-pack. He looked to be in good shape. She wondered what Tom would look like if he had lived. The black hair would be streaked with gray, probably. The laugh lines deeper around his eyes. Would he have put on weight? Or stayed lean as a greyhound?

"How old would Tom be now?" she puffed as they went up the first rise.

Barry appeared to think for a moment. "He was a couple years older than me, so shoot, I guess he'd be close to seventy by now."

It was such a sobering thought that Betty Ann didn't speak again until they reached the cabin. The door stood open in the silent afternoon.

"You leave it like that?" Barry asked, sounding bemused.

"Pretty damn sure we didn't. Lou, you remember us lockin' the door, don't you?"

Louisa shrugged.

"Okay," said Barry as he quietly put the cooler on the ground. "You girls stay here."

Betty Ann watched as he crept up the steps, crossed the porch and placed his back to the wall beside the door. He reached out and pushed the door wider open and looked cautiously into the front room.

"Why don't he just call out?" Louisa said irritably. "This ain't the wild west. Whoever's in there'll either answer or high-tail it out the back."

"Might be our shooter."

Louisa snorted but didn't say anything more. Barry disappeared inside. Betty Ann waited tensely until he popped up in the doorway.

"It's okay. Doesn't look like there's anyone around. Come look at this, though."

Betty Ann followed him through the front room and kitchenette to the back stoop. Yellow crime scene tape had been tied to one corner of the cabin and looped around a California Oak at the edge of the weedy back area, ending up at the opposite corner. She stepped down and went to inspect the wall.

"There." She pointed. "The cops have been here. Looks like somebody's dug out the bullets. Left some nice big holes to repair."

He stood with his hands on his hips, looking around. "You know, if you're thinking of fixing this place up, you sure got a hard fight ahead of you. There's a hole in the roof, and I don't know about you, but my outhouse days are over. You'd need to put in a septic tank and a good source of water. Depending on how deep you have to go, a well could run you major bucks. If I was you, I'd just put the place on the market."

"You're probably right," she said glumly, "but Louisa's got some idea she wants to live up here, be caretaker for me."

"Good God, she'd be as much use as a squirrel guarding a hen house. No, seriously, B.A. You probably couldn't ask much for it, as rundown as it is, but it would be money in instead of money out. I'd go ahead and list it in auction now before there's another real estate crash."

"I don't need the money," she said. She felt resistance to his disparaging remarks. They had had some good times at the cabin.

And it was Tom's land, whatever the deed said. Other than a couple of sketches stored in a closet in Vista, the land was all she had left of him. Somehow that had never bothered her before, and she didn't want to examine why it bothered her now after so many years.

Barry had raised his eyebrows at her last remark, but he said nothing.

"I can't get the cooler lid off," Louisa whined from the kitchen.

He went back through the screen door, leaving Betty Ann to listen to the quiet sound of something rustling in the underbrush. She went over to take a look, and a jackrabbit exploded out of a saltbush. She followed the trail he had dashed along. It struck upward through the trees, and with a vague memory of water, she climbed toward where a wedge of sky beckoned. Halfway up, a thicker copse of trees grew around a leaf-clogged pond. Even at the beginning of spring it looked brackish and would no doubt be dry long before summer.

Beyond it the path continued upward, twisting through the scrub brush. She followed it to the top of the rise and stood looking across a small meadow full of pale grasses and bright yellow wildflowers. On the far side of the meadow was a bench made of hand-hewn logs. Put there by some long-ago resident, it sat with its back to her at the lip of a deep arroyo, facing hills that rose and dipped away from her, fading from fragile spring brown to gray-blue. Beyond them was a valley so far away, it was just faint indeterminate smears of tan and white in the blinding sun, like an alien planet viewed from space.

The wind picked up, still chilly with spring. She drew her jacket tighter around her and approached the little bench. A memory bit into her heart, of a late warm evening when she and Tom had walked up hand in hand and ended up making rustic love on the bench in full view of anyone who might be hiking among the hills. At that age it had seemed daring to her and made her laugh. Now the bench looked full of spiders and splinters.

In front of it someone—likely the same forgotten resident—had built a platform of thick planks that extended out over a steep drop to the arroyo below. In the giddy aftermath of love, Tom had talked about bringing a blanket next time and spreading it on the platform so they could "make love at the edge of the world."

She walked over and peered underneath it, careful not to put her weight on the loose dirt at the edge of the drop.

"Makes you wonder, doesn't it?"

She jumped and turned around. Barry had followed her up the path.

"Wonder about what?" she asked.

"Why on earth someone stuck a bench out here, looking at nothing."

"It's kind of a peaceful view. I always wondered what this little platform was supposed to be for. It almost looks like a diving platform, but there sure ain't no swimmin' hole here. This arroyo wouldn't have any water except when there's a flash flood, and that's not anything you want to swim in."

"Maybe it was for some sort of crane to lower things to the bottom. Like miners used to make. Hey, maybe there's a gold mine around here." He stepped to the outer edge of the platform and looked around the arroyo. Then he bounced experimentally.

"Don't do that," she said, a little breathlessly.

He laughed. "It's pretty sturdy. Those four-by-fours are stuck hard into the cliff, with a bunch of braces running across, see? C'mon out, it's safe. You can see clear down the arroyo from here."

"I'll take your word for it."

"I don't remember you being afraid of heights."

"I'm not. I'm just not putting my faith in something like that. The last gold mines around here were played out a hundred years ago. Please," she added urgently, "come back off it."

He obeyed, stepping off with a grin. "Worried about me? So you do care."

"What are you guys doing up here?" Louisa called from behind her. She trudged up to join them. "I thought we were gonna search the cabin. I don't like being down there alone."

"I thought you wanted to live up here?" said Betty Ann.

"I mean I didn't like not knowing where you all went."

"Okay, you're right, we better get to work. We need to eat first, and then we can start seeing what's left in the cupboards and closets. There won't be a lot of light once the sun starts going behind the hills."

Three hours later they had eaten all of the food and dug into every closet and cupboard inside the cabin. Other than the questionable cans of food and tattered bedding, it looked like anything useful had been harvested by vagrants or hikers.

In spite of the season, the cabin accumulated heat from the sun. Betty Ann went outside in search of a breeze and sat down heavily on the top step of the porch. She hadn't noticed on their previous trip that the old picnic table was gone, probably one of the first things to be scavenged. She took the dripping bottle of beer that Barry handed her.

Louisa gingerly rested her broad hips on the sagging armchair. "What about Tom's paintings, anyway? Whatever happened to 'em? They might could be worth something today."

Betty Ann said pensively, "I never saw any of them again. I came up here when you were packing to leave, remember, Barry? You remember what he did with them?"

He shook his head.

"After you left I looked around for some clue to where he'd gone. None of his paintings were here, not in the shed or anywhere else. So I figured he'd taken them with him when he lit out. Or maybe he sold 'em all before he left, for the money." She frowned. "Could that be what he was killed for?"

Louisa scoffed. "How much could they have been worth? Back then, I mean. Now they might be worth something, since he's dead."

"Jesus, Louisa—" Barry started.

Betty Ann said, "Well, they're gone, so it doesn't matter much, does it?"

"You sure?" said Louisa. "Maybe they're way in the back of the shed, behind something."

"I don't think so. Last time I looked, all I saw was a lot of junk, some old paint cans and empty gas cans," Betty Ann said with a frown of thought. "Stuff like that beat-up bush-whacker we used on the yard. There might be some tools buried under other stuff. C'mon, might as well go see if we can get the padlock off."

She wiped her hands on her jeans and led them to the prefabricated metal shed.

"Sure ain't no padlock on it now," observed Louisa. "Looks like somebody's just about tore off the whole latch."

"Bent the hell outa the door, too," said Betty Ann. "They sure musta thought there was something valuable in here."

After considerable tugging and grunting, she and Barry managed to get the metal doors to grind through their tracks over years of accumulated dirt. They peered in together at vague metal shapes and large pieces of wood. Betty Ann pointed out the bush-whacker, now covered with old beach towels. Two broken shovels lay against the wall, their handles sticking up like bayonets. Loops of heavy sisal rope lay in the back, beyond a stack of twisted aluminum lawn chairs. A few dried up cans of paint remained against the wall, but everything else had been taken.

"Ugh," said Louisa. "What a mess."

"Looks like the back seat of your car," said Barry. He gingerly stepped onto the bush-whacker's frame and peered toward the rear into the shadows. "Nothing like Tom's pictures in here. Yeah, I think anything of real value is long gone, unless you got a use for that rope." He stepped back down and slapped the dirt from his hands.

"Maybe we should pull it all out and sort through it, though," Betty Ann said doubtfully. "Might be something worth salvaging,"

"Well, if you really want to do that, I'd hire a guy to do it for you and haul away what you don't want. Might save you a tetanus shot. Some of that old rusted stuff looks lethal. But I can't see that there's any rush."

"Alright. I suppose before we leave, we ought to check the root cellar under the floor," she said tiredly as they returned to the porch.

Barry looked startled. "What root cellar?"

"It's just a hole under the living room, just about big enough to store some sacks of onions and potatoes, not that we ever had any. Tom used to stash stuff down there in old surplus ammo boxes. Dunno if they're still there, but we ought to check, just to be sure."

"We could," Barry said doubtfully. "But you look pretty beat. Why don't we leave it for later? We can always come back on your next day off."

"No, it won't take much to just look."

Back in the front room, it took them a few moments to drag aside the cable-spool table and pull back the two indented slide bolts that kept the trap door secure. Barry stuck his fingers in the loop, pulled it up with a grunt and laid it back on the floor.

"Wow," he puffed. "I see why you didn't go down there much. Hernia in waiting."

"Ugh again," said Louisa, peering downward. "I don't care what's in it, I'm not going down there."

"Nobody's asking you," said Barry. He knelt down and probed with the flashlight he had brought with him. "Hey, it's really interesting down there! And I see some boxes or something. Here—" He thrust the flashlight at Betty Ann and lowered himself through the hole.

She handed the flashlight to Louisa. "Give me this when I get down there."

"You shouldn't come down." Barry's voice sounded muffled. "There's probably black widows, and it's really filthy."

Betty Ann lowered herself until she hung from the edge and felt gingerly for the bottom with one foot. Her fingers started to slip painfully on the rough wood, and she let go. She felt a sharp jab in her ankle and tumbled onto the cool earth floor with a gasp of pain.

Chapter Thirteen

"What happened?" Louisa stuck her head over the opening.

"Twisted my ankle a bit."

Barry helped her up and kept his arm around her as she gingerly tested it.

"Let me pull that table over," he said. "I'll help you climb back out. Louisa, get some ice out of the cooler to put on it. I hope you didn't break anything."

"No, of course not," she said shortly. She shrugged off his strong arm. "I'm fine."

"You sure?"

"Yes, really," she said, trying to soften her tone. "Sorry, I guess I'm not used to somebody fussing about me these days. I'm fine, and I want to see what's down here."

Reluctantly Barry ran the flashlight beam around the earthen walls. The space was perhaps twelve feet square and barely deep enough for her to stand upright. Barry had to keep his head down or hit it on the dark beams that supported the floor. There was a rickety table against the side and some empty wooden shelves. Piled in a corner were a cluster of metal boxes.

Barry squatted down and said excitedly, "Metal ammo boxes, like you said! Old military salvage. I remember these. Vets came home with them and used them to store lots of things. We had a stash of them at the SDS office. I'll bet Tom liberated them from there."

She counted. "Six of them. What did he want them for?"

"Who knows?" He picked one up. "Pretty heavy. Well, we can't see much down here, it's too dark." He yanked at the lid. "Besides, I think the hasps have oxidized shut. We're gonna need tools. I don't think you and I can lift them up outa here. Let's leave them until we can bring back somebody to help lift them out."

"No, I want to find out what's in them now. I'll stand on the table, and we can do like a bucket brigade, pass them up to Lou one by one."

"They're pretty heavy, you'll just twist your ankle worse. Why don't you and Louisa go see if you can get some of that rope out of the shed. I should be able to tie them together so we can pull them up."

Betty Ann hobbled to the trap door and explained to Louisa what they wanted.

"How'm I supposed to climb over all that junk?"

"Like you say—climb over. Throw those old towels over everything and grab the smallest coil of rope. Hurry up."

They listened to her walk across the floor and out the door. Barry poked around with the flashlight. "I don't see anything else."

Betty Ann sighed. "Y'know, I was kinda hoping some of Tom's paintings would be down here, in spite of the damp."

"Yeah, too bad," murmured Barry. "We'll probably need a knife to cut up the rope, but I don't have one, do you? There might be something in the kitchen, if you want to go look."

"No, we looked. Anything like that is long gone."

A heavy coil of rope dropped through the opening with a thud.

Barry lifted a box experimentally and began to tie it by the handle to another. He ended up with something that looked like a bulky fishing stringer.

"That's really good," she said. "You a Boy Scout?"

"Nope. I never cared for the quasi-military stuff. Free spirit, that's me. But I had some practice back in the day, tying up protest signs."

He gave the last knot a testing tug and handed the end of the rope up to Louisa. Then he dragged the wooden table across and helped Betty Ann climb onto it. With him steadying her legs and Louisa dragging on her armpits, she hauled herself up and out of the hole. For a moment she sat getting her breath, pulling cobwebs from her hair. Then with the two women hauling on the rope, Barry was able to stand on the table and thrust each box out of the hole. When all the boxes lay on the floor, Barry climbed out with no visible effort. He dropped the heavy trapdoor back in place. Dust puffed from its nearly invisible seams.

"Put the table back where it was," Betty Ann told him, "so nobody else'll be climbing down in there."

She set her teeth against the pain in her ankle and limped over to where Louisa had dragged all eight boxes into the shaft of light coming through the front door. The sun had dropped far down in the sky, and the orange tinge in the air made the olive-green boxes look acidic.

"It's getting late," Barry answered. "Why don't we load these up and take them with us?"

"Good idea. There's tools and plenty of light in my kitchen."

"I really think you need to put that ankle up tonight. It looks like it's swelling. I can help you with the boxes tomorrow."

A sharp crack made them both jump. Before Betty Ann could obey her impulse to duck, Louisa declared, "Look! I got this one open!" She brandished a screwdriver.

"Where'd you get that?"

"Found it in the shed when I got the rope."

The three of them bent over the box. It appeared to be stuffed full of folded papers. Louisa started to reach inside. Barry caught her wrist. "That stuff belongs to B.A., doesn't it?"

Betty Ann lowered herself awkwardly to the floor and lifted out a fistful of brittle documents. She flipped through them carelessly until one caught her eye.

"Here's a copy of a deed!" she cried. She unfolded the stiff paper and frowned. "Did Tom own something else up here? Similar property lot number. No, I think it's the same one I gave

Dorothy at Deeds and Records. Where's my purse? But, look, the name on this deed is 'James G. Garrett'. Who the hell's that?"

They both stared at her. Louisa swallowed. "Well, but what's it matter? Prob'ly the guy who owned it before."

"Tom inherited the place from his aunt and she wasn't married. Might be who she got it from, but I can't make out the date. Why would Tom keep it? I better stop by and check with Dorothy about this one. It just keeps getting nuttier." Betty Ann picked through the box and pulled out a dog-eared paperback book. "I remember this. It was Tom's favorite, he read from it most nights. T.S. Eliot's poems. Why'd he put it in here?"

Barry took it from her and flipped through the pages. "Nothing hidden inside. Here, this is underlined. 'Only those who will risk going too far can possibly find out how far one can go.' Yeah, that sounds like old Tom in his younger days. He mellowed out after a while, didn't he?" He tossed it aside.

Betty Ann searched through the rest of the box's contents, finding nothing of interest. A photo lay on the bottom. She pulled it out and said, "Oh, dear God. I remember looking everywhere for this. I always figured Tom took it with him."

Louisa leaned over to examine it. "Hey, that's you and Tom in front of the cabin! Who else is that? When was that taken?"

"One of the first times we ever came up here, right after we found out his aunt had died and left him the place. The cabin wasn't so beat up then. We even thought about living up here, sort of back-to-the-earth hippie commune style. We had no money to dig for water back then, or do any kind of improvements. We were just going to rough it. How young we were. Everything seemed so easy then."

Suddenly her eyes burned with tears. Embarrassed, she looked away. Barry put his arm around her. She stiffened but let it stay as she lowered her head and fought to control herself. Finally she sniffed, dabbed at her eyes with the handkerchief he offered and looked at the mascara on it.

"Sorry, it's a mess. I'm a mess."

Barry grinned. "That's more like it," he said. "When a woman starts to worry about her appearance, she's okay."

"No, it's not like me at all. It just caught me by surprise, that picture. I've been trying to remember Tom, or I thought I was. I think maybe I've been remembering the bad times and not the good ones."

"Seemed to me you'd forgotten about Tom entirely," said Louisa sullenly.

"Don't be an ass," Barry told her. "That's enough, B.A. Put it all back and let's get you home."

She slipped the photo in her back pocket and returned the rest to the box. He was helping her up from the floor when they heard crunching footsteps on the path. Barry stepped onto the porch and stood with the screen door open.

"It's a cop," he said.

She looked over his shoulder. "It's Lieutenant Kovacs. Seddleton police. Louisa and I went over there to report the shooting, and I ended up being interrogated about Tom's murder."

"Son of a bitch."

"You've met him?" she asked, thinking Kovacs wasn't that bad.

"No. I just don't like cops."

The two of them watched in silence as Kovacs walked up to the steps. He spotted Betty Ann and nodded.

"Wondered who might be up here. That your Ford truck down there, Ms. Beaumont?"

"It's mine," said Barry in a hostile tone. "Is there a problem?"

Kovacs didn't answer for a moment. Betty Ann saw his eyes narrow.

"I guess not," he said finally. "Not if you have her permission to park it there, blocking the bridge. Everything okay, Ms. Beaumont? He's with you, then?"

Before she could answer, Barry snapped, "Of course I'm with her. Do I look like I'm holding her hostage? On the other hand, this *is* private property. Why are you here?"

Betty Ann said quickly, "Barry, he was just checking. I did report a shooting. Why have you come back?" she asked Kovacs.

He said evenly, "I brought the County Crime Investigator with me to get those bullets out of the wall."

Betty Ann stood in stunned silence. Then she felt pounding rage move up from her chest and flood her face with heat. "Are you telling me you didn't take them out? First Pete Branson 'forgets' he's supposed to let Barry here know that his best friend is dead, and now you take a goddam *week* to get evidence of someone trying to kill me!" She limped across to the porch and held onto a support post as she leaned forward, pointing her finger at Kovacs. "Not to mention accusing me of murdering my husband!"

"I didn't accuse—"

"You as much as! Dammit, you cops are always the same! First you act like I'm some sort of bimbo when I try to report Tom missing, and then thirty-eight goddam years later you're lookin' to blame me for his murder! I want you off my property!" She spotted another figure coming over the rise from the direction of the road. It was a woman in a white lab coat carrying an equipment case. "And her too! Both of you get the hell out!"

"It hasn't been a week," he said with just a trace of defensiveness. "You reported a crime, and now we need to follow through. We'll go as soon as we collect the evidence—"

"Your goddam evidence is gone!"

Kovacs frowned at her. The woman came up beside him and paused to catch her breath.

"What do you mean, it's gone?" he asked.

"I mean," Betty Ann said with wrath, "that somebody already dug it out! If you didn't do it, then I guess whoever shot at me came back and dug those bullets out long before you ever got around to doing what I asked you to do!"

After her first words he had seemed to stop listening. He started to go around the building. Barry flew down the steps.

"Where the hell do you think you're going! She said to get the hell off the property!"

Kovacs turned and, ignoring the irate Barry, said to Betty Ann through his teeth, "I came up here the night you reported it and took a look. I couldn't see much in the dark, so I taped it off and decided to come back with a properly trained Crime Investigator, but I had to wait until she could drive over from San Bernardino." He waved vaguely toward the woman who stood watching them.

"Alright, Barry," Betty Ann said, "let him be. He can go see for himself that it's too damn late for his Crime Investigator. Then he can leave."

Kovacs disappeared around the corner of the cabin. The woman walked carefully around Barry and followed him.

Betty Ann went back inside. After a moment Barry came in. She sat down heavily on the makeshift backseat sofa.

"I feel like I could just cry some more."

"Go ahead," he said. "Maybe you should do it more often."

"Nah. Ain't never done me much good."

"I'm gonna go keep an eye on that guy."

"Don't worry about him—"

He was gone, through to the kitchen. Betty Ann sighed and followed, wondering if Barry's temper was a match for Kovacs' cold determination.

Louisa stood beside him at the kitchen windows, watching Kovacs stare up at the outside wall. "What's he think he's gonna do now?" she asked.

"I don't know," Betty Ann answered tiredly. "Hand me one of those beers, will you? I may just get drunk, since I ain't drivin'."

They watched as Kovacs and the woman had a murmured consultation. She knelt to open her case. He mounted the steps and entered the kitchen, patently ignoring Barry's smoldering presence.

"Casey's a tool mark specialist," he said, removing his hat. "She's going to cut out around the holes and take the wood back to her lab. She might be able to determine what they used to dig the bullets out."

"Fine," Betty Ann said with a show of indifference. "Is that gonna tell us who did it?"

"No. But if we get a suspect, maybe we can match the tool marks to something they own."

"So now I can repair the damage to my wall along with everything else?"

He shot her one of his piercing looks. "You planning to fix the place up? Live here?"

"Not me. Louisa wants to stay here."

He studied Louisa for a moment and turned back to Betty Ann. "I'd advise you to put up postings, whoever plans to stay up here."

"Postings?"

"Signs like 'No Hunting'. 'Private Property'. You can buy them at any hardware store."

"Christ," Barry said with a sneer. "Are there still *hardware* stores up here? No Home Depot?"

It was Barry's turn to receive the drawn-out scrutiny. Finally he said, "Not much business up here for something that big, but yes, you can find the signs at one of those. How are you with a hammer and nails?"

Betty Ann broke in. "I can manage a hammer myself. Thank you, I'll come back and post signs right away."

"Like that's going to stop anybody," said Barry.

"Well, it might make them think about it," Kovacs said mildly. "Place won't look so abandoned. Meanwhile I'll make a point of driving by on my rounds. The frequent sight of a police car can be sobering."

The technician called to him from the back yard.

"Okay," he said, "we'll be leaving now. I noticed you were limping. Anything serious?"

"No, I just twisted my ankle a bit."

"Need any help getting back to your car?"

Barry broke in harshly. "I can take care of her."

"I'll be fine," said Betty Ann. "But thank you."

"Got anything you need help carrying down?"

"I told you," Barry snapped, "I'll take care of it."

"Yes, you did say that," Kovacs agreed. "You need to want to watch the attitude, though, or you might end up being helped back down and taken into town on an attitude warrant." He turned back to Betty Ann. "Well, if that's all, I apologize again for messing up on the job. Here's hoping it was just a drunk hunter who won't come back, especially if you post those signs."

When the technician had finished putting the bits of wood in evidence bags, they left. Betty Ann limped back to the front door to watch as they negotiated the bramble-lined track and disappeared over the ridge. Her anger had not left her, but she had to admit that she liked the idea of an obvious police presence. A big man in a uniform did have a comforting effect.

There was nothing wrong with Barry; in fact, he was turning out to be competent in ways she never would have guessed. But he had a temper, and that could get them all into trouble. She refused Barry's offer to carry her back to the truck and fumed with helpless frustration while he and Louisa made several trips to take down the cooler and the ammo boxes.

"I'd say," he puffed when everything was gone, "that until you get that bridge fixed, you need to buy a wheelbarrow or some such thing. I've worked up an appetite, though. Is there a decent restaurant down in your town?"

"Can't we go to that cafe in Seddleton?" asked Louisa. "I'm hungry."

Barry scowled. "I'd rather not run into your friend the cop."

"Probably better if you don't. Never mind," said Betty Ann. "I'm going to need a bath and shampoo before I go into any restaurant, decent or not."

She braced herself on Barry's arm as they labored up and down the track to the road. All three were quiet on the way back to Vista de Copa.

"Let's leave the boxes in the back of the truck," suggested Barry as they climbed out and Betty Ann searched her purse for the key to the front door. "I'll get a room over at the Best Western and clean up. Then I'll come back and take you ladies to dinner."

"Okay," said Betty Ann, "but I don't want to leave those boxes in your truck. They're filthy and I think they're covered with mold. And dinner'll be my treat. I owe you both for the help."

"Why don't you guys go on?" said Louisa grumpily as she and Barry each lifted two of the heavy boxes and followed Betty Ann through the door. "I'm tired and I don't feel like going to some fancy place. When you finish with your date, you can bring me back something."

Betty Ann felt her cheeks turn pink. Barry looked intrigued by Louisa's remark, but he said nothing as he carried the rest of the boxes from the truck to the porch. When Betty Ann insisted that she wanted them inside, he put them on the floor in the hallway.

"I'll be back in an hour," he muttered as he left.

Betty Ann closed the door behind him and turned on Louisa.

"What the hell's the matter with you? This isn't any kind of a date! Like I told you, I owe you both for the help."

"Sure sounds like he thinks it's one. I thought you said you didn't like him."

"I got nothing against him, okay? I never did. And he and I need to sit down and go over what might have happened to Tom. If you don't feel like coming along, fine, but don't go making it into something it's not."

Louisa sniffed haughtily and went to her room at the top of the stairs. Betty Ann sighed and went to her own room and filled the tub in the master bath.

Chapter Fourteen

After a soak in Epsom salts, the throbbing in her ankle had nearly disappeared. With some clean clothes on, her hair piled high and fresh makeup, she felt like she could face the evening after all. She eyed the boxes still sitting in the hall, but her blood sugar was low. Before she did anything more, she had to eat.

Barry showed up in a button-down shirt and slacks, wet comb lines in his faded hair. It was so different from her memories of the young Barry in torn t-shirts and jeans, dirty hair falling to his shoulders, that she had to smile.

"What?" he asked as he helped her climb into the truck.

"Nothing. Just thinking how we've all changed."

"Thirty-eight years. It'd be pretty surprising if we didn't. You look real good, though." He got behind the wheel and glanced at her as he started the truck and headed down the hill.

"Thank you." She was tempted to say that she needed to lose some weight, but men were never interested in that kind of remark the way women were. Besides, it would sound like she was fishing for more compliments. "Where are we going?"

"No idea. Where's a nice place?"

"Lotsa nice places in Del Sueño, but most are pretty noisy, family places, fulla kids at this hour." She directed him south on the road to Escondido, to a restaurant that used to be Jackson's favorite. It was relaxing to let someone else drive while she gazed at the mountains that looked soft in the gray glow of evening.

"Nice place," he said as they walked in. "You come here a lot?"

"Haven't been here since Jackson died. They have good steaks."

The maître d' smiled at her in recognition. "A long time, Ms. Beaumont. We were devastated to learn of Mr. Beaumont's passing."

"Thank you."

He helped her drape her coat and scarf over the back of her chair. After he left, Barry looked around. "I'm impressed. You're remembered by the maître d', no less."

"He remembers Jackson. I think he came here a lot even before we were married."

Barry reached for her hand.

"I'm glad you chose a quiet place."

Remembering what Louisa said made her self-conscious. She slipped her hand out of his grasp to take a sip of water. "I figured it would be easier to talk. What all do you remember about the time around when Tom disappeared?"

He gave her a smile that curled one side of his mouth down. "Well, like I said, not much. I remember you coming up to the studio looking for him."

"You said you'd been down visiting friends. Anybody I knew? Or Tom knew?"

He shook his head. "Nah, just some folks I knew from Jersey."

"Sure seems like a lot of people from Jersey were floating around right then. Louisa says she was visiting some old friends from there, too, only she was up in Riverside. Everyone was out of town." *When I needed you.* She didn't say it, but to her horror, it seemed to float in the air.

Barry gave no sign of noticing. "Yeah, they invited me to come and live over their garage in Chula Vista. Once I got over feeling sorry for myself and my career started to take off, I realized I kinda ran out on you. But by that time, I figured you'd gotten through it and why rake it up?"

"Through what? Tom being gone? Or the cops not believing what I told them?" Her tone was sulky even to her own ears, and she quickly added, "I'd just like to know what you might have told me then, if we hadn't argued. Was there anything that would've helped me with those stupid cops?"

The waiter came up to take their orders, and Barry waited until they were gone before replying.

"Honestly, B.A.? For years I tried to think about where he might have gone off to. I never dreamed he was dead—I just thought, I guess like everyone else, that he decided he needed to get away. Like I said before, he'd done that enough times. Way back in our radical days, he'd get sick of the protesting and disappear for a while. Always showed up again, though, until one day he just up and took off for California."

"Louisa said he wanted to see Haight and Ash. Did he make it? I mean, would there be anyone in San Francisco he might have had ties to?"

"Doubt it. We were out of touch for a while, but as far as I know, he ended up here right off the bat. Never made it to San Francisco." He grinned. "He took one look at you and put down roots. Marriage, no less. That made me laugh. I mean, it sounded so far away from our days of wild anarchy. I could see him in a commune, maybe. But an actual establishment middle class wedding? What a trip! Was it church or courthouse?"

"Courthouse," she said curtly. "Neither of us were church-goers. I only mention his earlier times because I can't think of anyone around Del Sueño who might have had it in for him."

He sat back. "I can't think of anyone, anywhere, who had it in for Tom Stearns. Not anyone who would kill him, I mean. So, if you ask me, it was some bum he gave a lift to. He was always doing that. Giving lifts to strangers on their last pair of jeans, loaning money if he had it, letting them sleep on his couch."

Or camp out in his back yard in a hearse. "How about those artsy types he introduced you to? Any problems there?"

"B.A., I know you think he helped me a lot with the art scene here, such as it was. But the fact is, I can't remember him introducing me to anybody. I mean, I never had a show of my own or sold anything until I went down to San Diego. That's why I left when I did. His career seemed to be on the skids, and it looked like a good time to cut loose and go on without him."

The words sounded like vintage Barry, but she was glad to see that he had grown out of the whining tone. He was just stating facts, and she had to admit, with her limited understanding of the art world, he could be exactly right.

Their orders came out and they began to eat.

"Okay," she said. "How'd he look the last time you saw him?"

"I've been trying to remember ever since the cops came. But it's all mixed up with talking to my friends and then coming back for my stuff—that's when you were there—and moving into that loft they let me use. My paintings started to sell quick, so when they decided California was getting too built up for them and split, I took over their gallery. Moved in upstairs, and I've been there ever since. You should come down sometime and spend the day with me. San Diego is a great little city, lots to do. I'll take you over to the Gaslight District. Or Balboa Park. There's some great restaurants, and one of my paintings is hanging in the museum—"

"Didn't Tom say anything the last time you saw him?" she asked bluntly. "About going somewhere? Anything about me?"

He wiped his lips and put the napkin down. "Look, B.A., I want to remember what he said, maybe what he was up to. But the truth is, I was pissed the last day I saw him and didn't really want to talk to him. That's why I went down to spend some time with my friends. Of course he talked about you, he always talked about you." He flashed her the grin. "I do remember him saying that he wanted to get a job, find some money somehow, because you were getting tired of being the wage-earner. I was pretty shocked."

"What d'you mean, shocked?"

"He never wanted a real job once he quit college. Never wanted to pay income tax, support a wife, all that establishment crap. Hey, we were hippies, weren't we! We protested the war, the government, everything. We were going to change the world and live on our art and never be like our parents. It blew my mind when I found out he'd actually married you, all legal, like. He even owned property, f'Christ's sake, until he put it in your name."

She let her fork slowly descend to the plate.

"How did you know he put it in my name?"

For the first time, Barry looked unsure of himself.

"You said so. At the cabin."

She shook her head. "No, I was talking about the other deed. The old one with whatsis-name on it."

"Lou must have mentioned it when you were out of the room." Under her gaze he became uncomfortable. "I... she said she wanted to live up there and did I think she could do it."

"Lou was asking your advice?" she said, not bothering to keep skepticism out of her voice. "Tell me the truth, Barry. You knew Tom put it in my name a long time ago, didn't you?"

He chewed his lip for a moment, his eyes brooding. "Alright, Tom made me promise not to tell you, but I guess it doesn't matter now, does it?" He took a breath. "Tom had me be there to witness it when he put it in your name."

"I only found out it was in my name four days ago. And Lou was as surprised as I was."

He stared in amazement. "Y'know, I did wonder. I mean, I wondered why you weren't there with us when he did it."

"Did he say why he did it? Put it in my name and not both of ours?"

"He must have had his reasons." Barry looked unhappy. "Okay, the truth is—I mean, he didn't come right out and say, but I got the impression he was maybe planning to leave and wanted you to have something. That's why I didn't want to talk to you that day when you came up to the cabin looking for him."

"You knew he was planning to leave me and didn't say anything."

"I didn't really think he'd do it. Afterwards, I felt bad that he'd leave you without a word. But, honestly, I figured he'd come back eventually. He'd realize how stupid it was."

"Yeah, except he never left me, did he?" she said harshly. "Not voluntarily."

Barry picked up his wine glass and sipped at it, not answering. They finished their meal in near silence.

"So, when are you going back up to the cabin?" he asked as the waiter took their plates.

"I dunno. I guess I've got everything from there I might want. I should go up and post those signs Kovacs was talking about, though."

"That ankle doesn't need for you to be tramping around up there. How about if I pick up some signs tomorrow morning and go stick them around?"

"Thought you didn't want to run into Kovacs again?"

"True," he said ruefully. "But on the other hand, I'm not sure I like him being up there prowling around with nobody there. It sounds like a lot more than most cops would do. Makes me wonder what he's up to."

"Barry, you need to quit hasslin' him before you get your butt in trouble. He's just doing his job."

"Like not pulling those bullets out? There's something else going on there, B.A."

She said nothing for a moment, stumped. "Well, anyway, I like the idea of a cop being around, in case the shooter comes back. Someone in uniform might scare them off permanently. Otherwise, I wouldn't want Louisa living up there by herself. That's if I don't decide to sell it."

"I think you should do that. Let somebody else fix it up and pay the taxes. Why hang onto such a headache?"

"Speaking of taxes," she said abruptly, "who do you know named Abigail Hoffman?"

"Never heard of her," he snapped. "Jesus, could you sound a little less like a cop yourself? I'm trying to help out, here."

"Sorry," she said. "I know none of this is your fault. It's all so screwed up, and I guess it's making me edgy. And a little bit scared. People shootin' at me. Cops thinkin' I killed Tom. I don't mean to take it out on you. It was good of you to drive up here to help me. Maybe I will come down sometime to see what you've done with your life. I think I need to get out of town for a while. That is," she added ruefully, "if the cops'll let me."

This time when he took her hand in his, she didn't pull it away. The soft lights of the restaurant lay gently on his face, masking the lines of age, making him look more like the young Barry from so long ago. It was pleasant to sit in a restaurant while a man made love to her with his eyes. She had begun to think such days were over for her since Jackson had passed away.

"That'd be great," he said softly. "The sooner, the better. I'll come up and get you. We'll drive down, have lunch. I'll show you around."

Finally, she drew back her hand and touched her fingers to the nape of her neck. "I think I'd rather drive down myself. That way you don't have to bring me home."

His grin came back, and she realized how he may have interpreted what she had said. Angry with herself, she said, "You can show me around, and then I'll come home, okay? I'm not ready for anything more than that right now."

"Sure, B.A. Anything you say." He stopped grinning, but still looked slightly amused. Whatever he said about the old days, confidence with women did not seem to be something he lacked now. "I'm glad you're not writing me off completely. We can just spend the day exploring the park or walking on the beach. Whatever you like. Get to know each other again."

She wondered if she should tell him that she was thinking of hiring a search service to find the elusive Ms. Hoffman online. She had heard you could do that and it wouldn't cost too much. Or it might be worth the money to get an old-fashioned private detective, but they probably used the same services anyway. If the woman was somewhere in the area, she could drive down again to confront her. Maybe she could combine it with spending the day with Barry.

But the truth was, she felt somewhat nervous about facing the kind of woman who paid taxes for another man's wife. If Barry didn't know who she was, then she preferred to talk to the woman alone. There might be a very good reason Tom had never mentioned her to Barry. To either of them.

"So," he was saying, "when are you planning to try and open the rest of those boxes?"

"Tomorrow, I guess. I should be working on them right now, but after seeing what's in the first box, I'm not expectin' much in the way of clues. All the stuff in the first box looks pretty boring, like receipts and old registrations for the Chevy."

He cut a piece of steak and chewed, looking at her thoughtfully. "I meant to ask, who took that photo that upset you? I've been trying to remember, but I can't. Maybe if I looked at it again."

"Since you're staying in town, come over and look at it tomorrow. You know," she mused, "when Tom first inherited that property, we had gangs of people come up to the cabin. Sit around, drink beer, celebrate. Good times. That was before Tom decided he needed the solitude to paint." She let out her breath in a sigh. "If we can't get the other boxes open, I might drag 'em down to the End of the Line when I go in to work tomorrow. One of those guys will know how to pry 'em open."

"I might have a better tool than a screwdriver in the truck. Maybe we'll find something that can tell us if there was someone Tom was having problems with. I doubt if it'll be anything as obvious as a threatening letter, but who knows? And speaking of threatening, look who's here." He gave a discreet nod toward the door.

Betty Ann turned to see Lieutenant Kovacs walk into the dining area. He was wearing a suit and tie and towered over the young woman he was with, even though she wore the kind of ridiculously high heels that Betty Ann used to love to wear. Nowadays she shied away from them, to spare her aging leg muscles. While the maître d' seated his companion, Kovacs glanced around the room. He saw Betty Ann, gave her a slight nod of acknowledgement and then sat down himself.

"Nice." Barry smirked. "The old guy has better taste than I would have thought."

"He's no older than me," she said. "So much for avoiding running into him."

"Yeah," Barry said speculatively. "Interesting coincidence. You think he's keeping an eye on us?"

"Might be," she said with a show of bravado. "He suspects me of murder, remember? Maybe he thinks we're accomplices. I don't want any dessert. Let's leave, now that they've ordered."

Back at the house, he walked her to her front door.

"I'm tired," she said bluntly. "See you tomorrow?"

When he moved to kiss her, she turned her head slightly so that it was a Hollywood kiss, cheek to cheek. His lips were warm on her skin. She almost turned back, but he whispered, "Good night, my sweet accomplice," and drove away, waving a hand out the lowered window.

Chapter Fifteen

She opened the door to find Louisa laboriously getting up from the hall floor. Betty Ann looked at the screwdriver in her hand and then at the ammunition boxes on the floor.

"What are you doing? Did you open these boxes?"

"No, I tried, but they're pretty stuck. What're you doing home so early? Bad dinner?"

"Those belong to me." She tried to keep her voice level. "Lou, there might be some private stuff of Tom's in there. Things he wouldn't want anybody but me to see. You should've waited until I was here."

Louisa looked mutinous. "I was just trying to help. Doesn't matter anyway. I couldn't get any open except for the one we already did."

That box was sitting open on the floor. Betty Ann snapped the lid shut and picked it up.

"Just leave the others here. We'll get them open tomorrow. Good night."

Louisa remained in the hallway, looking up from where she stood amidst the boxes, as Betty Ann went up the stairs.

With relief, she kicked off her low heels, scrubbed her face clean of makeup, unpinned her hair and put on pajamas. Her indignation at Louisa's presumption roiled. Heedless of the dirt stuck to the heavy box, she settled on the bed and balanced it on her legs. As she had thought, it was full of very old documents.

Or rather, a lot of documents that were very old now, but not so old when Tom must have placed them in the box. She unfolded the title to the Chevy—*fat lot of good that is*—and a few receipts from places around Del Sueño where he had got it worked on. There were receipts for art supplies and the duplicate of a contract with an art agent in Riverside. She would show that to Kovacs, maybe the agent was worth talking to. She should probably show him the deed with the name "James G. Garrett".

There was nothing else from Tom's former life. But then, she remembered, he had arrived in town with nothing but some stretched canvases, some meager art supplies and his clothing in grocery bags, what he had called "Safeway Samsonite". She didn't even remember him unpacking the boxes, but maybe he kept them in the car's voluminous trunk until he could move them to the root cellar.

She sighed. If she had thought to search the cellar when Tom first disappeared, she could have taken everything to the police as proof that he wouldn't have left town voluntarily. Not, at the very least, without the title to the car.

She had propped the photo of the two of them against the lamp base on her side table. Now she took it and examined it, but though all the faces looked vaguely familiar, hers and Tom's and Barry's were the only ones whose names she could remember.

The doorbell pealed in the hallway downstairs. Betty Ann sighed. Did Barry really think such adolescent behavior was attractive? Maybe her judgment of his maturity needed rethinking.

She wrapped herself in her heaviest, most unattractive robe and stomped down the stairs in the dark. The porch light lit up the peephole and she looked through.

"Oh, for heaven's sake!" She yanked the door open. "What are you doing here?"

Kovacs turned back from his inspection of her front yard. He had removed his tie and rolled up the sleeves of his dress shirt.

"This was found under your chair." He held out her blue scarf. "I told the maître d' I was a friend of yours, and your place was on my way after I took Melissa home."

"Thank you." She opened the storm door and took the scarf. "I'm sorry if it spoiled your date."

"Spoiled it?" He looked puzzled.

"I mean, if you had to take her home early."

"Oh," he said. "It's been a long time since I had any say in her curfew, and I suppose this would be early for a grown woman. But a man usually prefers for his daughter to be safe at home at a reasonable hour."

"Daughter." Betty Ann felt a slight flush creep up her neck. "We assumed it was a date."

"I guess it was. We go to dinner at least once a month and exchange career updates. She's an accountant with a firm there in Escondido."

He spied the boxes sitting on the floor and raised an eyebrow.

"That's some old stuff we found up at the cabin. As soon as we can get them open, I'll go through and see if there's anything you should look at. I doubt it, but you never know."

He nodded. "You never know. Listen, could I come in? Just for a moment. It's, um, been a long drive, and it's even longer to Seddleton... "

"Of course," she said and clutched at the neck of her bathrobe as he entered. "It's down the hall to the left."

She refastened the door and went into the living room, turning on a couple of table lights. The cold room was helped somewhat by their soft yellow glow. When he returned, she was drawing the drapes to the large front windows.

"They always make me feel a bit 'onstage'," she said. "I've never been nervous at night, but since the shooting, I just feel more comfortable with the world closed out."

He looked around, hands in his pants pockets. "Nice room."

"Thank you." She sat down on the gray suede sofa and wondered what he had in mind, since he made no attempt to leave. There was a silence for a moment, and then she blurted, "Were you following us?"

"No. Should I?"

"Don't be silly. It just seemed like quite a coincidence. But I guess if your daughter lives right there. Sorry, but being suspected of murder does make you a little paranoid."

There was amusement in his eyes, but he answered seriously. "I told you I wouldn't go so far as to say you're a suspect. From what we can tell—so far—you didn't have any motive to kill him."

"Oh. Thanks again."

There was another moment of him studying her along with the room. She gathered her loose hair to the back of her neck and wished she had something to tie it with.

"Listen," she said, "I'm going to make myself a drink. You want one?"

"Not for the road. But I wouldn't mind a cup of coffee. To help stay awake."

She led him past the boxes, back to the family room and winced as he took in Louisa's dirty plates scattered around. She directed him to the leather couch while she went into the kitchen.

"Any news on the bullets?" she asked through the pass-through opening as she put a pod in the coffee maker. "I mean the wood she dug out, I guess."

"Nope. She found a couple 'flecks', as she called them. They've been sent to the lab, but even if they turn out to have come from whatever tool they used to dig the bullets out, it probably won't prove anything. They probably just used a common pocket knife."

She handed him a brimming cup. Self-consciously she poured herself a shot of bourbon over ice and sat down in the armchair.

"Thanks," he said. "I hope I didn't disturb anything."

"What do you mean?"

"Thought your friend might be here. The guy you were having dinner with."

"And me dressed like this?" she said angrily.

"You're a grown woman too. He's not upstairs, then?"

"No. If he was, it's none of your business."

"No," he agreed.

Almost in answer to his words, there came the sound of someone moving upstairs.

"That's Louisa," she said to his look.

"What's your friend's name?"

"I just said. It's Louisa Berringer."

"I meant the other one."

"Oh. Barry."

"Barry what?"

She had to think. "Freid."

He repeated the name, as if trying out the sound. His face had gone from cautiously friendly to showing nothing. *Cop mode,* she thought.

"Where's he from?"

"New Jersey, same as Tom."

"What's he do?"

"He's an artist, like Tom was. He has a gallery in San Diego. He's staying over at the Best Western tonight, if you want to go question *him*."

He nodded, apparently not registering her sarcasm. Or indifferent to it.

"How well did he know your husband?"

She described the old days for him, what she could remember from the lazy conversations on the cabin porch, plus Louisa's reminiscences in the car. Once more she felt as if she were getting lost in a soup of memories. The whiskey was stirring it up in her mind.

"He's changed a lot," she added. "'Course, we all have."

He put his cup down on the side table and was about to speak when the doorbell pealed again.

Betty Ann swore. "Why don't we just open the house up and have a party."

Unbidden, Kovacs followed her down the hall. She hoped fervently that it wasn't Barry this time. She was not in the mood for another testosterone tournament.

Without looking through the peephole, she threw open the door.

"Howdy," said Pete Branson. "I saw the lights on."

She opened the storm door, and he walked past her, looking astounded to see Kovacs in the hall. He did a slightly better job of hiding his astonishment when he looked at her bathrobe.

"The Lieutenant stopped by to return something I lost," she said. "What's up?"

"Thought you'd want to know," he said and added to Kovacs, "They tried to call you. The autopsy found a bullet embedded in his brain. Looks like Tom was shot through the open passenger window. That's why the bullet didn't go on through and into the lake—it spent most of its energy by the time it passed through his head and hit the frame."

She felt the grayness move in from the edges of her eyes and slowly take over her senses. Weakness flushed through her legs.

After a moment, she felt something cold at her lips and opened her eyes to discover that she was lying on the suede couch in the living room. Kovacs had one arm around her shoulders, supporting her while he pressed the glass of whiskey to her lips again. It was well diluted by the ice cubes, but it was enough to send a shock through her. She pushed the glass away and sat up, adjusting the robe where it had come loose.

"Maybe you don't want to move just yet," he said.

"I'm fine!" she said, and wondered how times she had said that in the last week.

Pete looked abashed. "Hey, I'm sorry, Betty Ann, I had no idea it might upset you that much. Just thought you'd want to know—whoever fired the gun wasn't in the car with him. Looks like it might have been just some wacko passerby or a hitchhiker he stopped to pick up."

"I'm not upset, Pete. I'm just tired. Tired of people dying, tired of old memories, tired of trying to understand why anyone would want to kill Tom, and I'm tired of not being able to figure out who the hell killed him!"

"I think you should leave that to me," said Kovacs gently.

"But if you don't get any other nominations, I win the election!" She felt her voice ramping up in her throat and forced it back down. Although Kovacs had on his inscrutable look, Pete looked ready to bolt for the door.

"Do they know the caliber of the bullet?" Kovacs asked him. "Was it from a rifle?"

"No," said Pete. "It's smashed—" He glanced at Betty Ann. When she glared back at him with no sign of fainting again, he went on, "but they were able to read the rim. It's from a revolver, a .38. That's why I came by, Betty Ann, to see if you remember anybody having a gun like that back then."

She stared into space and then sighed. "You know, I don't remember ever seeing anyone with a handgun back then. People didn't carry them around all the time, not like they do now."

Kovacs stood up to go.

"Have you talked with her friend?" he asked Pete. "Freid?"

"Not yet."

"She said he's staying over at the Best Western, so tomorrow morning might be a good time. Let me know and I'll go with you. I'd like to hear from him exactly where he was when her husband disappeared."

"You can't think he had anything to do with it!" Betty Ann exclaimed. "They were best friends since college. Marched together in protests, tried to change the world and all that. It killed him when Tom disappeared. He came up here right away when he heard, and he's been helping me."

He looked at her closely. "You seem real anxious to defend him."

Pete said to her, "We just need to cover the bases. My fault—I've been hung up on these meth labs we been trying to clear out." When she flashed him a look, he added, "Well, they're killing kids right now, and Tom Stearns died a long time ago."

"Branson," said Kovacs, "There's something else you might want to check into right away." He repeated what Betty Ann had told him about Nina Merryweather. Betty Ann looked away from Pete's searching gaze.

"I'm pretty sure Nina's just an old blow-hard," he finally said, "but I'll talk to her, see what she can tell me about back then."

She followed them both to the door. Kovacs worked the latch bolt with his thumb.

"You should get a better lock. A thief would be through this like a knife through warm butter."

Pete said as he walked past her, "I'll find you a good one and bring it up tomorrow before I go talk to Freid."

"I'm working at the Line tomorrow. Barry said something about meeting me there."

"What for?" asked Kovacs sharply from the shadows beyond the porch.

"Like I said, he just wants to help. We been talkin', to see if there's anything that he could explain. Something we could connect with Tom's disappearance." She still had trouble saying 'death' instead of 'disappearance', she thought. How silly. She said to Pete, "Thanks. And let me know what else they find out up at the lake, okay? I promise I won't pass out on you again."

He nodded and went down to where his patrol car was parked behind Kovacs' pickup. She watched as the two of them conferred with their heads close. Kovacs appeared to be speaking urgently. She closed the door without slamming it and made sure the lock was in place.

Chapter Sixteen

Sleep came with difficulty and didn't stay long. Morning was hardly more than a promise when she came down to the cold kitchen. She put biscuits in the oven just to warm the place up.

The olive-green ammunition boxes still sat in the hallway, tucked against the stairway. She got a sturdy screwdriver and sat down on the floor, stretching her sore ankle out in front of her. Several attempts at each lid got her nothing but skinned knuckles. She sucked at her knuckle and brooded. She was beginning to wonder if the boxes were really worth all the effort they were causing. Surely if they had contained anything important, Tom would have told her about it long before he disappeared.

"Any luck?"

Betty Ann jumped. She felt a twinge of pain in her ankle and cursed. Louisa had come down the stairs in her socks and sweats to stand behind her. "Not a bit. Should've asked Pete or Kovacs to help when they came by last night."

"What the hell they want?"

"Seems whoever shot Tom did it from outside the car, so it might have been a drive-by, or somebody he stopped to give a lift to. Or just about anybody, I guess."

"Well, that takes care of that," Louisa said cheerfully.

A delicious smell came from the kitchen. Betty Ann returned to the oven, put the biscuits on a plate, set butter and fruit spread on the breakfast counter and poured herself a mug of coffee.

"You don't look so good," said Louisa. "You catchin' somethin'?"

"I feel like I'm never going to sleep good again. I keep trying to figure out why Tom went to Blue Lake. I'm beginning to think I never knew him at all."

Louisa snorted as she bit into a biscuit. "Well, you never did, did you? When did you ever show any interest in knowin'?"

Betty Ann set her biscuit back on the plate. Usually she had to exercise discipline to keep from finishing an entire batch in one sitting. Now the soft bread tasted like dryer lint.

"What do you mean, Lou? You sayin' I shoulda asked Tom more about his former life? You think that would help now?"

"Mighta helped back then. Little late now."

Betty Ann looked at her thoughtfully. "How might it have helped back then? I didn't know he was dead. Cops thought he dumped me. Me knowin' more about his former life wouldn't have made them believe anything different, bein's it took 'em 'til now to find him."

Louisa shrugged. "Well, they found him. And they pro'bly ain't ever gonna find who killed him, so you might as well forget about tryin' to figure it out for yourself."

"How can I? Can you? I mean, sure, he wasn't your husband, but you knew him for years. How can you not wonder what happened to him?" She narrowed her eyes. "Or do you already know?"

"Know what?" Louisa stuffed the last of a biscuit in her mouth and went to the refrigerator for the milk.

"Know what happened to him."

Louisa poured a glass of milk and took a drink before answering. "How would I know what happened? I told you, I was in Riverside."

"Yeah. About that. What happened on that trip, Lou? Why'd you have to go there for two weeks, right at the time he was killed? Granny said there was blood on the seat of her car when you got back. She said it looked like you killed a chicken in there."

"I..." Louisa turned from the refrigerator, letting the door close of its own weight.

"Just tell me whose blood it was, Lou." She took a sip of coffee and waited.

Louisa's face began to blaze. "Jesus," she snarled. "I don't believe you! If you ain't the high 'n' mighty bitch just like you allus was! Here I been tryin' to help you out, and now you're sayin' what? You accusin' *me* of killin' Tom?"

"No, just wonderin' where the blood came from."

"Yeah. Okay. Fine." She took a deep breath and planted her hands on her hips. "You really wanta know? That blood came from me nearly losing my baby!"

Betty Ann gaped. "What baby? You weren't pregnant back then."

"Yes, I was. I barely made it to the clinic. They saved her, those people." She laughed harshly. "Here I was, thinkin' about gettin' an abortion after Tom tells me there's no way he'll leave you and marry me. Wa'n't so easy back then, but I was gonna do it 'cause that's what he wanted. Then when I almost lost her, I changed my mind. They told me my baby was okay and I could go home, but no way was I goin' back to your place again. So I went to my friends in Riverside and stayed with them. They can tell you 'zackly where I was when Tom was killed!"

Betty Ann barely heard the last of it through the rushing in her ears. "*Tom*? Why would he want to marry you? He was—"

"Chloe's father, that's what he was."

Betty Ann stared at her. "You were like a sister to him. To me too. There's no way he would—"

"Sleep with me?" Louisa shouted. "Cheat on you? Who cheated on who? You disappeared first, remember? Back in April! And okay, maybe it wasn't with Barry, but whoever you shacked up with that time, you let Tom think you'd left him for good. You never called or nothin' to tell him where you were. Not for three damn weeks!" She waved her hands wildly in the air. "He couldn't paint, he couldn't do anything! I picked up the pieces an' took care of him an' made him eat an' got him back to painting. Dammit, I was there for him! I held him when he couldn't sleep for worryin' about you. I *comforted* him! And then you walk back in, and it's like it never happened! So then, when he goes an' disappears himself, you think I didn't laugh 'cause now it was your turn to worry?"

Betty Ann spoke through a tight throat. "April was a big fight. Ramona took me to Mexico, we stayed at the beach. There wasn't a phone. I told him that when I got back."

"Who gives a shit? You took off. I was there. I thought he'd be with me from then on. Instead, he tells me to go get an abortion. He didn't need me anymore, did he? His precious little Betty-baby was back home. He told me he'd give me some money for it!" She snorted. "Yeah, right. Where was he gonna get money? Anyway, I didn't want money. I wanted a husband! I only ever wanted one husband, and you've had two! And you accuse me of killin' him! I would never have killed Chloe's father!" she shouted.

"Chloe," Betty Ann said dully. "Tom's daughter."

Louisa's sagging breasts heaved under her sweatshirt. "Yeah, maybe if you'd ever cared to ask him, you'd've known Chloe was his momma's name. I thought if he ever showed up, he'd like that. 'Specially when he saw her. He'd've taken one look at her and known she was his." She added mournfully, "If he'd ever got a chance to see her, he might've married me."

Betty Ann sat hunched and dropped her face into her palms. It made sense now, the feeling of familiarity when she was with Chloe. It wasn't herself she saw in the girl. It was Tom. His laughter, his rebellion, his love for every kind of art. His love for the warm colors of Mexico, the reds and golds and burnt oranges. "Full of life itself," he'd called them as he loaded up a brush and swept great swathes of flaming color onto yet another canvas.

Chloe had his gift for creating vibrant designs. She had her father's gift.

She pressed her fingers to her temples and rubbed hard. Betrayal burned in her gut, and the hurt began to ache in her bones. All those years, those cold childless years when she told herself she was glad she didn't have to raise a child alone. All those years, not only was Louisa raising a child, she was raising Tom's child.

Sure, she had been right all along. Tom hadn't left her like they all said. He had been cold-bloodedly murdered. But he had really left her when he crept into bed with the woman who shared their house. It was worse than all the abandonment she had felt throughout her life, starting with her father leaving her when she was five years old. That hadn't been his fault, either, and she had fought against the rage and the grief. She was tired of fighting.

She raised her head. "Get out!"

"What d'ya mean?"

"I mean get out of my house! Damn you! And don't ever come back!"

The look of scornful triumph slipped from Louisa's face. It was replaced by an uncertainty that Betty Ann might have found comical if it hadn't been so ludicrous.

"You throwin' me out?"

"I'm going for a drive. I need to get away from here. Away from you. I want you packed up and gone before I get back."

"Where am I s'posed to go?" Louisa demanded.

"My dear, I don't—" she started sardonically.

The front doorbell rang. Betty Ann stomped out, wincing at the renewed pain in her ankle, and flung the door open.

"Hi, Aunt Bee," said the tall woman standing on the sunlit porch. "Is my mom here? I saw her car in the drive."

"Chloe!" With a sob, Louisa ran past Betty Ann and flung herself into her daughter's arms. Chloe looked at Betty Ann over her mother's shoulder, absently patting her on the back. The gesture looked well practiced and dull from repetition.

Betty Ann stood holding the storm door open. Obviously Chloe's tallness came from Tom. And the black curls. She should have recognized it when Chloe visited as a teenager, but if she thought about it at all, she had assumed that it all came from the mythical Mr. Berringer. She had never asked what kind of man he was, how he and Louisa had met, how tough it had been on them, losing him to cancer. She had wondered sometimes if he had been just another nearly nameless dramatic interlude in Louisa's life. But she had never asked.

She prided herself on the fact that she didn't pry into people's lives. At the most, she had been a sympathetic if passive ear behind the bar. Maybe—the thought came to her now—maybe Louisa was the one in the right. Maybe she had just never cared enough to pry into Tom's life, his background. She saw herself, still a teenager technically. Passionate and demanding, self-involved, exasperating the man who had been so much older, yet so patient. Regret overwhelmed her anger and shock.

"Your mom and I had a disagreement," she said. When Chloe's eyebrow went up, she added wearily, "It's okay, but I think she needs to go somewhere else for a while. You're just in time to help her pack."

"Mom, are you being a pest again?" Chloe took her mother by the shoulders and shook her slightly, a parent to a misbehaving child. "Dammit, you can't spend your whole life doing what you please in other people's homes."

"I'm leavin'! She accused me of something awful."

"I didn't accuse her. I asked her a question. It doesn't matter. You can help her pack and drive her to a motel, or put her on a plane." She added, "Then come back if you want. We can talk and catch up. But it's best if your mom leaves now."

"I got a room at the Budget Motel last night when I got in late. I'll take her there." She swept her black hair back with one hand. "Is her car running?"

Louisa wailed, "All my stuff is upstairs!"

"Not all of it," Chloe said drily. "I looked in your car. There's probably enough in there to keep you going for a while."

"It's silly to keep standing here in the doorway talking about it," said Betty Ann. "Come in before we put on a show for the neighbors."

Chloe clicked the locks on the rental car that sat in the driveway. Betty Ann held the storm door wide as Chloe shepherded her mother through and down the hall. She left the heavy wood door open to get some fresh air through the storm screen. The ammo boxes on the floor were making the hallway smell like earth and fungus.

"You go up and get packed," Chloe told her mother. "I'll sit and talk with Aunt Bee for a while."

"No! Come up with me!" Louisa cried. "I don't want to be alone."

Chloe sighed. "Okay, calm down. We'll pack up your stuff, and I'll take you to the motel. *Then* I'll sit and talk with Aunt Bee."

"Take your time," Betty Ann told her. "We can catch up later. I need to go up to Seddleton for a while, and it's a three, four-hour drive. Would you give me a hand carrying those boxes out to my car? I want to take them to the police up there."

She wanted them gone, she was sick of them and no longer wanted to know what was in them. But Kovacs might. It was a good excuse to get away from Louisa and try to clear her head before Chloe started asking questions.

Louisa whipped around on the stairs.

"Oh, no, you don't!" she screeched. "Those boxes belong to Chloe just as much as you! We got a right to see what's in them!"

"Alright," said Betty Ann, feeling defeated and for once unable to cope with Louisa's drama. "I'll tell Kovacs about them later. He can decide if he wants to be here when we get them open." She added to Chloe, "Don't let her try to open the boxes 'til I get back."

"What are they? Why do we have any right to see what's in them?"

Betty Ann pleaded for silence with a glance, but Louisa looked mulish. "They got stuff in 'em that belonged to your father. Your *real* father."

"James Garrett?" asked Chloe.

Chapter Seventeen

"Dear God," Betty Ann said.

Chloe looked from her stunned face to her mother's. "You told me that was his name," she said accusingly.

"You knew," said Betty Ann. "You knew who that was, when we found that old deed."

Louisa came down to stand on the bottom step. "I knew that place up there could be Chloe's now, 'cause Garrett's the name I put on her birth certificate. First time she had to get a copy, I had to explain it to her."

"Why the hell did he change his name?"

Louisa hesitated, but she buckled under the weight of both their hard gazes. "He said the FBI might be looking for him. Might be still, but I don't guess it matters much now."

"Why not?" Chloe demanded. "Where is he?"

"Why was he wanted by the FBI?" Betty Ann interjected.

Louisa shrugged. "I don't know if he was, that's just what he said. There was a little thing. Back in the Sixties. Somebody planted a bomb in a military building or an apartment house. Anyway, some people got killed. Tom hated that, so he split for California. Barry might know, since they was both in the damn SDS when the Weathermen started settin' bombs."

"He never told me," said Betty Ann.

"Little straight-arrow Betty-baby? He prob'ly figured you'd run to the Feebies or somethin' an' cause all kindsa trouble. The

Weathermen took credit for the bomb, but they liked doin' that. Liked everybody thinkin' they was some kinda bad-ass revolutionaries, wanted by the FBI an' all. Most of 'em was just a bunch of screw-ups. Anyway, Jim Garrett's his real name."

There was a silence for a while, as Betty Ann tried to absorb yet another blow to her fifty-six-year-old vision of the world. Chloe seemed to be trying to decide what her next question should be. Only Louisa looked comfortable, like someone who had waited a long time and finally got the satisfaction she deserved.

Outside, the street was quiet. A car drove slowly away down the street, but other than that, they could have been the only people left on the planet.

Finally, Betty Ann went to the hallway table for her purse.

"I'm going—" She waved a hand vaguely. "I have to get out of here. Decide what to do. Your mother can explain it all."

The drive into the hills gave her time to think, if not make sense of it all. She went over old events and came to the conclusion that whoever killed her first husband, it was probably too late to ever figure it out, and besides, she no longer cared. That wasn't true, but saying it made her feel better.

The hills had decided winter was officially over and clothed themselves in tall grass crowded with orange wildflowers. When she started paying attention to where she was, she realized that even without the boxes, she had driven to Seddleton without making a conscious decision. The sidewalks along the two-lane blacktop were busy with people out shopping in the balmy spring air. The tang of fresh pine filled the car and blew out the sage and dust smells from down below.

As she got out of her car in the parking lot, a passing couple smiled and said "Good morning!" Dorothy of Deeds and Records peered out the window and waved like an old friend. Unlike Del Sueño, there were no husky unemployed men hanging out on the corner, watching her with carefully blank eyes. The children who grinned at her did not then throw glances at her hubcaps. She wondered if Seddletonites bothered to lock their cars. The habit was too ingrained, however, and she clicked the Thunderbird's locks before she went into the police station.

The woman in the glass cage still looked bored, but when Betty Ann stated her name, she raised an eyebrow and picked up the office phone. A moment later Kovacs held the heavy service door open.

"What're you doing here?" The question sounded only mildly hostile. His eyes held curiosity and something else she couldn't identify.

Her reasons for driving all the way to Seddleton seemed weak, even to herself. Betty Ann realized she shouldn't have been so wimpy with Louisa. It didn't matter who the boxes really 'belonged' to. They might have clues or evidence inside, and they should be turned over to the police.

She followed him to his office and said, to stall for time, "I wanted to ask if they've decided that it was a stranger who killed Tom."

"If who decided?" he asked.

She was pondering how to answer when she saw a slight twitching of his mustache.

"Have they decided *anything*?" she snapped, nettled. "And don't say 'who'."

"We're following a lead."

"Really? I mean, I didn't know you had one."

"You didn't get the memo?"

"Lieutenant—"

"No, we haven't decided who did it, so there's no arrest in the near future. But there is something that I'm following up on, and I'll let you know as soon as I can. Something you said last night got me thinking. And the lab is working on that piece of saturated paper in the watch. Looks like it might be a schematic of some sort, maybe for the watch itself. Meanwhile, Ms. Beaumont, I'm asking you to stay put. Don't go gallivanting around the hills any more. Don't go to work. Stay at your house and tell those friends who knew your husband to stay put for a while as well. Unless you have a special reason for driving all the way up here, I would prefer that you just call from now on."

"Now, look—"

"*Did* you have a special reason?"

"Actually, yes. I was going to bring you those ammo boxes that were in the hall. The ones we found under the cabin. But Louisa pitched a fit, and I didn't have the strength to argue. So instead, I came up here to tell you that if you want them, you can come on down and argue with her about it. You can probably intimidate her into handing them over."

The thick brows came together. "What have they got to do with anything?"

It all came out. Maybe as a cop he had learned how to be a good listener. Or how to make it easy for people to confess. She told him about the box they had been able to open, and about the deed in the name "James G. Garrett". Then she told him about the blood in Granny's car, about Louisa's confession, of Tom's infidelity and Chloe's conception. She had wondered if she would start crying. Instead, with every word, she felt herself breathing deeply for the first time in hours. Gradually her shoulders straightened. She had been carrying herself hunched, with her head bowed, without realizing it.

That ain't Betty Ann Beaumont, she thought. Hell, it ain't even Betty Ann Stearns.

When she got to Chloe letting slip that the real name of her father was the name on the deed in the box, Kovacs sat up, looking aggravated and stern. "You didn't tell me those boxes belonged to your husband. I need to see that deed and anything else that's in them. You say this Berringer woman claimed they were hers? And she's leaving the area?"

"I told Chloe to keep her from trying to open them until I got back."

"Doesn't mean she won't take 'em with her."

He propelled her to her car and followed her down through the hills to Vista de Copa, his patrol car a seething presence on the back of her neck.

Louisa's car sat like an abandoned barge in the driveway, and Chloe's rental car was gone. Betty Ann cursed under her breath as she got out of the Thunderbird. Kovacs rolled up behind her.

"Chloe was supposed to get her and her car out of here."

He frowned at it. "That thing even run?"

"It made the trip from Denver. I don't think she's tried to start it since. Maybe Chloe's making two trips. Damn, I wanted to give them enough time to get her shit together and get it out of my sight."

The front door stood open. Betty Ann stormed through the screen door with Kovacs close behind her.

"Lou!" she yelled, hoping the woman was packing and not watching television. Every painting on the wall hung crooked, as though someone had run down the hall sweeping them with a hand. She felt outrage again as she realized the boxes were gone from the hall.

"Lou! What d'you think you're doing?" She followed the trail of crooked picture frames to the family room. "Dammit—"

The dark red bloom on the rug was like a scream in the night, stopping her heart. A still figure lay on the floor, sprawled legs sticking out from under the shattered coffee table. Kovacs grabbed her by the shoulders and moved her gently back into the hall.

"Stay here. Don't touch anything. Don't contaminate the scene."

He left her leaning against the wall and moved carefully into the room. Betty Ann's eyes burned with the sight of the blood. She closed them, but she could still see it soaked into the carpet, splashed onto the leather couch. Splattered high along the wall, the drapes. Glistening in the dark hair.

After a moment he came back. "She's gone. I'm calling it in. How are you?"

"Fine," she said. Her voice sounded faint to her own ears, so she cleared her throat and repeated, "I'm fine. What happened to Louisa?"

"Don't quote me on it, but it looks like she's been stabbed. Multiple times. I didn't see a weapon. Let's get you outside. I'd give you some of that whiskey again, but the bottle's somewhere in there."

"I'll sit in the living room."

"The whole house is a crime scene." With his strong hand on her elbow, he took her out of the house, unlocked his patrol car and sat her sideways on the passenger seat. "If you feel light-headed, put your head down between your knees."

He walked a few steps away and pulled out his cell phone. In minutes two patrol cars slid quietly to the curb. With arm motions, Kovacs sent a brown-uniformed officer along each side of the house. He and a fourth man went in the front with weapons drawn. Finally he came back and said, "House is clear. Looks like our baddie took off."

Crime Scene technicians arrived in two white vans, and in moments her house was swarming. More officers started knocking on the neighbors' doors. One uniformed young woman took her fingerprints with a portable scanner that looked like an overgrown gamer's wand.

"For purposes of elimination," she said apologetically.

Kovacs said, "Looks like it might have been an interrupted burglary. You feel up to looking around, see if anything's missing?"

She nodded and he took her arm to guide her first through the downstairs rooms, avoiding the family room, and then went upstairs. All her clothes were undisturbed and her jewelry was in the lock box on the top shelf of her dressing room. No paintings were missing, and a brief glance into the family room told her the television and media set-up was intact. She shook her head as they re-emerged on the front porch.

A comfortable swing chair moved slightly in the breeze. It was where she loved to sit in the afternoon with a beer, watching the kids get off the school bus and go racketing down the street, shouting to one another about plans for the next day. It had been the only time the street had seemed like a real neighborhood.

Would she be able to do that again? Or would the neighbors see it as the front porch of a murder house and stare? They already looked askance at her, the lonely widow with no visitors, except for the crazy-looking woman with a car full of junk. Her lip trembled and she bit down on it, hard.

"They're going to be a while," said Kovacs with a nod at the technicians who buzzed like white-coated flies. "After they've finished with the body, the coroner will take her, but there's still a lot they'll have to go over. Is there anyone I can call for you? A friend you could stay with? Even when they're done, you're not going to want to sleep here tonight."

"Oh, my God!" The fog lifted, and she cried with her hand to her mouth, "Chloe! I've got to tell Chloe!"

"I'll have an officer take care of it."

She shook her head wildly. "No, I've got to do it. Now. That is, if you're not going to arrest me."

"I may arrest you for pouting." He glanced away. "I need to get this Chloe's statement."

"About what?"

"About where she's been."

"Jesus Christ! You can't think she killed her own mother!"

"I need to get her statement," he repeated. "I'll drive you to the motel. I suggest you get a room there too."

"I need to take my car. Unless that's evidence too."

He sighed. "I'll follow you over. You're going to get a room and *stay put.*"

She didn't answer. It swept over her. Louisa surely told Chloe about Tom being found. Within hours of finding out that the father she had never known had been murdered before she was born, Chloe had now lost her mother as well. To murder again. She shuddered.

Pete Branson pulled up in his own patrol car.

"Jesus, girl," he said as he walked quickly to them, scrubbing his face hard with one hand. "They called in a homicide. I thought—you alright?"

"It's her friend," said Kovacs. "Woman who was living with her. Daughter's missing."

He walked away, and Pete followed. They spoke in low voices. Betty Ann sat and stared at the busy techs she could see moving inside the house. Kovacs led Pete in the front door. She waited, watching a fly buzzing around the windshield looking for a way out. Groups of people had gathered on lawns and in driveways, and she felt their stares. The neighbors, she thought bitterly, had finally found a reason to leave their cushy fortresses. After what seemed like a long time, but was probably only a few minutes, Kovacs came back out.

"Branson's got it now. I'll fill out a report, but it's his investigation. He said he'll be okay with coming over to the motel later to get your statement." He handed her the purse she'd dropped somewhere on the hall floor. "They're done with this. Is there anything else you need?"

"No. Can we go now?"

She didn't spot Chloe's rental in the motel parking lot. Kovacs went into the office to get the room number, and Betty Ann followed him to the unit. The thin motel door opened immediately to his knock. Betty Ann thought, *I should faint.* But evidently she had had shocks enough to dull her senses.

"Lou," she said stupidly. "You're here."

Chapter Eighteen

Louisa stood with one hand on the door, the other on her hip. "Where else would I be, since you threw me out? Where's Chloe? She went back to the house, said she had to talk to you about the property. Says she doesn't want it. I don't know where she expects me to live, then."

Betty Ann walked past her without speaking, unable to think.

"What'sa matter with you?" Louisa demanded.

"You're Louisa Berrenger?" asked Kovacs.

She nodded, looking fearful.

"They weren't finished with identification when we left." He held up a finger and stepped back outside. Betty Ann watched as he spoke on his cell phone. After a long moment he put it away and came back in.

"It's not Chloe. Fingerprints say it's someone named Greta Marshall. Who's she?"

Betty Ann couldn't answer.

Louisa said, "Hey, ain't that the psycho bitch tryin' to take your house? Why? She under arrest?"

"She's dead," he said bluntly.

Betty Ann sat down on the nearest bed and dug her fingernails into the chenille cover. To Kovacs' questioning look, she managed to say, "Greta's—was Jackson's sister. My sister-in-law. How'd she get in my house?"

"Killer may have let her in."

BA started to laugh. "And who would that be? Chloe? Or me, I suppose. Maybe I killed them both."

"Stop it."

She gulped and stopped laughing. It hadn't felt good anyway.

"Neighbor said they saw a taxi come by about the right time. She must have sent it off, figuring she'd be there a while."

A long while, she thought. The house would always be Greta's now, I don't ever want to go back there. Betty Ann closed her eyes, but it was worse than laughing.

"I'll get you a room for the night," said Kovacs.

She stood up. "I can get my own room. Then I'm going down to the End of the Line. Lord, how appropriate. I feel like I'm already at the end of the line, or getting there. What next? I can't just sit around here. Besides, I'm supposed to be at work tonight."

"You're not going anywhere. I told you, you're going to just stay put for a change."

"Who you givin' orders to?" she demanded. "Am I under arrest?"

"Don't push me!" he roared. "If you force me, I will arrest you! At least that way I'd know where you are!"

"Well, it'd be cheaper in jail than stayin' here! I intend to go back to work, so if you're not going to arrest me, get the hell outa my way!"

Louisa watched them with wide eyes. "Why's he arrestin' you?"

"If I didn't have any reason to kill Tom or Chloe, I sure as hell had a good reason to kill Greta!"

Kovacs stood blocking the door, his hands on his service belt. Then he took a deep breath. "Alright! Might be the best thing, with people around. Just don't go anywhere else. I'm going to get Branson to put a man to watch you. When you leave, he'll follow you back here, and I better not hear any different! But first, both of you tell me your exact movements since this morning. You first."

He pointed at Louisa. Looking suddenly nervous, she told him a rather lengthy version of their conversations, Chloe's arrival and trying to start her car after Betty Ann left. "Battery's dead. Chloe brought me over here with some of my stuff. She was supposed to go back to the house for the rest."

He looked back at Betty Ann. "How about you?"

She glared up at him. "I already told you."

He made her go over it again.

"See anybody hanging around when you left this morning?" he asked. "Anyone unusual?"

"*Anybody* hanging around in that neighborhood is unusual. I would've noticed."

"How about you?" he asked Louisa.

She shook her head, an accusing scowl on her face. "Lissen, how come you ain't out there looking for my daughter? She could be th' next one murdered."

"Branson got the plate number of her rental from their office. He's putting out an APB for it. We'll find her. So who's got the boxes?" He looked around the room, seeing nothing.

Louisa shrugged. "Maybe Chloe's got 'em."

"Why would Chloe take them?" Betty Ann demanded.

"Prob'ly because they belong to her," she answered with a trace of triumph.

"They've got nothing to do with her—" Betty Ann began hotly.

"They belong to her more'n you! Just like that property up there!"

"I was his wife! He never even knew he had a daughter!"

Kovacs fixed her with one of his looks. "Sure woulda been easier if you'd let me know about those boxes right off the bat."

His tone made her burn. "I... yes, I should've told you before, but I honestly didn't think they had anything to do with anything. And I guess I wanted to keep something all to myself. They're just about the only thing I have left that was Tom's. You've got his watch, and he took all his paintings with him when he disappeared. I'd forgotten those boxes even existed until we took Barry up there to search the place. We found an old picture in one, and I was going to go through the rest myself, as soon as I could get them open. The only thing in that first one that might have any significance was the old deed, and that turns out to be Tom's name, not anything mysterious. Up to then, I never heard that name before, and Lou never told me what it meant until this morning." She threw a look of disgust at Louisa, who looked impassively back. "Christ, even Barry lied about it."

"This Barry," said Kovacs. "Where is he today?"

"How should I know?" she said, bristling. "He told me he might go up and post those signs you said we needed, and then he'd come to the End of the Line, but I don't know where he is right now."

Kovacs tucked his fingers under a pocket flap and pulled out a card, handing it to her. It was pine green with a gold badge emblem taking up the center. At the top were the words "Seddleton Police Department" in white lettering, with desk and cell phone numbers. Below it were his name and rank. In spite of herself, she was impressed.

"As soon as you see him," Kovacs said, "give me a call. Immediately. I'll be here in town for a while, coordinating with Branson. I want to get to the bottom of this."

She didn't reply. There was nothing wrong with his request, but his arrogant tone was annoying. And once again she had been told to do something that smacked of turning in a friend. It felt worse than telling him about Nina Merryweather. She dropped the card in her purse, putting off the decision until she saw Barry and had a chance to talk to him herself. He had to have known who "James Garrett" was when he saw the deed, and she wanted to know why he had said nothing. Was he protecting Tom after all these years? Or had he been protecting her?

"I'm surprised she ain't told you all about Barry," said Louisa. She was standing with her arms crossed. "Them bein' such sweethearts an' all."

"Dammit, Lou—"

Kovacs said harshly, "What's this now? I sure as hell wish you'd tell me these things before I have to pry them out of you. So now you're having a relationship with a man I need to question about your husband's murder?"

Betty Ann gasped. "It's not any such thing! Lou sees sex everywhere, don't listen to her! Barry's been trying to remember anything that might help you asshole cops do your job! It's thanks to him that we got those boxes out of the cellar!"

"Why'd you ask him to go up there and help search?"

"I didn't! He volunteered."

"I'd ask him why it didn't occur to *him* to report them to the police, but I got a taste of his helpfulness the other day. He's pretty protective of you. Almost as protective of you as you are of him! Honor among thieves?"

"I keep telling you, he's an old friend!"

They were standing a mere two feet apart, chins jutting out, hands on hips. Louisa stood apart with her arms still crossed, relaxed and smirking at the emotions she had stirred up. He looked over at her, seemed to register her satisfaction, and took a deep breath.

"Alright. You've got my card. Call me the minute he shows up. And when you leave work tonight, Branson's man will follow you back here, so no late night dates!"

"Just who the hell do you think you are?"

"I'm the *asshole* cop who's doing his job! The *asshole* cop who's going to catch Tom Stearns' killer!"

He let the motel screen door slam behind him as he left.

The End of the Line was unusually busy for a Thursday night. One reason was a birthday celebration for Mason, who had just turned thirty. He sat glumly while his friends toasted him with black plastic cups of beer and congratulated him for joining the "Over the Hill" club.

The other reason, Betty Ann was sure, was the rampant curiosity after the killing of Greta Marshall hit the local news station. Pete Branson had called and warned her not to go near her house, as the media geese had flocked onto her front yard.

When she had parked and got out of the Thunderbird, she saw the patrol car Kovacs had ordered to follow her around. It pulled in next to the curb behind the media vans. She expected the officer to follow her inside, but after killing the engine, he appeared to settle in behind the wheel for a long watch.

Reporters recognized her, and a cry went up as if from hounds after a fox. They ran to shove microphones and cameras in her face, shouting wild questions.

"Did you kill your sister-in-law?"

"How's it feel to be a suspect in another murder?"

The locals had suffered media frenzy before and were feeling protective of one of their own. They had formed a solid phalanx between her car and the front door of the saloon as she scooted in, turning her head away from the cameramen who were belatedly catching on. Cowboy and the others then took turns standing in the indented doorway, ostensibly smoking, but denying the media access to the bar.

The reporters, male and female, were still protesting their right to enter a business establishment and "have a beer". There had been some pushing and shoving, but so far none of them had gotten up the nerve to take it to a higher level. Or maybe the presence of a patrol car parked at the curb had a sobering effect. She hoped none of the reporters had realized that the officer had been ordered to watch her, not protect her.

Someone suggested that she turn the television to the news channel so they all could watch themselves on TV, but that had been shouted down. At the moment it was playing a sit-com with the sound off.

Even though Winston had called Patsy in to help, Betty Ann deliberately stayed busy behind the bar and avoided their questions. It helped that everyone kept ordering drinks so as not to lose their front row seats to the show. Some threw out remarks that she might — "Ha, ha!" — poison their drinks. No one laughed, and it didn't stop anyone from ordering more, so she did her best to ignore it.

"You're pretty brave," said Marilyn from her usual bar stool where she had been for the last four hours. She glanced over her shoulder at the doorway. "If it was me, I think I'd head on outa town for a while."

"Cops want me to stick around, and anyway, I couldn't face sitting in a goddam motel room. I needed something to do."

"Well, Winston's happy, anyway. The joint's prob'ly made more money tonight than it has all winter. Cops think you done this one too?"

"I don't know," Betty Ann said shortly and wondered if Marilyn would look so impressed if it were her that was being followed around by police. The officer hadn't come in, so she guessed she couldn't exactly call it harassment.

She looked up as the door bumped open and a large camera tried to push its way in. The crowd outside surged. The crowd inside the room posed, laughing, for the camera. A few waved and yelled, "Hi, Mom!".

There was a scuffle and a shout outside. Several men got off their bar stools with looks of glee, eager to join the scrum at the door. Intimidated, outnumbered, the cameras backed off into the darkening street. There was applause in the barroom.

Betty Ann sighed. "Maybe this wasn't such a good idea. Somebody's gonna end up in a fist fight or in jail, just tryin' to outfox Fox News."

"Won't be the first time," said Marilyn. "Some a these folks think it's been a dull night if somebody don't get in a fight. And anyway, after the murders last year, they kinda like bein' a bunch of reality TV stars."

The door opened again. Betty Ann saw dull blond hair in the struggle beyond Cowboy's shoulder.

"Hey, you guys!" she shouted. "Let that one in! He's a friend!"

Barry shoved through the small opening the men made and stopped to straighten his sports jacket. The massive lens of another large camera glanced off the back of his head. He whipped around and raised a fist, his face flushing visibly in the light over the doorway.

"Barry!" she shouted again. "Let the boys take care of it! Come have a drink and talk to me."

She led him to the far end of the bar, out of the cameras' angle of sight. On the way, she dipped into her tips jar and handed Joey Blankenship a dollar bill. "Go play some music and let Barry here have your stool. I need to talk to him."

Joey obligingly took the dollar and moseyed over to join the crowd around the juke box. Betty Ann dug out a bottle of Corona and popped the cap off. Barry took it gratefully and drank like a man in the desert. Two dark patches still showed on his cheeks.

"Those guys over there take a lot on themselves," he said with a small burp. "I've seen crime lord compounds back in Jersey that weren't as well defended."

"They're my friends. And they don't think much of reporters, especially from out of town, except to have fun with them. We've had trouble here before, and some folks got their words twisted in the news."

"What kind of trouble?"

"Murder," she said dismissively. "It's good to see you here tonight."

"Christ, what kind of town do you live in, B.A.? They're saying somebody got killed right in your house. I came over right away because you said you'd be working. I wanted to make sure you're okay."

"It was my sister-in-law. She was there alone for some reason. They think maybe it was a burglary gone bad. Lou and I had a big fight and she left the house this morning. She'll probably be going back to Denver in a day or so."

"Well, I can't say I'm sorry, but that means you're alone at the house? The police have left?" He looked deeply concerned.

"Cops're gone but the news people are still hanging around like cockroaches. I got a room over off the freeway, at the Budget motel where Lou is at right now. For a few nights. Then I'll decide what to do."

"You shouldn't be here."

"I couldn't sit in that motel room. I might go down and try looking for that Hoffman woman again."

"I think you should forget about her," he said sternly.

She laughed. "Forget about some ghost who keeps paying for what belongs to me? I got to find out why, Barry. By the way, Louisa told me about James Garrett."

His arm paused on the way to lifting the bottle again. "What about him?"

Chapter Nineteen

"Come off it," she said. "That was Tom's real name, wasn't it? That's why it was on that old deed. How come you didn't say anything then?"

He made a face and set the bottle down. "Sorry, B.A. I shoulda said something right away. I guess I was thunderstruck when you didn't seem to know. I always assumed that Tom got around to telling you about it, same as telling you about putting the deed in your name. I was still thinking what to say when that cop showed up. After that, I forgot."

"Forgot. Forgot to tell me I used to be married to a man with a fake name."

"Well, yeah. There didn't seem to be a rush. It's been so many years, and what difference does it make now? He was your husband no matter what name. But that's probably why he put that deed in your name. In case somebody came looking for Garrett."

"If he was going to put a fake name on it, why not Tom Stearns?"

"Well, he couldn't, could he? Like you say, it was fake. He never changed it legally. He just started living a new life with a new name, like lots of people do."

"Most don't have a very good reason."

He scratched his head. "I don't know if his reason was exactly good, but it wasn't any of my business to spread it around.

Somewhere along the line I guess he realized that having a land deed in his old name was just as dangerous as the name. He was always worried he'd go up there some time and find the Feds waiting for him. And, like I said, seemed to me he was getting ready to split again. Maybe change his name again. So he had me witness him putting it in your name. The point being, it put another layer between him and anybody that might be looking for him."

"Yeah, Lou told me about that. Why in hell would the Feds be looking for Tom? She said he wasn't involved in any bombing."

He looked away from her. "Not that he'd tell her about it. B.A., you gotta understand what it was like back then. In the Sixties, J. Edgar was on a rampage against anyone remotely connected to a radical group. Tom could've ended up in prison because of—" He glanced around and lowered his voice. "There was a bomb that went off in an Army Reserve building and killed some poor fool. Tom did tell me that he hadn't been part of that, but why else would he have split so fast? Changed his name and everything? Anyway, sure as hell nobody was looking for a Betty Ann Stearns. He made me swear not to tell you, said he was going to tell you himself when the time was right. I guess he didn't get around to it before—" He paused.

"Before he died. He didn't trust me. He should've told me all this right away, when he did it," she said stubbornly.

"He should have, dammit. I know you thought the world of him, but in a lot of ways old Tom was something of a shit. He didn't mean to be. But—and this is from someone who was his best friend—sometimes he got too wrapped up in himself to realize how he was hurting people."

He sounded so incensed on her behalf that she felt better. She swallowed an impulse to tell him about Chloe. Tom's physical betrayal with Louisa weighed larger in her soul than a fake name, and it was something she was still trying to deal with. She wasn't ready to share it, not even with a sympathetic ear. Maybe someday it would stop mattering. After all, as Barry said, it had all been so many years ago. Of course, she thought wryly, maybe he'd find out about Chloe anyway, when Louisa tried to get the property away from her, based on her daughter's blood kinship. Or, she thought with a jolt, maybe he had always known about that, too. She studied him narrowly, searching for the words to ask.

"I told him he ought to level with you," Barry was saying earnestly. "But he thought he was protecting you."

"*Protecting* me! From what?"

"Well, if he did get caught, you could deny all knowledge, that kind of thing. He thought putting it in your name instead of his would make sure you could always keep it, no matter what happened to him."

"Except for one little thing. Betty Ann Stearns is a fake name, too. On the deed and on the marriage license."

At least, she thought, *if the marriage wasn't legal, Greta can't claim I was a bigamist.* Then she remembered that Greta was dead.

He said comfortingly, "Hey, you didn't know it was fake, did you?"

Betty Ann leaned an arm on the bar. "I don't know," she mused. "Since Tom is long gone, I wish now I hadn't told Kovacs his real name."

"What?" Barry said, startled.

"Well, when I told him them ammo boxes belonged to Tom, he wanted to know what was in the one we got open. So I told him about the deed we found and the name on it. By that time, Louisa'd told me what it was."

After a moment he said, "That's not good, B.A."

"Why?"

"Well, I witnessed him putting your name on the new one. He knows now that I knew Tom's real name too."

"So what? He already would know that, wouldn't he, since I told him you guys were friends since 'way back in the protest days."

He shook his head emphatically. "No, Tom changed his name even before that. I always knew him as Stearns, didn't I, until I witnessed that deed. That's when I started realizing he'd never really work hard on being a success – for fear of pictures and recognition, you know? For fear somebody might make a connection with the bombing. I kept his secret, even from you, like he wanted. But if that cop connects me with the name Garrett, the son of a bitch will probably call in the FBI to look at me too."

Seeing the look on her face, he added with a shrug and a grin, "Aw, hell, B.A., I'm kidding. Who knows, the publicity might be good for selling my own stuff."

"Speakin' of which, I never did tell you how nice your gallery looks."

Something uneasy shadowed his light eyes. It was the first she had seen of his old insecurity. He said, "You've been there?"

"Stopped by the other day after I tried to find that Hoffman woman."

"You did? Any luck?"

"Found out that address is just a postal annex, and they wouldn't give me her home address. I gotta find out who she is, Barry. Maybe I'll hire a private detective. They still exist, don't they?"

"Wish you'd let me know. That you were going down, I mean." He set the empty bottle on the bar and shook a negative at her offer of another one. "I might have been able to help, and anyway, I'd have liked to be there to show you around the gallery. Brandy never told me you were there."

"I didn't leave my name. I did get the impression you haven't been so all alone and pining for me, after all."

"Dare I hope that you're jealous?" He relaxed. "Brandy does like to give that impression. She's a nice kid, but, actually, she's just a kind of helper. And she comes cheap—what other kind of job can you get with a degree in 'Art Appreciation'?"

Betty Ann didn't answer. A group of ranch workers had taken over the pool tables, and several were starting to look like they had topped off their limit of alcohol. With a frown she eyed one man in particular. A thin wife-beater undershirt stretched across his burly chest. Too often it went with a male ego bigger than Marlon Brando's. His voice was getting louder, and his face more flushed, and she made a mental note to tell Patsy to start making his drinks weaker.

"So," Barry pressed, "what did you think of it?"

"Of what?"

"The gallery. My stuff."

She shrugged, still watching the burly rancher. "I saw such a lot of it, didn't I, when Tom was doing it." She considered asking him why he hadn't tried painting in some other style instead of continuing to mimic Tom's. But what did it matter anymore?

"So," he said harshly, "What about the rest of it?"

"What d'you mean?"

"I've been doing well with the photography for years. A whole different kind of thing. My own thing."

"Oh. Those are nice. I could see hanging them in my living room." So could a lot of other people. Now that she thought about it, they were rather typical of the standard large-framed scenic ocean photography that she had seen in a thousand homes from San Diego to Carmel.

She opened a beer for one of Mason's friends. Barry's face had gone somber. For the first time he seemed as discouraged as he had been when he was hanging around the cabin thirty-eight years before.

"The photography is really good," she amended, trying to give him the encouragement he obviously wanted. "When did you decide to stop painting and do something else?"

"Who said I stopped?" He said angrily. "I can do both."

"That girl, Brandy. She said you wanted to try something different. Right? I got the impression you stopped doing the painting altogether."

He looked at her for a moment. "You and Brandy seem to have had quite a chat while I wasn't there. Anything else you need to tell me about?"

"Don't be silly." His anger confused her. A call for a refill came from the other end of the bar, and she used it as an excuse to walk away and think. She handed the man his white russian and looked back. The tail of Barry's sports coat flashed out the door.

She bit her lip and wished he hadn't gone. In spite of his moods, it had been nice to have one person in the room who wasn't wondering if she had committed murder.

The burly rancher came careening out of the men's room and stumbled past the pool tables. He slapped a meaty hand down on the bar and bellowed, "How's a man get a drink in here? And where's our murderess? I wanna meet the killer bartender I saw on TV!"

"Shut up, George!" Marilyn yelled at him. "Don't be a jerk! Leave her alone."

"Ain't bein' a jerk," George said thickly. "Ain't never met me a honest-ta-god murderess, is all. Maybe she'll sign her autograph for me. I ain't gonna bother her. But I sure ain't gonna marry her neither!" He roared with laughter.

People around the bar looked uncomfortable. A few echoed Marilyn's order to shut up. Gleefully Nina Merryweather walked over to George and pointed in Betty Ann's direction. "She's right there at the end of the bar, asshole! Where d'you think a damn bartender'd be, murderess or not? If I was you, though, I'd open my own bottle! Just in case. And watch out for knives!"

Her cackling ran up Betty Ann's nerves. She opened a beer bottle with more force than she had intended. The glass neck broke, and beer and blood ran over her hand.

"Look out!" George shouted with a barrel laugh. "She's on a rampage!"

"That's enough!" Winston said sharply from his seat on a banquette against the wall. "Next person makes a remark like that gets eighty-sixed right outa here!"

"C'mon!" said George as he wavered on his splayed feet. "You ain't never eighty-sixed nobody, no matter what they done!"

"There's always a first time," said Winston. "You gonna shut up or not?"

"Tell ya what. I'll shut up if you mix my next drink yourself. Like the Injun broad says, it might not be a good idea for a man to be served by somebody what killed her husband. And her sister-in-law! Man, she musta hated that family!"

His har-har laughter rocketed upward. There were nervous giggles. Patsy stood with her hands full of beer bottles, looking appalled and uncertain. Betty Ann felt her heart beat beating in her throat as she used a bar towel to staunch the cut on her hand. Winston clenched his small fists and started through the crowd. The young girl who had been sitting with him grabbed his arm to pull him back. He jerked it away.

"Cowboy!" said Betty Ann urgently. "Get Winston to come over here. I need to ask him something."

While George's buddies gathered around, attempting to distract him, Cowboy steered Winston to the other end of the bar.

"Listen, Win," she said, "you're gonna hang around tonight, right? You got Patsy here, and Mason can refill the cooler for you when you need it. I think it's gonna cause more trouble than it's worth for me to stay here."

Winston bit his lip and then nodded. "Yeah. You go on home."

"I don't guess I got a home right now, but I got a room up at the motel. Don't tell anybody. I'll call you from there tomorrow."

Winston glanced at the door which had been firmly closed for some time. Now that night had settled in, the porthole was a black circle, showing only an occasional flicker of movement in the scant street light, like something spotted deep in the depths of a black pond.

"Assholes still hangin' around," he said. "Gimme your keys and I'll have Joey drive your car away. He's good behind the wheel, he can lose those vultures and then sneak back to the rear door. You wait for him there."

"Nobody's used that door in months. Will it open?"

"I'll go make sure." He grabbed the ball of keys from behind the cash register. "You wait a few minutes, tell Cowboy and Mason to help Patsy if she needs it. Then come to the back."

She watched him go to Joey Blankenship, slip the boy her car keys and whisper in his ear. Joey grinned at her as he went by.

"Don't you go layin' rubber down the street!" she hissed. "And just do what he told you, y'hear? You take it for a long joy ride, I'll bust your butt!"

He dangled the keys above his head as he slipped out the door.

After whispering Cowboy and Mason their instructions, she grabbed her purse and pretended to be walking toward the women's restroom. At the last moment she dodged quickly down the hallway that led between age-blackened walls to a padlocked door in the shadows. The light over the door was out. For decades it had been a popular rear entrance from the municipal parking lot, but now Winston kept it locked.

He grimaced with effort as he twisted the key in the lock and dragged the door open. The parking lot was empty in spite of the crowd. No one ever wanted to leave their cars there with nothing but far-away spastic street lights to protect them. Betty Ann was relieved to see that the reporters had been lax and not discovered the back entrance yet.

"Thanks, darlin'." She gave him a hug and pecked him on the cheek. "I'm really sorry about this."

"Not your fault," he mumbled, visibly pleased. "Where'n hell's that kid? If he don't get here damn soon, I'll cut him off for the rest of his life."

A shout came from the barroom behind them. Patsy called down the hall, "Winston, the boys're havin' trouble with George! He's gettin' outa control. You want us to call the cops or what?"

"Shit." Winston hesitated. The Thunderbird flew up and screeched to a halt, sending up a cloud of dust that spat grit in their eyes. There was no sign of followers.

"You go on back," she said. "I'll give Joey the keys, he can lock the door."

Joey jumped out and saluted as he held the door for her. "What, no tip?"

"Try 'Yo Mama' in the third race at Santa Anita." She relented and gave him a peck on the cheek too. He scooted in the back door and slammed it. She heard the screech of the key in the lock.

Out of the corner of her eye she thought she saw movement. She strained to see anything, hear any kind of sound. Nothing but shadows and the muted sounds of music. So it wasn't reporters. She waited for another silent moment, shivering slightly in the night air, hoping Nina wasn't playing Apache just to scare her.

Then conversation drifted down the alley. Deprived of access to the restrooms inside, male reporters unzipped and faced the alley wall. She slipped in the Thunderbird, pulled the door shut with a slight thump and clicked the locks. And then had to move the seat back to its forward position to reach the pedals, but in a quick moment she was rolling out onto the street and heading for the motel, certain they'd had no time to pursue.

Chapter Twenty

The room she had secured was at the far end of the motel, with nothing beyond but rough sand extending out away from the town. It halved the chances that she would have to listen to neighbors all night, so she had made a point of asking for it. Now its isolation felt ominous.

Her tires crunched through the lot to the end, past Chloe's rental car halfway down. With a sigh, she parked in front of the last door and trudged back up the lot to knock on their door. Her morale was too depleted for much conversation, especially with Lou in the room. But she wouldn't be able to sleep until she saw Chloe and knew she was alright.

"Hey, Aunt Bee," Chloe said sleepily. She was in a long shirt and leggings. Louisa had made a chenille nest in the far bed and didn't look up from the television.

"I won't keep you from your sleep," Betty Ann said. "I just wanted to check on you. Did the cops find you?"

"Yeah, over at the grocery store. Scared the shit outa me until they said there'd been another murder and I might be at risk. What's that about? Mom said some woman got killed in your house after I left?"

"Jackson's sister. We're still trying to figure out how she got in. I'm just so glad you were gone when it happened."

Chloe sat on the empty bed and yawned. "I brought Mom over here and carried her stuff in. Then thought I'd pick up some food before I went back to get the rest. The cops jumped me standing in the checkout line. Those folks got an eyeful. I'm sure glad I don't have to go back there again."

"So you never went back to the house?"

"No, I rushed over in a panic to check on Mom, and she wouldn't let me leave her alone again. I knew you were working, so we stayed put. You're not going to the house now, are you? You should stay here."

"I got a room down at the end. I didn't want to wake anybody up, but I needed to ask you what you did with those ammunition boxes."

Chloe wrinkled her nose. "The boxes? You said not to touch them. They were there when I left."

"Shit, they're gone now. I was hoping you put them in your car for some reason. That must mean whoever killed Greta took them."

"I don't get it. Why was Uncle Jackson's sister killed in your house? Why would they want those boxes?"

"The police think she may have interrupted a burglary. So maybe they thought there was something valuable in them. Maybe they took other stuff, too, but I couldn't spot anything missing. What gets me is why they'd take the time to steal those boxes and not my jewelry first. They were heavy and dirty and sure didn't look like they were worth much."

"Lotsa people keep old wills and deeds in them, don't they? I mean, they're pretty much fire-proof. So maybe they figured there might be some personal info they could use."

"Deeds," Betty Ann mused. Deeds were supposed to be straightforward documents, but hers seemed to be the cause of a lot of puzzles and questions. "You doin' okay, Louisa?"

"Just ducky," came the sullen reply.

Chloe rolled her eyes. "I'm going to buy her a ticket to Denver tomorrow. My place has a big screen TV, and she can walk to the grocery store."

"Actually," Betty Ann said with guilt, "I don't think she can leave after all. I think the cops want to talk to her. To get the timeline straight," she added as Louisa looked alarmed. "What happened when."

Before her mother could object, Chloe said, "I'll take her over to talk to them and *then* put her on a plane. I'll hang around here for a while. I still have some time off coming. When you can get away, why don't you and I take off for somewhere? Mission Bay, maybe? Or Laguna Beach? Kick back in the sun and relax?"

"Sounds heavenly. I don't know how long Kovacs wants me around, though. They may never solve—the first murder." Just in time she remembered that she was talking about Chloe's father.

Chloe didn't seem to notice. And after all, Betty Ann thought, Tom was dead before she was born and she hadn't known he existed until years later. It was hardly a surprise if there was no emotional involvement.

Chloe said, "Surely the cops don't expect you to live cooped up for the rest of your life. Give them your cell phone number and tell them right where we'll be staying, so they can find you if they need you."

"Yeah," said Betty Ann, feeling a small prickle of pleasurable anticipation for the first time in what seemed far too long. "We can talk about lots of things. How your job's going. Even your father, maybe, if you have questions."

Louisa shifted in the bed and scowled, but she didn't say anything.

Betty Ann threw her a wave, hugged Chloe and tramped back across the stony lot to her own door, looking forward to a long hot bath and something mindless on the television. It wasn't until she approached the Thunderbird that she remembered she had no clean clothes with her. She hesitated, tempted to run to the Super Walmart for some fresh undies, at least, but decided to wash hers in the sink and hang them up before she fell into bed. There was a vending area outside the dark office, with an ice machine. Wishing she had brought a bottle of whiskey as well, she turned her key in the lock and pushed the door.

A deep voice spoke from the shadows at the corner. She jumped in terror, and the nerves that had begun to relax raced back into high gear.

"We need to talk," said Barry.

"After the day I've had, I ain't got word one left in me," she said gruffly. "Come around tomorrow, and we can all go to breakfast."

"We need to talk now," he repeated.

She pulled the door shut and turned to face him. "I'm not inviting you in, Barry," she said firmly. "And I ain't standin' out here. I'm tired. Whatever's on your mind will have to wait."

He glanced around the quiet parking lot. His light eyes reflected the overhead lights like bits of glass. He stepped closer to her and pushed his finger into her ribs. She looked down and realized it wasn't his finger, it was the muzzle of a gun.

"What—?"

"Just get in the car. You're going to drive us out of here." With his free hand he shoved her toward the passenger door.

"I'm not going anywhere—!"

"I've already killed once today. If you do what I tell you, you'll be fine, and so will that moron and her daughter."

She looked wildly around. The office windows were dark. No lights showed behind any curtains, including the ones in Chloe's room. Suddenly she remembered the police officer who had been sent to watch her. The scheme to get her out the back door had worked too well. He was probably snoozing in his patrol car, out on the street in front of the End of the Line.

Nevertheless, she said, "Kovacs has a police car following me. He's probably parked out on the street."

"Not even close, B.A. I took care of him before I followed you out of town."

"What did you do to him?"

"Nothing fatal. Unless he dies from that crack on the head. Now unlock the door. If you try to yell, I'll shoot whoever comes out after I shoot you."

As he shoved her toward the car, she let her purse slip down to drop near the bumper. He picked it back up.

"Nice try."

Out of ideas, she clicked the locks and opened the door.

"Get in and move over behind the wheel."

She did as he said. He grunted with impatience as she wedged herself over the gear shift console and under the steering wheel.

"I'm not a skinny girl anymore," she snapped.

"Shut up." He got in and slammed the door. "Just drive out of here."

The street was deserted when she pulled out.

"Where the hell are we going?"

"I think up to the cabin would be a good place. Head for the turn-off."

"Why go all the way up there? And it'll be black as pitch this time of night."

"We'll manage." He was quiet as she turned onto the road that wound up toward the hills, and she tried to think hard of somewhere she could drive the car into a ditch and maybe knock him sideways without killing herself. Or without him killing her. Her headlights shone forward, blacking out everything to the right or left.

"You broke in to get the boxes, didn't you?" she said, more to distract him than to elicit information.

"I've been watching your house. I saw you take off, and then the other two left, so I figured I had time to bust in and grab them. Didn't take much get in the door. Not a very good lock."

"Yeah, I've heard that. Why kill Greta?"

"Who?"

"The woman in my house."

He laughed, a high-pitched sound full of stretched nerves. "She really threw me, walking in the door like that, like she owned the place. I tried to pass myself off as a lover of yours who stopped by to pick up some clothes. But she'd seen me taking the boxes out the door, and turned into some kind of maniac. Said everything in the house belonged to her, and I'd have to prove the boxes were mine. I tried to reason with her, I really did," he said rather plaintively. "Just like with Tom. Some people are just too bull-headed to live. But then I was afraid you'd come any time. So I picked up a screwdriver that was on the floor and tried to conk her with it, knock her out, you know? It just pissed her off and she screeched like a banshee and came at me with her nails. So I stabbed at her with it, just to shut her up."

He raised an arm to wipe his face on his shirtsleeve. "I didn't want to kill her. I never wanted to kill anybody. But she ran away from me into that back room and I had to stop her before she got out the back way. Christ, the screaming. Total wacko piece of work." He paused for a breath. "Who the hell was she, anyway?"

"Jackson's sister. My sister-in-law. She wanted Jackson's money and his house. She didn't deserve to die for it."

His shrug was a faint movement in the dark car. "Like I said. Wacko."

She listened to him talk and slightly increased her pressure on the accelerator pedal, letting the speed build gradually, hoping he wouldn't notice. An idea had formed, that somewhere along the way she could use the Thunderbird's power and her driving skills on a sharp curve to throw him off aim, off balance, or even scare him enough to drop the gun. She had already seen that in spite of his machismo act, he was actually a coward, uncomfortable with speed. She used her contempt to steady her nerves.

The further they got from town, the more he seemed to relax.

"I got all those boxes open finally," he said chattily as they left the last light of civilization behind. "What a waste of time. Tom told me he hid stuff on the property 'someplace safe'. Said it was buried, so I figured he meant under a tree or the porch. I've been digging around up there for years. Never thought about a cellar. Never knew it was there."

"Weren't you afraid you'd be seen?"

"I parked the truck up in the woods so nobody'd notice and used a rifle to scare away any hunters who wandered in. At first I was expecting you to show up. Always looking over my shoulder. But it looked like you forgot all about it. That's when I started paying the taxes so it wouldn't get sold."

Her hands jerked on the wheel. "*You're* Abigail Hoffman?"

"Good old Abbie Hoffman. He was a hero of ours back then, you know. It just popped into my head."

"You set all that up and paid money just so you could look for something?"

"California was booming back then. If somebody else bought it, they might have decided to build on it. Some bulldozer might've dug it up. In any case, that would be the end of me searching. So I paid the arrears first, thinking it wouldn't take long for me to find it." He sighed. "Then it was every damn year after that. You coulda knocked me over when I saw you and that dipshit Louisa walk up to the cabin after all that time."

"So you shot at me too. Why didn't you just kill me?"

In the dim light from the dash, he looked shocked. She almost laughed.

"I never wanted to kill you! I was only trying to scare you away so I could keep looking in peace. But then you told me you were going back up, so I had to come along. Good thing I did. Funny, in all this time, I never found that stupid cellar. If you had just let me have the boxes then, B.A., everything would have been fine!"

"Don't call me B.A. I always hated it. If you've got the boxes, what do you need me for?"

He laughed raggedly. "I told you, there's nothing in them! Stupid waste of time, just junk he thought meant something. News clippings that don't show or say anything. Some pictures of us together, back in the old days of the SDS. I burned those. He told me he'd kept the plan we made for the bombing, *with our names on it*, but I didn't find anything. So I figured we must have missed one of those damn boxes. You're going to show me where he hid it."

"*Me*? I don't know where it is. I forgot about that cellar myself until the day we were up there."

"What did you take with you when you moved up to that snooty house? Thanks to the wacko, I never got a chance to search. Tell me now, and we can cut this short." He shoved the gun muzzle into her side painfully. "And slow the fuck down."

She lifted her foot slightly. "After Tom disappeared, there was nothing left to take anywhere. He took his paintings and everything else with him."

His laugh was harsh and jeering. "He didn't take shit. He was heading over to the FBI office in Palm Springs with nothing but his pure and noble soul. And his big mouth. So I went along, trying to talk sense into him."

She downshifted to go around a corner and then pressed the pedal again, trying to hold her foot steady, and said through her teeth, "Why kill him?"

"The bastard was going to 'come clean', he said. Turn himself in. Which would've meant turning me in, too, you know, but do you think he gave a damn? Christ, I'm the one who set that stinking bomb!"

"Not Tom?"

"Oh, shit no. He never had the guts for any of that."

Betty Ann kept her hands steady on the steering wheel, wishing she had something she could bash his head in with.

Barry was mumbling, "I was practically begging him not to be a fool all the way up to Blue Lake. Even had my old gun with me from our radical days. But I couldn't scare him. He was too full of himself and his noble gesture. Said all our old pals were talking about turning themselves in. Bill Ayers, Bernardine, Hoffman. Tired of running. So he says, come with me and turn yourself in and we can both start new lives. That's what he kept talking about, starting a whole new life with you. He was doing it for you!" This time his laughter was on the edge of hysteria. She saw the gun tremble in his hand, but he didn't lose his grip on it.

"So that was what was bothering him that summer," she said. "I thought it was another woman."

"Old stick-up-the-ass Tom? Always was stupid. He never believed I would shoot him. He never believed we were really going to set that bomb. He thought it was just talk, to make a statement. When he saw we were serious, he backed out and ran. But that wouldn't cut any ice with J. Edgar. Somebody died in that bomb. He would have fried, and me with him."

"Maybe not. Maybe they wouldn't have connected you with him."

"Told you, he had some diagrams or something with our real names on them. His and mine."

"What's your real name?" she asked, mostly to keep him talking. The turnout to the rickety bridge was coming up fast.

"Richard Nickson. Yeah," he said in answer to her look, "not spelled the same, but you can see why I was happy to change it. That's partly why I got so pissed. All the way over the mountain, Tom kept calling me 'Dickie'. I never once slipped and called him Jim in California. We were different people, but he wanted to go back and dig up the old ones, like some ghoul in a graveyard."

"But why kill him?" she cried. "Why not just run?"

"Actually, I got out of the car with that idea. Just split for Mexico. Stood there shaking. Then I guess I lost it. Turned around, and the gun came up, and I fired right through the window."

"And then you shoved him in the lake," she said dully. Her hands gripped the wheel and she tensed to twist it, run the car into a tree, anything. She bit her lip until the blood ran but she couldn't make herself do it. *Maybe if I was still young,* she thought, *but now I'm old and scared.*

Then she thought of the path to the cabin, pitch-black in the night, the moon barely a whisper behind spring clouds. Maybe she would have a chance to bolt before he could shoot. He might miss in the dark.

"I searched the car before I pushed it in," he was saying. "That's when I knew the nightmare wasn't over. There wasn't anything in it. No papers, nothing. It was all still buried. That's why I took all his paintings. He goddam owed me. I made a lot of money on 'em."

She glanced at him in shock. "You sold Tom's paintings?"

"Still selling them. You saw what's left on the wall. A couple are mine, but it was just easier to hang his up than make more of the same shit."

She thought it through. "You've been selling them as yours."

He looked at her quizzically. "Thought you figured that out." He shrugged again. "It was an impulse, believe it or not. I hitchhiked to the cabin from Blue Lake and started throwing anything I could grab into the hearse, including all the paintings. Didn't want to take the time to separate his from mine. You remember, you were there when I left, but it was all under that mattress in the back. Couldn't look for what he buried, not then. I stuck his crap in a storage unit in San Diego. Should have burned it. Then one day it occurred to me that he didn't need it anymore."

Suddenly he screamed, "Stop the fucking car!"

Chapter Twenty-One

She barely kept the car from twisting across the gravel cutaway into the ditch. When it came to a stop in a cloud of dust, she sat with her hands frozen on the wheel, waiting for her heart to stop pounding. He had been thrown sideways, one arm clutching the seat back, the other hand white-knuckled on the sissy bar of the dash. The gun in his hand drooped.

She leapt across and grabbed for it, missed it as his arm whipped up and the metal cracked against her head. Stunned, she fell back. The gun pointed at her again, steady now.

"Don't try that again," he panted. "Next time I'll kill you."

"You're going to kill me anyway."

He sighed with exasperation as he used his left hand to open the door and backed out, the gun muzzle unwavering. He motioned for her to follow.

"I keep telling you," he said as he moved back to keep room between them, "just do as I say and you'll be fine."

She wouldn't be able to start the car and drive before he could shoot. He'd done it before. She climbed out the passenger side. He motioned for her to cross the bridge.

Picking her way across the loose planks during the day had not been a problem. In the dark, under trees and a moon lost in the cold clouds, she felt her way across. One plank shifted and her ankle twinged sharply. At first she bit her lip against the pain, but then let out a hefty moan.

"What's the matter?" he asked, his boots making soft careful sounds on the wood behind her.

"My ankle. I think I sprained it again." She balanced on the other foot as though unable to put her weight on it.

"Too bad. It'll be a long trip to the cabin on all fours."

"I can manage." Exaggerating her limp, she started up the first rise. She had been so intent on reaching the cabin the last time that she hadn't paid much attention to the terrain. Now she tried to remember just how overgrown it was, if she could run through it and back to the road. Not that reaching the road would do much good. They hadn't passed one car on the way up, and the wide tarmac would just give him a clear shot.

Summer homes had started cropping up on the hills in the last twenty years, but there weren't any within shouting distance of the cabin, which was why hunters had not stopped coming around. Then she remembered that for at least twenty years, the only hunter around had been Barry. He had long since scared off anyone who might be inclined to be a knight in shining armor.

And no one would be hunting at this time of night anyway. No one would hear a scream and come running before he shot her. She trudged on, limping heavily, making a point of gasping out loud when her sore ankle turned on the shadowed ruts, having a vague idea of convincing Barry that she was unable to run away. At one point she did trip and went down on her hands and knees. The hard stones bit into her hands and into her knees through the jeans.

As she paused there, braced to come up in a sprint like a runner, Barry said into the darkness, "If you can't get up, start crawling. I can't miss from here."

She got up. The long day of insanity, physical and emotional, was beginning to creep in, making her legs feel like they each weighed a hundred pounds. Even if her ankle wasn't as bad as she wanted him to think, she was beginning to wonder if she could run very far before her strength gave out. It was still early in the year, but the winter had been dry and she felt the desiccated brush grab at her pants legs. He would only have to follow the noise she would make crashing through it in the dark.

She topped the last rise. The cabin was indistinct in the veiled moonlight. Beyond it was the hillside where the little pond lay hidden in a tree copse. Above that was the meadow where she and Tom made love in front of God and everybody. Weary tears burned her eyes, and she tried to blink them away.

"Ankle better?"

"No," she said shortly and went back to limping.

"Too bad. But in a minute you can sit down and rest." He prodded her forward and at the porch went quickly around her and up the steps. He shoved the door open and stood back with the gun steady.

"There's a lantern on the table and some matches. Go in and light it. Oh, and watch where you walk. I left the trap door open, so if you step in the hole, there'll be more than your ankle messed up."

Her feet felt their way across the floor. The hole in the roof barely gave enough light to show the contrast between the dark wood floor and the black square of nothingness that was the cellar. She bumped into the cable spool table, groped and found a box of kitchen matches and the lantern. It was an old style and she had to prime the tiny pump several times. "Been a long time since I used anything but battery-powered ones. Where'd you find this antique?"

"In the tool shed this morning. There was even some fuel to put in it. Sorry, but I never got around to buying a better one. This'll be enough for you to go down and look for another box."

"You're crazy," she said as she finally got the mantle to light up. She adjusted the gas and the room filled with soft light and the nostalgic hiss of kerosene gas. "We gave that hole a good going-over the other day. If there was another box, we'da seen it."

"Maybe. You're going to go down and look anyway." He had moved around to stand behind the trap door, and she saw his expression in the light. He was sweating with avid anticipation.

She froze. "There's nothing for me to find down there, is there?"

"*Get in the goddam cellar*!" he screamed. The sound jarred and horrified her. She started to shake and fought against it.

"No," she said stubbornly. "You'll have to shoot me first. Why didn't you do that before?"

"What, and carry you up here?" He was back to sounding reasonable. It made her skin crawl. "Like you said, dear, you're no little chicken anymore."

"But why come here at all? You could have shot me anywhere."

"Too many bodies, they keep looking. But if you just disappear like old Tom did, they'll figure you're the one who killed what's-er-name. Maybe Tom too. Anyway, they'll stop looking for anybody else."

"I get it. Another thirty-eight years before I'm found." She blinked away the infuriating tears of fright and braced herself with one hand on the lantern. "Get it over with, then. Just shoot me."

"Jesus, I keep telling you, *I don't want to do that*!" He took a deep breath and spoke with childlike reasonableness. "If you don't do as I say, I will have to shoot you, just like Tom. Please don't make me. I've always been crazy about you. You don't know how much I wish things could be different. And who knows? Maybe that moron will come up here looking for you right away. Oh, no, that's right, you said she's leaving town, isn't she? Well, maybe you can dig your way out. Eventually. Otherwise they'll find you some day and figure you accidentally shut yourself in."

He took a step toward her around the trap door. The handle of the lantern was still in her hand, and she swung it as hard as she could.

Barry yelled. The lantern bounced off his shoulder as he ducked, and the force of her pitch sent it crashing against the wall. Glass shattered and the lantern thumped to the floor. Liquid fuel splashed out and ignited. Tongues of flame began to crawl across the floor toward Barry. He leapt back in panic, tripped on the trap door and fell crashing to the floor. The gun went skittering across the floor into the shadows.

The kitchen door was behind her. She turned and ran without thinking. A moment's fumbling with the door and she was out, flying down the steps, running flat out across the dirt and up the path. Her shoulders contracted, feeling a bullet aimed at her back, and she pushed more speed into her legs.

The copse of trees surrounding the pond was a darker shape against the sifting clouds. Briefly she thought of throwing herself in the water to hide, but she had no idea how deep it was. The bottom mat of rotted leaves and muck could be just under the surface. She fled past it and up the hillside, sometimes grabbing at tree branches or scrambling on all fours like a hounded rabbit.

Where the trees stopped, she paused. The meadow was so exposed, everything in plain sight even without a moon. She looked over her shoulder. At first all was black, but then a faint light grew inside the cabin. Slowly it blossomed, and she saw Barry's silhouette as he stumbled across the yard searching for the path. He was screaming at her, sounding demented.

Why couldn't he have fallen in the hole? her mind cried. *Why couldn't he fall and die?*

He found the path and came charging upward. Behind him flames licked up through the cabin roof. The lantern had set fire to the old dry cedar-shake walls. She saw a gout of flame leap to one of the old California Oaks. She had watched such fires sweep through trees faster than any human could run.

She fled across the meadow to the bench. No place to hide, and it would burn. From the platform it looked a long way down. But maybe the fire would leap over the arroyo.

Ugly screaming came from the path. Terror drove her to grip the side of the platform and swing herself over the edge. Into nothingness. She flailed wildly for a foothold in the steep dirt and felt the whole construction shift. Crazily she flung herself forward to cling like a bat to the nearly perpendicular earth beneath the platform. She reached up and yanked at the nearest brace. It slid easily. She pulled it free and let it drop to the soft earth below. Before she could tug on another one, she heard his footsteps, his panting breath, coming too close.

She let go and slid gracelessly down to the floor of the arroyo. Grit dragged up under her shirt, and she came to a stop in a jumbled painful heap. Heedless of her ankle, she leapt to her feet and fled down the narrow arroyo floor. Rocks and shadows loomed around her in huge patterns of black and gray.

She slammed into a hard stone surface and fell back. It was a boulder higher than her head, obviously washed down in some forgotten flash flood, and it neatly blocked the arroyo, halting her flight. Hearing his boots on the platform behind her, she dove to the side behind a loose avalanche of rocks. She peered over the edge of it, and her breath stopped.

The platform looked high up from where she was. Barry was a black silhouette against a sky now filled with throbbing red light. Smoke billowed up behind him, underlit with red and gold and burnt orange. It was Tom's painting. It was a backdrop from hell.

"I can see you down there!" he shouted. She cringed from the menacing figure who stood with his arm extended, the gun in his hand catching shards of evil light. He moved further out on the platform and stopped.

Betty Ann dragged air back into her lungs and ran for a lit-up patch of the arroyo wall opposite him. She began climbing upward, grabbing at rocks, roots, scrambling, sucking the dust in with each gasping breath, knowing she couldn't reach the top but she had to keep moving to spoil his aim.

"*Stop*!" he cried. "I will shoot you in the back if I have to! You can't get away!"

Then she heard a weird groan, not a human sound. She whipped around, clinging to the crumbling earth, pressing against it. Barry took another step, aimed at her and fired. Dirt exploded next to her shoulder.

With a despairing moan, the platform tilted itself and plunged downward in a rocketing avalanche of dirt, metal and chunks of wood. Barry screamed and fell with his arms outflung. He hit with a sickening thump, rolled once and was still. The gun clattered to a spot a few feet from his hand.

She dashed unthinking and grabbed it. She pointed it at him as she backed away.

He lay in a slough of rubble and stones that slowly skittered and settled to a stop. His eyes were open but he was motionless.

She waited, breathing heavily, holding the gun in both hands, ready to shoot if he moved. But his neck lay at a heart-stopping angle. He wasn't going to move. Ever again.

With a sob she sank to the ground, cradling the gun in her lap.

"Betty Ann!" The cry came from above. In a moment Kovacs had slid down to the floor of the arroyo and ran to kneel beside her. "My God—I saw him shoot—are you hurt?"

She shook her head wordlessly. Gently he worked the gun from her fingers.

"There's fire," she mumbled.

"Trucks are already up there. If California fire troops don't know how to respond quick, nobody does. I saw the flames from the road and called it in."

"How did you—"

"I saw your car and started up to find you. Saw the fire, thought you were inside and nearly lost my mind. Then I saw Freid running up between the hills yelling your name."

"He's dead."

"Yes."

"He killed Tom. And Greta."

"I know. When you told me his name, it rang a bell. I, well, I took the glass he used at the restaurant and had it tested for fingerprints. Finally connected Garrett and Nickson and figured there was a falling out among scoundrels. Listen, we need to get you out of here. Can you walk?"

"Think so."

She managed, but when they had climbed back to the meadow, her legs decided to quit. He picked her up in his arms and carried her through the trees and back down the hill, skirting the furious activity at the fire. Beside the road a paramedic ambulance waited with the gathered firefighting trucks.

Kovacs stood aside while her ankle was taped, then sat down beside her on the tail of the ambulance.

"I can't believe you were up here at this time of night," she said.

He was silent a moment. "We found Barker. That is, Pete Branson found him. That's the officer he set to watching you. Freid must have quietly walked up to his cruiser window and got him to roll the window down. Barker's head was smashed in, looks like with a handy piece of rebar concrete. All those media-types were cooped up inside their own vans, staying warm. Didn't see or hear anything. Anyway, Branson got it from the bar owner that you'd left for the motel. But when he got to it, there was no sign of you. He called me and I was heading down the mountain when I saw your T-Bird sitting beside the road. I wasn't sure if I should go up. If Freid was with you, I didn't want to interrupt a—well, a love session—"

"Oh, my God!"

"Well, but then I saw the flames and came running up anyway. Heard him screaming your name like a lunatic and followed him. Couldn't believe it when I saw him just disappear down into that canyon, and there you were at the bottom too. Who set the fire?"

"I did. At least, I threw a lantern at him. Everything caught fire then, and I ran. Lieutenant—"

"Jim."

"Jim. He tried to force me down in the cellar. He was going to shut me in down there, lock the trap door, and leave me there to die and everyone would think I ran away because I killed Greta. And Tom. So I had to do something."

"Of course you did."

"Didn't mean to set fire to the whole damn hill."

There were tired but jubilant calls between firefighters.

"There you are," said Kovacs. "The fire is under control."

Crime Scene Investigation technicians arrived in their van, and Kovacs gave them directions to the arroyo. Carrying their equipment cases, with huge flashlights creating a light show through the trees, they swarmed up the hill, well to the right of the firefighters' cleanup efforts.

Kovacs came back to sit beside her. She leaned gratefully against his warm shoulder. Whether from sheer reaction or the chill of the approaching dawn, she had started to shiver.

"What did you mean, the name rang a bell?" she asked.

Kovacs snorted. "The man was arrogant. When Garrett changed his name, he picked a poet. Nickson took the same name that his hero, Abbie Hoffman, used when he was underground. 'Barry Freed'. Just changed the spelling and thought no one would ever be smart enough to make the connection. Hoffman, Freed, revolution. He couldn't let go of the past."

"You were smart enough to figure it out."

He chuckled. "Just his luck. The Raging Sixties are a hobby of mine."

"Took you long enough, though. I thought you thought I was a murderer."

He was quiet for a moment. "You know, when I ran after him up the hill, I thought he was hollering your name. But it was something else."

"It was 'B.A.'," she said bitterly. "I told him I hated it. I always hated it."

"Nothing wrong with Betty Ann. I like it."

"It's a good name for a bartender."

He made one of his inscrutable grunts. His face turned upward to where the black smoke plumes were beginning to be combed by faint fingers of dawn. She gazed pensively at it.

"What are you thinking?" he asked.

"I was thinking maybe after I get this whole name thing straightened out and if I still own the property, maybe in a few years I could build a new cabin up here, a place to come to in the summer."

"No bad memories?"

"No," she said firmly. "Just memories."

Enter the World of Eugenia Parrish

The Last Party in Eden

Welcome to the middle of the turbulent 1960's.
Kennedy's been dead for two years, while the
Summer of Love lies three years in the future.

Five young women come to Washington to
share a townhouse while they chase their
dreams in the offices across the Potomac.

Some want to find a husband, just as their
mothers did. Others pray that there's something
more to life besides being a housewife.

What they find, on the eve of the sexual revolution
and at the death of the staid 50's, will shatter their lives
and destroy the last of their innocence.

The pages that follow provide a glimpse into
the world of *The Last Party in Eden.*

Print and eBook Editions available
at all major eBook retailers.

THE LAST PARTY IN EDEN

EUGENIA PARRISH

CHAPTER 1

Berdie watched through the Captain's open window as the Jeep rattled by on Constitution Avenue, boiling over with young men in green uniforms, each one with a rifle balanced on his knees. It was a sharp reminder of how much Washington D.C. had changed in the two years since Jack Kennedy's assassination.

The window let in the Jeep's exhaust along with the humid summer air. Across the street small birds flew loops between the skinny trees. A squirrel hurried up one trunk and back down again.

She lifted her pencil from the steno pad and used her wrist to brush back her hair, feeling the sticky hair spray cling to her skin. Then she scribbled to catch up with the Captain's dictation. Her pencil flew across the paper while Captain Jackson droned on, a somnolent sound in the warm room.

Her mind wandered. It was a trick she'd learned easily, taking dictation with one ear. She often wished the Captain's office was on the other side of the Navy Building. It would be nice to glance out at the reflecting pool, maybe even see a monument or two instead of the dusty street. When she'd arrived two years before, D.C. had enchanted her like a fable city, white with eternal marble, glowing with the vitality of the people striding its streets. Women's faces were smiling or intent on their purpose.

They were beautiful in stylish clothes and more makeup than she'd ever seen in the small town where she'd grown up. The city had seemed so full of eagerness and adventure that Berdie's heart lifted every time the bus brought her across the river from Alexandria. After the assassination it hadn't taken long for everyone to settle back into business as usual. But there was an undercurrent now, a frisson under the skin of the city that made her shiver if she dwelt on it. America had recovered, but many believed that D.C. would never be the same. That the country would never be the same.

Her pencil paused. Captain Jackson had ceased pacing and stood gazing out the window. His silence was unusual. Most of the officers were uncomfortable with dictation and drove the stenographers crazy by stuttering and repeating themselves or wandering off the subject of their letters without warning. Many preferred to type out rough drafts with two fingers, leaving it to the stenos to clean it up. Captain Jackson could fire letters off the top of his head as he roamed the room, hands in his pockets, head bent as though picking the right words from the faded carpet. Her shorthand speed had been the best of her class, and unlike the other girls, she had no trouble keeping up with him. The two of them were a good match. In fact, after two years she could take his dictation with half her mind and let the rest of it go where it pleased. Now she watched him from under her bangs and dug the eraser end of her pencil under her headband to scratch an itch.

"What is this Berdie thing?" he asked the window abruptly. "What kind of name is that?"

She stared at him blankly and then said, "My last name is Berde."

"So what's your first name?"

"Nothing I want to be called by. I've been Berdie since the first grade."

He moved his shoulders irritably. "I suppose you know that Elizabeth's getting married."

"I heard something. Nothing official."

"It's official. She'll be leaving, of course. But not till the end of the year." There was tension in his back. "I'll need someone to replace her."

Berdie stopped breathing. Elizabeth held the exalted title of "Secretary" and ran the stenographers like a drill sergeant. She oversaw everything outside the Captain's office, and most things inside it as well. To have that job would be a dream come true.

He turned from the window.

"Well?" he snapped. "Do you think you'd be interested? Do you think you could handle it?" He frowned as if he personally doubted it.

She took a breath. "I'm sure I could. I help her with a lot of it already, and with five months till the end of the year, there's plenty of time for her to teach me anything else I need to know."

"You understand," he began, and coughed, cleared his throat. "I can't promise anything. It would have to be worked out. Things. Would have to be worked out. Between us. Before I could say for sure. I need to know that you and I can work together."

* * *

He stared at her. His face had gotten thinner in the last year. His eyes were sadder. She'd heard rumors that his wife was difficult to live with.

"Of course we could," she answered. "We've done fine the last two years, so why not?"

He started and gave her a half-smile, causing a warm feeling deep in her stomach. "Two years. Has it been that long?" He turned away again to gaze out the window. "Why don't you meet me tonight after work? We'll have dinner and discuss it. Get to know each other a little better."

Berdie's warmth turned to ice.

"Dinner?"

"Well, we might as well eat while we're at it. In fact, I'm spending the night here in town. I have to get something to eat anyway, so why not join me for dinner there at the hotel?"

"The hotel?" Her mind had frozen, surely it had.

He snapped, "Well, we'll eat in the restaurant, of course."

"Of course. It's just – I can't stay in town tonight. I promised to help a friend. Tonight."

"A sick friend?" He looked genuinely amused. "Very well. You go home and help your sick friend."

"Maybe some other time? We could go for lunch."

He said dismissively, "I don't have time for…lunch. If you're afraid of a simple thing like dinner, then maybe we wouldn't work together that well. Just forget I said anything."

"Captain, I really do have to be home tonight. I promised. I'm not afraid at all, not of a silly thing like dinner." She fought to keep her voice steady as she felt him slipping away. Felt the promotion slipping away.

"Never mind. You can go back to your desk. We're done here."

A sharp rap on the door made her jump. Elizabeth came in carrying a stack of typed letters and dropped them on his desk. She was a thin and bitter woman, with colorless hair scraped up in a tight French twist that pulled at her eyes and made them cat-like. The steno pool had been stunned when word spread that the resident old maid had found herself a beau. Berdie wondered what it was like, not to get married until you were too old for romance.

Captain Jackson gave Berdie a curt nod of dismissal. She gathered her pad and pencils and crept from the room. His invitation had frozen her ability to think. The heat of embarrassment was thawing it out. Her mind screamed at her, telling her that she'd just boxed herself forever into the steno pool. That she'd never make it, just like her father had said. But her father would never have allowed her to go to dinner with a married man, no matter what the reason. Her father hadn't wanted her to leave home right after school, but she'd hardly waited to take off her graduation robe before getting on a Greyhound bus and saying goodbye to the hills of Pennsylvania.

Elizabeth followed her out of the office. Berdie flashed her a grin with nothing but desperation behind it and returned to her tiny typing desk. The other girls were bent over their typewriters, fingers flying.

"Hsst!" Furtively, Alice beckoned to Berdie. She was part of the group that had flooded the steno pool right after the last wave of high school graduations. The government people had gone to Alice's school just like they'd come to Berdie's, those men and women in suits, breezy and brisk, with their typing tests and their air of Mighty Mouse to the rescue. Certainly the towns had seen it as a rescue, those poor towns looking at tidal waves of high school graduates flooding the job market, hundreds, thousands of baby-boomers who were no longer corralled safely in school but cut loose, aimless and surely looking for trouble. The government had delivered "billets" for jobs in every state.

Berdie swallowed a sigh. After only two years, she already felt dryer and older than these new, apple-faced children.

"Hey, Alice," she said.

"I messed this up again. What should I do?"

Berdie longed to tell her to take it to Elizabeth. Her own desk was piled with letters to type. She was in no mood to save this girl's job. But if she wanted the Captain to consider her for Elizabeth's job, dinner or no dinner, it would help if she started paying attention to the problems of the whole office. Helping these helpless girls was something Elizabeth had been doing for a long time. Get used to it, she told herself, or go home to Daddy. She leaned over Alice's shoulder.

"What's wrong?"

"I switched the headings – I put Captain Jackson where the Senator should go. Should I try and erase both addresses and retype them?" The girl plucked nervously at the velveteen bow that anchored her enormous bouffant.

Berdie shook her head. "An erasure here and there might be okay, but this is copied to three congressmen. Erasing six lines – you'd never keep the carbons straight. Sorry. You're gonna have to re-type the whole page."

Tears welled up.

"But I've already done it twice! Elizabeth said it had to go out tonight, and it's already four o'clock! There's too many big words. I'll never get it done in half an hour, and Lizard Liz will have a cow!"

"Okay, tell you what. You do one of mine, and I'll see if I can finish this one."

Alice swelled with damp gratitude. Berdie chose one of the shorter letters that the Captain had dictated and handed the girl her steno pad. Alice stared at it blankly.

"I didn't learn shorthand too good. Just typing. I don't think I can read this."

Berdie pressed her lips between her teeth and scrabbled through the projects on her desk.

"Here – this is one I typed up but the Captain made changes. See? Just re-type it for me with the new wording."

Alice clutched the sheet of paper to her plump chest.

"You're a doll, kid. I owe you one." She turned happily to her typewriter and fed a fresh sheet into it.

"Four copies," said Berdie.

"Oops. Forgot!" Alice yanked the sheet of paper out of the typewriter and started forming a packet of letterhead, carbon paper and pastel onion-skin sheets. Berdie made up her own packet and fed it into her IBM Selectric. Her fingers flew over the keys.

She was the only one besides Elizabeth who used an IBM Selectric. The other girls' fingers were too rough for electric keys. This, more than anything, had helped Berdie get the job when the government representatives came, offering jobs in Washington, D.C. to girls who could qualify. Girls from the swelling first wave of baby-boomers.

At first her father had refused to let her accept the job, certain that she wasn't ready to be on her own so far away from home.

"Dad," she had said desperately, "I didn't get one single reply to all those applications I put in. Not from the department stores or the lawyer's office or any of the car dealerships out on the highway."

All that spring before graduation she had trudged around to the telephone company, the electric company, the gas company, to fill out multi-page applications and fumble through interviews, feeling like a twelve-year-old instead of a high school senior, certain that she looked that way as well. The secretaries smiled their flat smiles and said they'd call. No one ever had, even though in shorthand and typing she was one of the top ten in a graduating class of four hundred. The job market was flooded with high school graduates, and many were sons and daughters of the business owners, boys needing a start on a career, girls needing to save up for a hope chest and hoping to spot new husband material. A factory worker's daughter didn't have much chance. Berdie's only offers had been to work the register at Halley's Drug Store or waitressing at Eberhardts Root Beer stand. Her feet had taken on the weight of a dull future, wearing a cheerleader's skirt and roller skates, delivering trays of hamburgers to the cars of her friends. And spending weekends at home helping her mother with the cleaning and cooking, presumably until she married and had a husband to cook and clean for herself.

Her father had sat stiffly on the living room couch while the government people told him his daughter had not only passed all their tests, she had given some of the highest scores in the country. His surprise had been obvious to the sleek woman who'd come to offer Berdie work as a clerk-typist in the Navy Office Building in downtown D.C. In a quick pounce she informed him that there would be chaperones for all the girls, a week's stay in a women's hotel, and lists of apartments, along with written instructions on negotiating the bus system. His daughter would not only be taken care of, she would be prized.

Doubt had warred with grudging pride in his eyes, and pride had won. He'd gruffly told her that she had two years to "get it out of her system" and that was only if she and her friend Maggie went together.

That had been over two years ago. With a gust of exhaust, the Greyhound had dropped Berdie and Maggie at their hotel. The next day they were brusquely introduced to their new jobs and given the phone numbers of girls who were looking for roommates. It had been the adventure of a life time, riding the bus around the beautiful marbled city, finding the townhouse to share with three other girls on the other side of the Potomac in Alexandria. With their first paychecks, she and Maggie had bought sophisticated seersucker suits so they would match the crowds of girls who stood at every bus stop in the mornings, chirping like the birds that filled the small trees. Berdie had worked to forget that the adventure had been given a time limit. Until recently, when telephone conversations with her mother started to concentrate on when she was coming back home.

When the office clock struck four-thirty, she clipped the finished letters together and took them to Elizabeth, who threw a cursory glance over them, nodded and strode into Captain Jackson's office. Berdie had never seen Elizabeth leave before the Captain. She wondered if it would be required of her, covered her typewriter, grabbed her Jackie Kennedy pillbox hat from the coat tree and hurried out to the bus stop.

Maggie was already there holding a place for her in a line of girls. Maggie had started the day with her doll-like black hair teased high and swept down into a wide flip. The heat had flopped the flip, and it hung down her back in a shapeless mass. Her bangs were stuck to her heavy mascara, and her frown did not bode well for the rest of the evening. Berdie sighed and hoped she would snap out of it. It was Friday night. She had questions to share and needed Maggie's calm head.

She squeezed in line and ignored outraged looks from people behind them. Maggie said, "Do you believe that jerk asked me out again?"

Berdie hopped on one foot to adjust the T-strap on her shoe and noticed a new run starting in her left stocking. She'd have to throw another one away. There were only so many times you could stop a run with a dab of nail polish.

Maggie went on, "He can't get it through his thick head that I don't date married men. What is it with guys here?"

"Come on. They're the same everywhere. They'd be the same back in Pennsylvania, and you'd probably be working at Burger Slop instead of in an office."

"So being chased around a desk is better than being chased around a hamburger grill?"

"Well, it pays more. Speaking of which–"

"Criminee! There goes another full bus! We'll be late getting home again. I'm dying and my feet are killing me."

The overloaded bus swam past. The driver averted his eyes from the unlucky ones stranded on the curb. His passengers stared out the windows at nothing, their weary faces not yet softened by thoughts of the weekend. Berdie heard a savage curse at the back of the line, but most them were stoic and silent. It was the price of working in the most powerful city in the world.

"What?" Berdie asked Maggie. "You got a hot date or something?"

"Yeah, right. When was the last time any of us had a hot date? Unless you count the swarms of guys who will probably show up again tonight. They seem to have made our place an auxiliary base to Quantico."

"They're lonely. But no, they hardly count as romance. More like a couple dozen little brothers."

"Exactly." Maggie sighed and added in a less belligerent tone, "I don't blame them, I really don't. I know they just want to get away from base, and I guess our place is better than being in the bars all night. If they just wouldn't keep bringing more and more of their buddies. I'm gettin' real tired of getting up Saturday morning and having to step over guys passed out on our living room floor. Last week Ilona said she deliberately stepped on some guy's chest to get across, and he didn't even wake up."

"Was she wearing heels?"

"Sharing the bathroom is bad enough with five of us girls. We can't even sleep with the doors open because the guys will see us in our shortie PJs."

"Everybody's seen Annette Funicello in baby-doll pajamas."

"That's in the movies. I am not going to have those guys see me in my baby-dolls. It's barely the end of July, Berdie. It's gonna get hotter. The only way to have any air at night is to leave the door open, and we can't with them running up and down the stairs all night."

"They're pretty good about hollering before they come up."

A bus wheezed up and stopped. They shoved their way up the steps, past damp crushed people to stand in an aisle space halfway back. Maggie grabbed at a pole as the bus lurched forward. She wiggled one three-inch spike-heel and moaned, "I'm gonna start wearing flats to work."

"You keep saying that, and you never do. It would be easier being chased around the desk if you were in flats."

Maggie gave her a reluctant smile. The bus stopped again and they were forced further back. Berdie gazed out the window and ignored her own sore feet. The sun was late afternoon bronze and set the white marble buildings on fire. The slice of sky she could see over the river changed from blue to purple even as she watched. Its beauty reminded her why she loved the city so. It never failed to spark a bit of the excitement she'd felt when she saw it for the first time. On their second day, Maggie had asked what monument they should go see first. Berdie had replied, "Just lead me around on a chain."

City workers were like a tide washing out each evening, leaving the streets damp and hollow except for an occasional dark shape moving in the shadows. Then it all surged back in the morning.

Having run out of pickup points, the bus plunged across the Arlington bridge and into Virginia. When she saw their corner of King Street, Maggie pulled the cord and they struggled past the crush to get off. There was no breeze in the street, but the air was soft on their damp skin. Sometimes Berdie liked to stand on the sidewalk and gaze dreamily southward toward the tip of the high tower of the Masonic Temple. It seemed a rather absurd mid-western tribute to ancient architecture, yet she found it strangely uplifting to see it thrusting into the sky, above the shabby row houses and tired shops.

But in mid-summer it was too hot to linger outside. They hurried up the walk and through the back door to find a day's accumulation of heat filling the hallway. Berdie let the screen door bang behind them as she called out, "For heaven's sake, didn't anyone turn on the fan?"

"It's on!" called a young male voice from the living room. "It's all that cooking heating up the place!"

The hallway was thick with the odor of frying meat. Maggie's nose lifted like a Pekinese. "What smells good?"

Ilona's silver-blonde head appeared around the door of the kitchenette.

"Y'all timed that just right. We are serving sloppy joes."

"You made sloppy joes?"

Ilona raised her eyebrows. "Good heavens, no, Ah certainly did not. My mama would have the shivers if I cooked up such low-class food. Y'all can thank the new girls."

Berdie followed Maggie into the kitchenette. It was like diving into a Swedish spa. Connie and Joanna stood at the stove, their heads together over the largest skillet from Maggie's "hope chest" set. They'd changed out of their work dresses into shorts and sleeveless blouses. Connie's thick yellow hair was pulled up into a pony tail with loose wisps clinging to her neck.

Two boys sat at the dinette table eating from stained paper plates. Both wore cotton dress shirts with the sleeves rolled up over the fresh muscled arms of the military.

"Hey, Nick," Berdie said to the older one.

He took a deep swallow from a misty bottle of beer and waggled it at her in greeting. Over a dainty belch he said, "This here's Lenny. He just finished boot camp."

The other boy nodded, chewing. His crew cut looked close and painful. He slipped looks of dumbstruck adoration at the girls at the stove, and Berdie marveled that one of them, or both, already had a conquest. She couldn't remember devastating anyone so easily at that age. The girls were barely two years younger, just the age she and Maggie were when they left home. A stab of bitterness hit below the belt, and she felt a wall grow up between herself and these youngsters. A wall not of years but of experience.

She said abruptly, "How long you been coming here, Nick?"

He showed no surprise at her question, but then he never showed surprise at anything.

"Since right after you and Mags moved in, I think," he said.

She nodded. A month ago two of their original roommates had married and moved out, leaving them with Ilona and an empty bedroom. Berdie registered with the government agency as needing two more to share the rent. The next day Connie and Joanna had showed up on the stoop like a pair of puppies. Ilona called them "Salt 'n' Peppah". Connie was a honey blonde, Joanna a dark brunette, and they never seemed to be far apart. They'd even managed to get jobs as filing clerks in the same government building downtown so they could ride the bus together.

Lenny drawled, "You girls are lucky Connie and Joanna moved in. They can cook."

Maggie fixed him with a look. "I think I could manage to throw ketchup over hamburger, thank you."

"Didn't mean nothin'," he muttered.

At the stove, Joanna said, "That's enough ketchup, Con. What are you doing now?"

"More Tabasco. It needs something." Connie licked her finger.

Ilona said from the doorway, "Y'all keep dumpin' that stuff in, you'll need an ambulance." She shrugged and walked out of sight.

"Hi, you guys," Connie greeted Berdie and Maggie. Her face was pink and moist, her blonde head enveloped in steam. "I hope you don't mind, it's not our night to cook, but it was getting late and the guys were getting hungry and we thought this would be easiest. We're gonna need to buy ketchup, though. We used up all you had."

Maggie's eyes widened. "You used all the ketchup? There were two bottles in there."

"That's not going to feed everybody," Berdie said, pointing at the skillet.

Connie smirked and pulled the oven door down. "There's a whole huge pan of it down here. The guys took up a collection and bought pounds of hamburger and about a hundred buns."

Nick grinned. "We figured it was time we paid for dinner."

Joanna pushed her hair off her wet forehead. "Guess it was a waste to put my hair up last night. Look at it, it's just frizzing out." She held out paper plates with sandwiches on them. "Some of the guys have had theirs, but you better move fast before the rest of the thundering herd comes in."

Maggie said, "I'm not eating sloppy joes in these clothes. I'll be back down in a jiff."

She left. Berdie took a Coke from the refrigerator, accepted the offered plate, dumped some potato chips beside the sandwich and carried everything out to the living room where Maggie's record player was sobbing out the Beach Boys.

CHAPTER 2

The living room was marginally cooler than the kitchen. Someone had propped the front door open with a chair, to act as a draft and pull fresh air through the hallway from the rear entrance. A round fan sat on the floor, turning with an exhausted rattle. The one large window framed a view of the quiet front street lined with townhouses. In the middle of summer it was a breathless brick canyon but safe from the noise and dirt of King Street behind them. Sunset made a silhouette of the roofs across the street. Someone flipped on a table lamp, and it threw a mellow glow on the living room walls.

Berdie counted at least six young Marines relaxed around the room and sighed.

Joanna was saying, "I'll get married someday. I don't guess there's a real rush."

"You got that right, sweetheart," said Pete. "You broads are always in too big a hurry to rope some guy in and tie him down."

Pete had a skinny nervous body that weeks of boot camp had not built up. He'd eaten at least four sloppy joes, and Berdie had lost count of the beers. Now he lay stretched out on the carpet, drumming his fingers on his stomach in time to the music from the record player. Connie sat cross-legged next to him with her paper plate between her knees. When Berdie had come in, one of the boys moved and sat on the floor, giving her the armchair, which offer she accepted gratefully. She slipped off one shoe and rubbed her foot in time to the music.

"That sounds familiar," she said to no one in particular.

Rabbit said from the floor, "It's 'Daisy Petal Pickin'. Same guy that did 'Sugar Shack' so it sounds a lot like it." His round face was gleeful as he burrowed through the girls' record collection, organizing a stack to play. He was the only plump Marine Berdie had ever met. She looked away as he gnawed on his sloppy joe. He chewed quickly with his front teeth, and it made his ears wiggle comically.

"Jeez, buddy," dark-eyed Tony said. "Can't you find something new? Something that ain't that high school stuff? Play the Kinks or the Stones, maybe."

Ilona made the ice cubes clink in her glass. "Why ya'll want to listen to that nasty stuff?"

She sat enthroned on an armchair, disdaining the cooler floor. Her silvery hair fell smoothly across her forehead without a hint of the damp that softened everyone else. The glass of Canadian Club and Coke in her hand had its ubiquitous mint leaf. She claimed it was a poor excuse for a mint julep, but better than none.

"The Stones are big, babe," Tony answered her. "They're real music."

"Naw," said Jim from his seat on the couch beside Maggie. He had burst in weeks before, brash and excitable, having invited himself along in Rabbit's car, an iridescent purple Plymouth known as "Moby Grape". Jim had thrown his heart at Maggie, and Maggie had seemed happy at first to catch it. Lately she'd been discontented.

"He won't let me talk to anybody else," she complained late at night in their room. "And he follows me every time I leave the room and watches me every time I talk to somebody else. You'd think we were married or something."

Berdie figured she'd work it out; she just wished Maggie would hurry up. She had gotten rid of enthusiastic boyfriends before. Only once had she been dumped herself, and she refused to talk about it. Berdie suspected that things had gone too far. Some boys dumped you as soon as they got what they wanted. It was a fact of life, but it wasn't something you asked about, if the information wasn't offered.

Jim settled his arm around Maggie, ignoring her irritable shrug. “Elvis,” he said. “Now that’s real music.”

The boys hooted.

“Elvis is done, man,” said Tony. “He’s makin’ them girlie movies now. All that fifties stuff is over. Get with it, will ya? We wanna hear ‘Louie, Louie’, somethin’ like that.”

“Jeez, Tony, nobody wants that stupid beatnik stuff,” said Jim.

“Beatnik stuff? Man, that’s fifties. Whatsa matter with you? Ain’t no beatniks anymore!”

Joanna had a finger in her mouth, probing. “I think I need to find a dentist. You guys got a phone book?”

Berdie pointed to where three thick phone books were serving as the fourth leg of the couch. Their spines said they were for Washington D.C., Arlington and Alexandria. Joanna’s face fell.

Ilona said, “Ah got one in mah room.” She went up the stairs.

Connie pulled the rubber band from her yellow pony tail and ran her hand up the back of her head, holding the warm weight of her hair higher. Hairspray made it resemble corn-colored cotton candy.

“I’m not getting married for years and years,” she said. “I’ve got too many things I want to do first.”

“Like what?” Pete scoffed. “What you figure on doing so special?”

“Oh, I don’t know. I want to travel, see things. Get a better job. I think working in an embassy somewhere would be fantastic.”

Maggie said, “One of our old roommates went to work at an embassy in the Middle East for a while.”

Connie squealed. “Did she love it?”

“Hated it. Said they couldn’t leave the building without being followed by crowds of creepy men staring at them, and that’s after they put on clothes that cover everything. She even covered her hair up, but she said it doesn’t help.”

Tony swallowed and wiped sloppy joe off his mouth with a paper napkin.

"Bet she's a blonde," he said. "Nothing'll help. Those Ay-rabs are nuts about blondes."

"My sister went to the Middle East with the Peace Corps," Rabbit said. "One day all the girls went into town together to shop, and she had to use the head. It was in a back room of the store and when they walked in, there was just this hole in the ground. She said there was these two little blocks you put your feet on, and you squatted down over the hole, and there was no paper or anything. And when she looked up, some guy was watching her through a hole in the wall."

Joanna blushed. Ilona came back down and handed her the phone book for Alexandria, and she busied herself with it.

Connie grinned at Rabbit. "See? Now I know what to expect. That's what I want to learn, stuff like that so I can never be taken by surprise. I want to learn all the languages and customs there are, so I can blend in."

Nick gave a soft laugh from the corner where he sat against the wall. "Honey, you're an American. You'll never blend in. We all stick out like sore thumbs, no matter where we go."

Connie made a face at him. "That's 'cause we don't make the effort. Anyone can do it if they try."

"What's wrong with just being an American, Conzie?" asked Joanna. She looked around for a place to put her empty paper plate. Lenny jumped up and carried it out to the kitchen. Berdie hid her smile. He'd obviously made his choice, and the other boys had given him the field, turning their attention to Connie. Joanna seemed oblivious of the shift. She went on, "Why not just travel around and be yourself?"

"Because you don't see the real country or the real people. Only what they want you to see."

Ilona gave a great shudder.

"Ah can't imagine wantin' to see anything they don't want you to see. There's bound to be a reason, and I for one don't wish to delve. I certainly have no intention of squattin' over no hole. If I nevah go anywhere but heah, I'll be quite happy, thank y'all." She sipped delicately at her glass.

"But," Connie protested, "don't you ever want to know how other people live? What they talk about? The exotic way they do things?"

Ilona didn't bother to answer.

Tony yawned and stretched, then scratched his glossy black curls. "I'm going to Okinawa in six months. That's exotic enough for me."

"Okinawa!" Connie breathed. "Will you send me some postcards? I'm just dying to get mail from some neat place like that!"

Their laughter confused her.

"Where you from, honey?" Tony asked.

Connie stiffened. "Ohio. Why?"

He threw up his hands. "Just askin'. What's wrong with Ohio?"

She said in a rough tone, "It's a great place to be from."

"Oh, come on!" said Joanna. "It's not that bad. Don't you want to go back and settle there after you're married?"

"What for? And maybe I'll never get married."

They all laughed again.

"You will," said Maggie from the couch. "You'll meet a great guy and that'll be that."

"You sound like my mother," Connie said. "She's old and tired and never been anywhere or done anything."

Maggie said nothing. The rest looked embarrassed.

Nick said, "How 'bout you, Berdie? You're the oldest of the girls, aren't you? When do you figure on getting married?"

"Just as soon as you ask me, Nick."

They all laughed, including Berdie. She'd meant it as a joke, but she wondered why it should be that funny. Berdie liked Nick's quiet maturity and the way the younger boys deferred to him. Most of them had bulked up when they joined the Marines and wore their muscles like a brand-new suit they were proud of, but not yet used to. Nick seemed comfortable in his body. He'd never shown her any more attention than he'd shown Maggie or Ilona, but sometimes Berdie wondered what life would be like if he did.

"Maybe I could join the Peace Corps," said Connie.

Rabbit shook his head. "You gotta be a college graduate."

She looked at him with suspicion. "You're kidding."

"Nope."

"But that's just stupid!"

Joanna said, "There were only about ten people in our class that went on to college. Where they gonna get everybody?"

Nick said, "Me, I guess I'm goin' places, too. It just isn't my idea to go there."

"Like where?" asked Connie.

"Like maybe Viet Nam."

"Where's that?"

"Who knows?" said Tony. "Who cares?"

"Do you figure any of us'll have to go?" asked Lenny. He'd come back from the kitchen and sat next to Joanna, who paid him no attention.

"I'll go," said Pete. He sat up and cocked his arms as though aiming a rifle and swept the room with it. "I wouldn't mind shootin' me some gooks."

"Some what?" said Connie.

"Never mind," Berdie said. "That's an ugly word, Pete. Don't use it here."

"What? Gooks? That's what they are. Gooks from gooks-ville."

"Well, where is it?" asked Connie before Berdie could speak.

Tony said, "It's on the other side of the damn planet somewhere. I joined the Marines 'cause they said I'd go to Europe or Africa or someplace somebody maybe heard of. It's the Army that's s'posed to go to goo—" He shot a look at Berdie. "To dumb ugly places ain't nobody ever been before."

Connie looked dreamy-eyed. "I'd love to go places nobody's ever been."

Pete scratched his raw crew cut and scoffed, "How you gonna live in some place where there ain't no people?"

"I mean there'll be people. Just nobody I know."

Nick asked with a smile, "What've you got against people you know?"

"They've never been anywhere!"

"What's wrong with that?" Tony reached into Rabbit's shirt pocket, pulled out a lighter and flicked at a fresh cigarette. He dragged a glass ashtray across the carpet to bring it within reach.

"Leave her alone," said Joanna. "I wish I had her nerve. Strange people scare me."

"Better stay away from us, then," said Tony. He waggled his eyebrows at her. "We're pretty strange."

"You certainly are," said Berdie. "Where you guys from, anyway? Jim's from Louisiana, aren't you?"

"We call him the crazy Cajun," said Pete.

Jim scowled. "Not for long, you don't."

"How about you, Lenny?"

Lenny blushed and glanced at Joanna. "Ohio, like you and Connie."

"No kidding," said Joanna. "Where at?"

Connie interjected, "Who's from farthest away?"

"Why?" asked Tony. "You gonna give a prize?"

"Tony," said Berdie. "Be nice."

He looked hurt. "I am nice. I'm just askin'. I'm from Brooklyn, myself, darlin'."

"Okay," said Connie. "New York and Louisiana. Anybody farther?"

"I'm from Florida," said Pete. "How 'bout you, Rabbit?"

"Massachusetts. Nick's from Chicago, ain'tcha?"

"Just as far away from it as I can get."

"What's wrong with Chicago?"

"Nothin'. Like she said, it's a good place to be from."

Connie had scrunched her face up in thought. "I gotta look at a map. I'm not sure which is farthest from here."

Tony hooted. "She is givin' a prize! I think you got it, Nick."

"Cut it out," he said. He scooted over to their tiny television and turned it on. He played with the rabbit ears and then turned the dial until the news came on. Stuttering images in black and white flickered on the screen. Berdie watched young soldiers grin as they carried enormous duffle bags on their shoulders or looked determined beneath their helmets as they felt their way through a flooded field of head-high grass. It didn't look at all like the pictures she'd seen of World War II or Korea. For one thing, the soldiers looked a lot younger. Especially with their heads and arms bandaged after an attack by something the newscaster called the "Viet Cong".

"See what I mean?" said Pete. "Man, I'd like to go shoot me some of them dick-heads."

"Pete," said Nick.

"Sorry. Some of them re-tards."

Rabbit spoke. "Jeez, Nick, get off his back. You called 'em same thing the other day."

"Not in front of the girls."

Ilona spoke from her chair. "Ah don't understand why y'all want to watch people dyin' and such."

Tony laughed. "What do you wanta watch, honey, 'Bewitched'?" He took his nose between thumb and forefinger and wiggled it.

"How 'bout 'Bonanza'?" said Lenny.

"It ain't Sunday," someone said.

"Anyway, 'Bonanza' ain't no fun without color," said Rabbit. "Black and white stinks."

"So buy 'em a new TV," said Tony. Rabbit didn't bother answering. Buying hamburger was one thing. Color televisions were expensive.

Lenny reached for the channel knob.

Pete protested, "Leave it alone. I wanta see how them…re-tards fight. Better to know what we're up against before we get there. We're blowin' em to kingdom-come, and I wanta see how we're doin' it."

"If they don't blow us to kingdom-come first," said Nick.

"Oh, now, that's real cheerful. Whatsa matter, you don't think we can beat 'em? Buncha little jerks in black pajamas?"

Birdie studied Nick's face.

"You think it's that bad?" she asked him, nodding toward the TV. "They're saying it'll be over soon. Maybe none of you will have to go."

He smiled. "Yeah, it'll probably be over quick."

It was what her father always said when the union went on strike. It was what men said to women, not what they said to each other.

"Man," Pete moaned. "Don't say that. We gotta go. I don't want to miss it!"

"It's so far away," Joanna mused. "Does it really matter?"

"Honey, the Commies are tryin' to take over everywhere!" Pete cried. "We let it happen, an' boom – it's World War Three. We gotta go 'n' kick 'em outa there now. We'll bust their…behinds and come back heroes."

Some of the boys nodded. Nick checked his empty beer bottle and went to the kitchen. Pete watched him go.

"He thinks a lot of his own opinions. Doncha get tired of it?"

"Yeah, sometimes," said Tony. "But he thinks 'em through real good before he says 'em, so I keep my mouth shut. Might be, you should do the same."

Through the screen door they heard young male voices in the street. Someone yelled clearly, if raucously, "Hey, Maggie! C'mon out!"

"Hey, Maggie-pie! Come out 'n' play!"

One cried in falsetto, "Here, Berdie, Berdie! Come fly with us, Berdie!"

The boys on the floor had stiffened.

"What the hell?" snarled Pete as he started to get up. Berdie went to the screen door.

"What d'you guys want?" she called out.

"Who is it?" asked Maggie from the couch. She made no move to get up.

"It's the guys from the townhouse down the end of the row. I think they're mostly Navy."

"They live down there?" asked Lenny.

"No, that's just where they hang out."

She felt Nick's presence behind her shoulder.

"You know any of 'em?" he asked.

"I've seen that big guy," she said. "But we've only gone up there a couple times. Their parties get too wild, fights and things.

People have called the cops on 'em. They've got a bad rep, and we don't want to get caught in it."

"I think some of the guys actually live there with them," said Maggie. "I mean, they actually sleep in the bedrooms with the girls. Not something we feel comfortable with."

"Ah should say not," said Ilona.

From the street came, "Hiya, Berdie! Whyncha come out! We got a great party goin' up the street!"

Nick stepped around her and pushed open the door. He said nothing, just stood looking down at the newcomers from under lowered eyelids. Berdie followed him onto the concrete stoop. Pete stood behind her holding the screen door open.

"Whoo-hoo!" yelled one of the boys in the street. "Looka there! She got some big bad Marines with her."

Berdie felt the heat radiating from Nick's muscled arm. His posture was relaxed, but he made her think of a cat watching a flock of small birds. She called out quickly, "We might come up later, Butch. We're just finishing up eating."

"C'mon, Butch," said a slim blond boy with hair long enough to fall onto his forehead. He looked like one of the Beach Boys. "These broads ain't int'rested."

Butch gave the waistband of his corduroys a hitch and ambled toward the steps. Then he stopped, looking up at them. Nick had not moved, but the other boys were crowding into the doorway. Pete pushed the screen door open further.

"You need any help out here, man?"

Nick shook his head without looking away from Butch. "Nah. Everything's cool. These guys just came to invite the girls to a party."

Pete called harshly, "Like the man said, they ain't interested. G'wan back home."

The others stepped up behind Butch in a menacing wedge. He glowered and said, "Who asked you? They can decide for themselves. Can'tcha, Berdie?"

She said, "Pete, it's okay."

"Yeah," the slim blond yelled. "You hear that? It's okay. Anyway, ain't none a yore business, jarhead."

Berdie felt Pete move. She whipped around and put her hands to his chest. To her relief he froze. In his face a man's anger fought with the child's habit of obeying women. He sent glares past her at the boys in the street.

"Forget it," Nick said. "They ain't comin' up here."

"Then we'll go down there."

"No!" Berdie pleaded.

Nick said under his breath, "If we get in a fight, somebody might call the cops. The girls'll get in trouble, and you'll get busted back down to Private. You just made Lance, man. Hang onto it for awhile."

Pete hesitated, visibly weighing the options. Berdie stayed in front of him. She saw Maggie standing in the screen door.

"Maggie!" she hissed. "Go back inside. They'll leave if they don't see you. Tell the other girls to stay out of sight."

Maggie disappeared.

"Hey, where'd she go?" asked Butch, sounding more petulant than belligerent. "Hey, Maggie!"

"She's still eating," said Berdie. "We all are. So maybe we'll be along later, after dark. It's still too hot."

After a moment Butch stepped back. "She's right, man. It's hot out here. Let's go back and get some more beer. Who needs these broads?"

The others made sounds of agreement. As they drifted away, the blond boy called, "Just leave your boyfriends at home, okay?"

Berdie gave Pete a little shove, and he stomped back inside. The others followed him. Nick stood watching the group as it ambled drunkenly up the street.

"Damn sailors," he said. "Always looking for a fight."

"I didn't notice you backing down," said Berdie.

He grinned and held the screen door open for her.

"Did they leave?" Connie breathed as they walked in. Someone had turned off the light, and her eyes shone like a cat's in the darkened room. "You scare 'em away, Nick?"

Berdie turned the light back on and said, "They got thirsty. It's too hot out there to fight."

"I didn't see 'em comin' up the walk after we went out there," said Pete sulkily.

"Nobody invited 'em up," said Nick. The other boys laughed.

"How crazy," said Connie. "Have you guys been up there before?" She was looking at Berdie and Maggie. "Up to that townhouse? What's it like?"

Maggie shrugged. "Looks just like ours, only backwards, like this whole row. Every other townhouse is a mirror-image. We been to their parties a couple times, but it gets too nasty. Always a fight, either between the guys or the girls."

"The girls?" Joanna looked stunned. "Why would girls fight?"

"'Cause they're mean," said Jim. "You girls stay away from there."

Connie said stonily, "I'll go where I please."

Nick said, "He just means you'd be better off not mixing with them. The cops have been there more'n once. It could cost you your jobs."

Connie laughed. "Oh, sure."

"He's not kidding," said Berdie. "All of us except Ilona work for the government. If any of us gets a bad rep, we could get fired. A friend of ours was a typist for the FBI. She went to a party and it got too loud and someone called the cops. Turned out there were some guys there from some embassy who were really drunk and got nasty with the cops and really ticked 'em off. And some of the girls were underage. So they took 'em all downtown. The embassy stepped in and got it hushed up, but Dee-Dee got fired, and so did her roommate, who wasn't even at the party."

Connie and Joanna stared at her, mouths open.

Maggie pursed her freshly-lipsticked mouth around a cigarette and accepted a light from Jim. She blew the smoke out. "They're always afraid you'll do something or get caught in something that you could be blackmailed for."

"Blackmailed?" Joanna looked astounded. "Blackmailed for what?"

Maggie shrugged. "Information."

"Holy cow," said Connie. She'd gotten back her shining-eyed look. "You mean like spies and stuff?"

"Yeah, baby," said Nick tiredly. "Just like James Bond."

"More like Alec Leamas," said Berdie. "And he died."

Connie frowned. "Who?"

"Never mind. If you want to go to their party, go ahead. But don't go alone, and leave if there's any trouble."

"'Kay," said Connie surprisingly. She took a big swallow of the drink in her hand.

"Conzie," pleaded Joanna. "Take it easy. You'll get sick."

"No, I won't. It's nice. Try it." She offered the glass.

Joanna took a sip and handed it back. "Ick. It's too sweet."

"I like it," said Connie and took another big gulp. Berdie noticed two of the boys watching her. It was the girl's own fault if she got drunk, but Berdie hoped nothing bad would happen because of it.

CHAPTER 3

"Wow. Secretary. That's pretty neat, I guess."

Maggie sat at their dressing table, listlessly winding her black hair up in rollers. Berdie pulled her shortie-pajama top over her head.

"You guess? Maggie, it would be fantastic! It would pull me right out of the steno pool. I'd make tons of money."

"Sure, but." She stared earnestly at Berdie's image in the mirror. "Does it really matter? I mean, eventually you'll get married like everyone else and quit your job."

"I don't see why."

Maggie scoffed, "You don't see why what? Get married? Or quit your job? No decent guy's gonna let you keep working after you're married."

Berdie pulled back the chenille cover on her bed and climbed under the sheet. "Then maybe I won't ever get married. No law says I have to."

"Oh, you." Maggie pouted. "I'm being serious. Soon as you find a nice guy, you'll be ready to get married like everybody else. You don't want to be an old maid, do you?"

Berdie was silent for a moment. "I guess not. Not permanently. But, Maggie, what's wrong with waiting until you're older. Maybe thirty?"

Maggie shuddered. "Who knows what we'll look like by then? I'm not taking any chances."

Rain burst on them in the middle of the week and stayed, soaking them Friday night on their walk from the bus stop.

Music thumped in the living room, disguising all sounds but the watery roar from the roof gutters. Maggie fled to their room to repair the damage done to her hair. Berdie greeted Lenny in the kitchenette, poured herself a glass of Coke, added a little rum, looked into the lukewarm pan of floating hot dogs and went out to the living room to join the others. She stepped across the boys sprawled on the floor.

"What're y'all doing here?" she asked a little grumpily. "I thought you had duty this weekend."

Their look of surprise made her blush. There were a few new faces, scrubbed with the boot camp look. One boy dwarfed the window behind him. Rabbit introduced him as "Big Bill". She sighed and tried to think of something to say that didn't sound like she wished they'd all stayed on the base for once. Nothing came to mind. Maggie came down in dry clothes with her face freshly made up. She sat on the couch, and Jim scooted over next to her. She ignored him.

"Hey," said Tony. "Any more of them cookies your mom sent?"

Rabbit dug in the bag. "There's only one left."

"Good. That's all I need."

Rabbit gave him a dirty look, turned the cookie over, gave it a big lick on the bottom and handed it to him. Tony contemplated it, turned it over, gave the top a big lick of his own and handed it back to Rabbit. Holding it with two fingers, Rabbit placed it carefully on a paper plate that someone had left on the end table. Lenny came in from the kitchenette.

"Hey! Who had cookies?" He scooped it up before the girls could stop him and popped it in his mouth. "What's so funny?"

"Nothing," said Berdie before Joanna could speak.

"Everybody likes cookies," said Tony.

Their laughter froze on Maggie's shrill cry. "Don't do that!"

Jim removed the arm he'd thrown around Maggie's shoulders.

"Just gettin' comfortable, doll."

"Get comfortable with someone else. Or I will."

Dark anger washed over his face.

"Nobody else better even try," he snarled.

"That's for me to say." Maggie started up from the sofa. Jim grabbed her arm, but with one glance at her face, his anger dissolved into something begging and ashamed.

"I'm sorry, doll. I won't do it again. Stay here with me. Whatcha need? I'll get it for you."

"I need some air," she snapped, wrenching her arm from his grip. The screen door slapped behind her with a crack that broke the air in the silent room. The others started a quiet discussion of the merits of Motown music, keeping their heads down. Jim glowered from the corner of the sofa.

Berdie found Maggie under the spindly tree that anchored the patch they called the "front yard". The rain had stopped and the street was quiet and empty. Maggie leaned against the wet trunk.

"He's really just gettin' crazy," she said. "I swear, he started right out pawing me. Right in front of everybody."

"I guess he likes you a lot," said Berdie.

"Guess so. He asked me to marry him."

Berdie looked at her in surprise. "I didn't know that. When?"

"Last weekend, before the guys all left."

"Did you say yes?"

When they'd first arrived in town, Maggie had been determined to get married as soon as possible, and she'd welcomed Jim's attentions. They'd gone out to movies and to the Hot Shoppe, just the two of them. Whenever Maggie crept back into the bedroom after everyone was asleep, Berdie said nothing, believing that if anything happened, it was what Maggie wanted anyway. Maggie always knew what she was doing. Now she seemed to carry a forest of indecision around with her.

"I thought we'd get married, back when we started," Maggie said. "It seemed okay, and I didn't want to get away from him or anything. But then he started pushing at me, wanting me to promise crazy things, like never talking to the other guys or sitting near them. He acts like I'm some kind of wind-up doll and only he should have the key. He follows me everywhere and watches everything I do. Berdie, the other day he said he'd shoot anybody else I went out with. Then he said he'd kill himself. Or me. When he says that, he gets all – I don't know – weird in the eyes. And if I say 'calm down', he just gets madder. I guess I should be flattered, but I hate being around him anymore, and I'm afraid what'll happen if I go out with somebody else. Sometimes I just want to be with somebody else, someone fun. Only now I can't. What'll I do?"

"Well, don't cry – your mascara will run, and I don't have a hankie. Don't worry about the guys. They can take care of themselves, and they know Jim. Anyway, he's not that crazy."

"I dunno," Maggie said softly. She turned doe eyes to Berdie. "Will you tell the other guys to make him stop coming here?"

"Good grief, Mags. Even if they agreed to try, Jim wouldn't listen. Not now. He's drawn a bead on you. He's not gonna just walk away."

"They've got to make him stay away." Maggie sounded more desperate than Berdie had ever heard her. "I don't think I can take this much longer."

A crash came from inside the house. One of the girls screamed. Berdie ran inside with Maggie close behind her. Nick had his fists bunched in the front of Jim's shirt, pinning him to the wall. The others stood frozen, staring at them. Maggie gasped.

"Nick," said Berdie.

He made no sign of hearing her. Jim hung limp against the wall, and Nick's shoulders heaved with the effort of holding his weight.

Tony said with disgust, "Let 'im go, Nick. He's shot his wad."

Nick opened his fists. Jim slid with a thump to the floor.

"He punched a hole in the wall." Nick's anger reverberated in the air. "Crazy drunk Cajun."

Berdie saw the ragged gap in the plaster. Another thing to fix before the landlord saw it. Big Bill said from his seat at the window, "He didn't move after you two left. He just sat there mumblin'. Then all of a sudden he rears up and cocks his fist and smashes it through the wall. Dumb sonovabitch. Sorry, Berdie."

"Forget it."

"Maggie," Jim murmured from the floor. His unfocused eyes searched the room for her. Maggie fled up the stairs and they heard a door slam.

Ilona went to Jim and looked at his hand.

"You're bleeding," she said.

"He's gonna bleed a lot more, he pulls somethin' like that again," Nick said harshly. Berdie watched as he shoved the screen door open and walked out to the street.

Jim moved his head from side to side. "Maggie? Doll? I'm sorry. I dunno what I was doin'. Guess I had too much to drink."

Tony snorted. Berdie said to Ilona, "Take him in the kitchen and use the first aid kit."

Ilona tugged at his arm. Jim followed her from the room like a docile dog.

Tony said, "Boy's definitely a quart low sometimes."

Into the silence, Connie said, "What's is this again?" as she peered owlishly into her glass.

"It's called a Purple Jesus, sweetie," said Big Bill with a grin. "Grape juice and grain alcohol."

She made a face. "That's not a nice name. What's grain alcohol? I don't feel anything."

"You won't. Not till you try to stand up."

Joanna said, "Conzie, stop drinking that." She grabbed for the glass. Connie pulled it out of her reach.

"I'm fine. I'm tired of sloe gin. I wanna try something else."

Berdie heard Ilona's voice getting higher. She sighed and went to the kitchenette. Jim was crouched at the dinette table, picking at a fresh bandage on his hand. Ilona jammed the gauze and mercurochrome back into their first aid kit. Her porcelain face was livid.

"What's the matter now?" asked Berdie.

Ilona said, "Will y'all please tell him ah'm not Maggie, and she ain't comin' back down?"

"But why?" Jim cried. "Ain't I been good to you? I love you, doll."

Ilona thrust a hand through her silver hair and made a sound of disgust. "Y'all are just stupid, you know that?" She left the room.

"God, I love her so much. We belong together. Hell, I'd marry her tonight if she wants. Tell her, Berdie." Jim crossed his arms on the table and dropped his head into his elbow. He burbled words onto the table top. Berdie wondered if she should talk to him. She decided she was too tired and went back to the living room.

"Any of you guys going back to base tonight?"

"Yeah, I got duty," said Rabbit morosely. "We just wanted to get away for awhile, but I gotta be back by ten."

"Be sure and take Jim with you, okay? He's just a mess, and he's gonna keep making trouble."

Rabbit looked alarmed. "What if he don't want to leave?"

"Why don't Maggie just go out with him?" asked Pete. "He's okay, when he ain't drinkin'."

"She don't want to, okay?" said Rabbit. "She's got a right."

Berdie knew Rabbit had asked Maggie out himself and she'd rejected him with affectionate humor. It followed a pattern, she thought. They made passes, Maggie turned them down with a sweet smile, and from then on they protected her from her other pursuers. But no one seemed inclined to dispute Jim's claim.

"I don't get it," said Big Bill. "I thought she liked him."

"Liking is one thing," Berdie answered him. "Being constantly bothered is another. He won't leave her alone."

Pete belched into his beer and snarled, "Aw, f'Christ sake. You broads want us to chase after ya, and you let us catch ya, and then you scream rape. It ain't like any of you are virgins. Hell, my girlfriend back home told me she's a virgin, 'n' when I finally get to third base, I nearly fall in, it's so big."

A couple of the new boys laughed. Connie gasped and then began to giggle uncontrollably.

"Pete, shut your damn mouth!" Nick snapped. Berdie jumped. She hadn't noticed him come back in the room.

Pete stared at him through alcoholic haze. "Wha?"

"We don't talk like that in the girls' house."

"Well, hell. Scuse the shit outa me."

"Yeah," Connie said through her liquidy giggles. "Scuse the shit outa him!"

"Hey, man," Tony said to Pete. "Nick's an a-hole, but he's right. It ain't nice. Not around the girls."

"What? I'm talkin' about fake virgins to somebody who's maybe a real one. Gimme a break." Pete shoved his bottle to his mouth and drank deep.

"Okay, pal," Tony said, not without compassion. "You've had enough too. Gimme the keys to Moby, Rabbit."

Rabbit threw a bunch to him. Tony helped Pete up and took him out to the car. Then he went to the kitchen and gathered Jim up.

"Pete don't mean nothin', Berdie," said Rabbit as he followed them out. "Don't pay him no nevermind, his smartass overruns his smart sometimes. You know we don't think of you girls that way."

"I know," she said, and wondered. She listened to the old car rumble away and breathed a sigh of relief.

"Is he gone?"

Berdie looked up to where Maggie leaned over the banister. "Yeah, he's gone."

Maggie came downstairs and took her place on the couch again. Her freshly lipsticked mouth trembled. When the phone rang, she jumped. Joanna picked it up.

"For you, Berdie."

Berdie took the receiver. "Hi, Mom."

"Hello, love. How's everything?"

"Just fine. How're you?"

Joanna turned the record player down.

"Who was that answered the phone?" said her mother. "It didn't sound like Maggie or that other girl, what's her name."

Berdie knew her mother remembered Ilona's name. But she'd decided it was too foreign and refused to use it.

"That was Joanna, Mom. One of the new girls. I told you we were going to get some new girls. We were lucky to get them so soon. We can't afford this place with just the three of us."

There was a meaningful silence and then a sigh.

"Well, that's good, I guess," said Gladys. "We don't want you spending all your money on rent. Will these girls stay, then, if you leave?"

"Me? Why would I leave?"

"Well, you'll have to come home sometime, love."

Berdie heard a suck of air through the receiver. For most of Berdie's childhood her mother had puffed on cigarettes without inhaling, happy with just the appearance of sophistication. After one of the wives in her euchre club made fun of her, Gladys had forced herself to start inhaling. Now she never seemed to be without a cigarette.

"Mom, I'm doing fine here. No reason to leave."

"Your father gave you two years, remember."

"Two years to 'make it', Mom. I'm making it just fine. In fact, I'm in line for a promotion–"

"You know what he meant. If you haven't met a nice boy yet, maybe it's time to come back home."

Birdie heard her mother shush someone. Her father continued to make comments in the background. Gladys came back. "It's good for you to have this experience, love. We just want you to know that you can come home any time. Don't be afraid to tell us when you've had enough."

"It's nice to know that. But I don't need to come home."

"Even if you just get tired of it. I'm sure it's been fun, but it's got to be hard, a girl on her own."

"How's Dad?"

Berdie listened while her mother started a long list of medical events. She pulled her feet up onto the chair to get comfortable. Maggie shot her a questioning look. Berdie put a hand over the receiver and mouthed 'wants me to come home'. Maggie rolled her eyes.

Joanna whispered, "Anything wrong?"

Berdie shook her head and whispered back, "My parents think this is like some kind of summer camp. Just a fun thing to do and then I'll go back home."

Joanna and Connie giggled. The boys listened avidly.

"Did you hear me?" her mother said in her ear.

"Of course." Berdie ran her mind back over what she'd half-heard. "Dad might have to have an operation, maybe next summer."

"You should be here when that happens."

Berdie could feel a headache coming on. Again in the background she could hear comments. From the sound of it, her father was denying that she would be coming home just for his sake. He wanted her to move back, she was sure, but he would forever resist the idea of anyone doing anything solely for his benefit. He was the giver; everyone else had to be the receiver and properly grateful. Her mother had perfected the role and brought Berdie up to do the same. In her senior year at high school, Berdie had suffered from constant migraines. Until the government people had come and offered her a way out.

She forced her jaw to relax. "Well, if he does go in the hospital, Mom, I'm sure I can get time off. It's called family emergency leave, or something. Just let me know when it's scheduled, and I'll catch the first bus."

A pause. Her mother said in a furtive whisper, "Your father's gone into the TV room, so I can talk. Listen, they say it'll be a long drawn-out thing, love. They don't know how long it'll take him to recover. It's some kind of heart surgery and it's new. People die. He'll never admit it, but I think he's worried about it. Your father depends on you a lot. You know that."

"He's never depended on anyone," Berdie snapped. "He's done everything he can to make sure we're dependent on him, helpless without him. I have a life here, Mom, and I'm making it work. I'm not going to quit my job because he might have an operation a year from now!"

"Lower your voice, young lady."

"Sorry. But Mom, this is not some kind of summer camp–"

Connie and Joanna smothered more giggles. Maggie shushed them.

"It's a job, Mama." Berdie twisted to put her back to them. "I can't just quit. I might not be able to get it back."

"You can always find another one. Later, after he recovers. Somewhere closer."

"Like I found one before? Mom, I looked everywhere, you know I did. Listen, for Thanksgiving I have four days off. I'll hop the bus and come home for a visit, and we'll talk about it then."

"Well, I don't know," said Gladys doubtfully. "Buses are dangerous. Hold on while I ask your father if it's okay."

Berdie said through her teeth. "I wasn't asking for your permission."

"Don't talk to me that way. You may think you're all grown up now, but I'm still your mother."

"Sorry," Berdie said again.

"Now you listen to me," Gladys said, her voice a mixture of harshness and pleading. "Your father has spent his whole life working jobs that tired him out sick so that you'd have nice clothes and plenty of food and a roof over your head. The least you can do is be there for him when he needs you."

"I'll be there, Mom. I just can't quit my job. Not yet," she added as a conscious peace offering. "It can't be that bad, or they wouldn't be waiting a year. So I'll see you Thanksgiving, ok? And we'll talk then. This is long distance, we're running up a bill. I'll let you know what time the bus gets in."

ABOUT THE AUTHOR

Eugenia Parrish has mined her stories from her travels and a variety of pay-the-rent jobs. She's had short stories published in small magazines, the anthologies *Turning Leaves*, *Elemental*, *Eugenia Parrish's Baker's Dozen +2*, *He Had it Coming*, and a well-received essay in the *Journal of The Romance Writers of America.*

Her most recent book tells a startling tale worthy of 'Sex and the City' – but set in our nation's capital, circa 1965: *The Last Party in Eden.*

You can find out more about
Ms. Parrish and her other works at:
www.EugeniaParrishAuthor.com.

OTHER BOOKS BY EUGENIA PARRISH

The Last Party in Eden
Eugenia Parrish's Baker's Dozen +2
He Had it Coming
Murder at the End of the Line
The Tattoo Murders

THE DEL SUEÑO FILES

Murder at the End of the Line
The Tattoo Murders
A Cold Blue Killing

Made in the USA
San Bernardino, CA
19 April 2017